THE DANCING DETECTIVE

THE DANCING DETECTIVE

A.N. WIDDECOMBE

Also by Ann Widdecombe:

Fiction

The Clematis Tree
An Act of Treachery
Father Figure
An Act of Peace

Non Fiction

Strictly Ann: The Autobiography
Sackcloth and Ashes: Penance and Penitence
in a Self-Centred World

ISBN-13: 9781500247621

FOR Anton Du Beke and Craig Revel- Horwood. It was fun!

CHAPTER ONE

IN WHICH WE MEET SOME OF THE CAST AND DO NOT HAVE TO WAIT LONG FOR THE MURDER.

He meant her to fall, was going to let go, was enjoying her fear now that he was sure she realised. She looked down, down to where she must land and then into his eyes. They were surprisingly normal eyes, greyish blue, clear, guileless, not orbs glittering with evil intent. Her own, she knew, were fear-filled, pleading but not weeping. She could not weep because there was no time before she was spinning through the air and falling.

She waited for the impact but he caught her with the deft assurance which never failed to bring that roaring cheer from the audience. Damn him, she thought, damn Cobb Grainger, the conceited brute. And there were still five weeks of this competition to go.

"You don't trust me," he had reproached her as they waited to be called back for the judging. "You were so scared the cameras must have picked it up."

"You just like power."

He smiled mockingly. "Of course, sweetie. I'm a politician. But you are a dancer, a *professional* dancer and you were scared."

"Yes, because you are not a professional and you take risks I don't agree to. This time, last time and probably next time."

"The risks pay off, don't they? And you need to win this time, don't you?"

He was certainly right about that, she thought, as she applied a third dose of cleanser to the screen make-up Angela had put on. Maybe she should give in and go for the fake tan after all. *Lively Toes* had been a disaster from the start.

The phone rang as she emerged from the bathroom.

"Darling, you were wonderful!" Her mother's voice filled the room with uncritical delight. It would be no good asking if she had looked scared because Gillian Hobbs would have noticed only what she was wearing, not what she might have been feeling. It had been her father, not her mother, who had cautioned against her wild craving for success.

Of the three sisters it was Amy who had always been the most nakedly ambitious despite being less clever than Laura and less pretty than Sarah. At six she discovered the joy of dancing and at ten the much greater joy of winning. By sixteen she was helping with the teaching at local dance classes and was determined that one day she would have her own studio.

At seventeen she announced that her professional name would be Beautella LaReine and her father choked on his Yorkshire pudding. Her mother thought it romantic.

"You might wish you had gone for something a bit more ordinary later on," had been Laura's counsel. It had not been difficult for Amy to interpret *later on* as *when you are older.*

When, ten years later, Amy opened her own studio she proposed to call it Happy Feet after the film then making such an impact but it was Laura who said "No, call it after you. Call it Studio LaReine."

"What a marvellous idea," cried her mother.

"Have you really done the sums?" asked her father who did not say "I told you so" when, two years later, he advanced a small loan to help the recession-hit business.

Then the Family Broadcasting Corporation announced it was to introduce a new talent show in which celebrities would learn to dance and compete with each other. The programme would partner each amateur with a professional dancer and the audience would determine the winner. Eventually they might have the viewers doing so but not until success was assured.

Beautella, who by this time had all but forgotten she was ever called anything else, applied to be one of the professionals and won against heavy competition but the first series of *Lively Toes* saw her eliminated in the first round. There was nothing wrong with her partner's dancing but he chose that week to make headlines over an extra marital affair and was punished by an audience which thought his pretty, tiny, timid –seeming wife a woman wronged.

"They don't have to listen to her nagging all day long," was his bitter farewell to Beautella.

In the second series she was partnered by a gentle, charming celebrity hairdresser with two left feet. Early elimination was inevitable but she was so engaged with his disappointment that she felt little on her own account until the producer casually remarked "You have been unlucky, haven't you?"

Programme makers wanted lucky people and Beautella knew her contract was in danger. When the same producer said "better luck this time" as the third series began it was not hard to imagine the unspoken addition of "three strikes and you're out."

And they had given her every chance, partnering her with a popular politician from a minority party whose good looks made him a media favourite. Never likely to see power and live with the fruits of his pronouncements, he said only what he believed tuned with the prevailing mood and was hailed as a model of common sense and compassion. At 65 he was the oldest celebrity but looked 50 and knew it.

He could certainly dance, thought Beautella gratefully, until it became obvious that he was interested only in excelling and performing feats which would have been beyond the abilities of most professionals and that she, as the one who was thrown in the air, spun until she was giddy and caught again at the last millisecond, bore all the risk while Grainger basked in the glory. When she found that his dancing was exceeded only by his arrogance and undisguised disdain for lesser performers, she hated him and, but for the imperative to win, would have walked off the set.

It was a driving imperative. Studio LaReine was struggling as people in turn struggled to economise. The roof over their heads was essential while dance classes were not. If she could claim to have trained the winner or the runner-up of *Lively Toes* she might just save her livelihood and, anyway, the programme paid well.

Beautella sighed and fell into a sleep which was haunted by a now recurring nightmare in which she was dropped by Cobb Grainger and paralysed for life. When she woke to find herself in a soft bed instead of immobile on a wooden floor the relief drenched her in sweat and she, who once began each day with an almost childish delight, began this one in tears.

Cobb Grainger had thrived on fear all his life. Other people's fear. Cowering, miserable, sobbing fear. It had begun with that snivelling little brat Phillipson who hid from him so clumsily and who, when confronted in whatever refuge he had crawled into, looked back at Grainger with huge pleading eyes. He had since seen that look in so many eyes: in his little sister's when he found her stealing fifty pence from their mother's purse, in the chief whip's when he mentioned the name of the man's mistress, in Beautella LaReine's when she thought she was going to fall from the height at which he held her.

He had developed an unerring instinct for the straw that was about to break the back of whatever human camel he was tormenting. He learned it from the mistake he made with Phillipson, pushing him so far that he broke and told a prefect all. The prefect had marched both boys to the Head's office and the humiliating punishments which followed had taught Cobb not that he should not bully but that he must do so with more finesse, that he must cease at just that moment when his spiritless victims were about to appeal to higher authority, that he must learn to recognise the imminence of a breaking point.

Janet had been far from spiritless. She paid the blackmail of half her week's pocket money the first time he asked but when the demand was repeated a week later she went to their mother. Both parents looked at him with disappointment in their eyes but the only lesson he learned was to choose his victims more carefully.

From the time he left prep school to the time he passed his Oxford entrance exam Cobb was not caught once. His approach to dominating others had grown subtler and surer but he no longer craved the fear in another's eyes: it was enough to know that he could cause it, no longer necessary actually to do so.

He resented it only when he could not read someone and puzzled long when, many years later, he read that Captain Sam Phillipson had been awarded a posthumous medal for bravery in the Falklands conflict. Stupid little Phillipson couldn't even survive and there was hardly any surprise in that but *bravery*? What had *bravery* to do with the snuffling little toad?

Fortunately everyone on *Lively Toes* was transparently easy to read: Beautella was frightened of him but too desperate to win to do anything about it; Jos Lewison, the senior judge, merely played at being rude; Fred 'n Em thought they were going to win but were not quite sure; Rashid Ahmed wanted to win the ratings war and Jess was in love with Ahmed which was bad luck as he was a devoted husband.

Jos Lewison yawned and immediately glanced at camera number six but Chris was fiddling about with a cable, not filming his momentary indiscretion. Relieved, he shuffled the papers in front of him, noting that the first to dance would be Fred n Em. They had begun the competition as Fred and Emily but a high circulation red top had decided Fred n Em fitted the space of a headline better.

Em was popular because she was overweight and played a somewhat scatty nursery nurse in a soap and Fred because he was a courtly soul who dealt with her clumsiness as though she had the grace of a sylph. They would probably win, reflected Jos gloomily.

The public voted for faces not footwork. Why else was Fred still dancing at seventy?

Beside him his two fellow judges were organising their own papers. Later he was to say that all three of them froze at exactly the same moment although in reality they saw the name a few seconds apart. It was written in large red capitals on plain cream card. JESS.

The judges looked at each other in puzzlement. Was this some hint from the producer? A clumsy canvass for an uninspiring dancer? But the director had signalled the beginning of the programme which was recorded as live and it was impossible to enquire.

Fred n Em turned in a passable performance which the audience cheered as if it had been of virtuoso quality. His own caustic comments were booed, Serena's score of eight wildly applauded, Liz's of six greeted with groans. Em watched the scores unfold with an expression of agonised suspense while Fred appeared to regard them with the benign curiosity he might have bestowed on the mothers' sack race.

Cobb Grainger took the usual risks and Jos wondered if he were the only one to notice that Beautella was afraid. Hal and Leonie retired after thirty seconds when Leonie twisted her ankle and, with a cry of anguish, sank to the floor. She limped off set to sympathetic cheers.

Probably did it deliberately, thought Jos. She hadn't been going anywhere in this competition and now at least she had a headline. Jess and Matt came next, then Belle and Bruce. Finally Ru and Tatum raised their game sufficiently to make survival possible.

Jos stifled another yawn, admitting to himself that this must be his last series, that he had grown bored with his own rudeness, that he must find some new outlet for his way with words. During the interval he would ask the producer why Jess's name had appeared in front of the judges.

But it was Serena who asked, not Jos, because he was rather enjoying the performance of the Honeycats, who sang two of their hits to entertain the audience while the dancers drank water in their dressing rooms and Angela and her team refreshed their make-up for the second half of the show. Rashid Ahmed frowned and shook his head. No, of course it had nothing to do with the show. None of the production team would dream of trying to influence the judges. And why on earth would they pick Jess?

The Honeycats left the stage to loud applause, the judges took their seats and the dancers began to line up in the wings.

"Where's Jess?"

The question came from Ahmed as he cast his eye along the queue of contestants. Leonie was there, her ankle bandaged, her face white beneath Angela's efforts.

"Matt, have you seen her?" Ahmed's voice sharpened as the warm-up man began preparing the audience for part two. At any moment they would be recording and Venetia would come on to present the dancers for the results show.

"I'll go and see," muttered Ed the runner but Ahmed snapped at him to send the work shadow instead because he needed Ed to check that the dancers were in their right places in the line-up and Helen flew off to do his bidding.

Helen ran along the corridor and, ignoring the lift, down the stairs and along the next corridor before realising she had no idea which dressing room was Jess's.

"Don't panic, Captain Mainwaring," she muttered as she slowed to a walk and began checking every door for the name it bore. She had never watched an episode of Dad's Army in her life but it was a favourite catchphrase of her father. Even now Ahmed was probably hissing into Venetia's earpiece that she must keep talking, that the dancers weren't ready. Knowing her luck, it would be a miracle if Jess's room wasn't the last.

Fortune rarely smiled on Helen although it was also true that she hardly ever frowned on her. She just seemed to ignore her. Helen was the last word in average: average looks, average height, average brains, average redbrick university, average two- two degree, average very small flat shared with two other unremarkable girls, average surname - Brown. It didn't even have an "e" she often reflected glumly. Her one piece of luck had been landing this job for the duration of the show, although she never fooled herself that work experience led necessarily to work.

Jess's room was the second to last. The pre-penultimate, she muttered aloud, as she knocked on the door. There was no answer so Helen pushed it ajar "Jess?". There being still no answer, Helen opened it further and entered the room, whereupon she let out a well above average scream.

Nobody heard. They did not hear her further screams as she ran along the corridor and began to race up the stairs. By the time she neared the top she was panting too much to cry out again but Helen would not stop to catch her breath as long as she knew she was alone. Instead she ran the length of the next corridor, pausing only to look fearfully over her shoulder. Then, as she saw the studio door ahead of her, the lights went out. Helen screamed again, a cry of pure, abject terror but nobody heard.

After the scream there was silence as deep as the darkness around her. Helen stood with her back pressed against the wall, her ears straining for any sound, willing the return of rationality, of the triumph of twenty - first century thought over primeval fear. It came slowly, enabling her to creep forward until her hand finally encountered the studio door. In vain she sought for the metal box beside it which contained the code to open the door, her hand meeting nothing but door and wall.

Forcing herself to move methodically she began to slide her hand down the wall until she knew herself too low and then to slide it up until she was too high. If she did this carefully enough she must surely locate the box.

As she found the metal on the fourth attempt it occurred to her to wonder for the first time why nobody had come to look for her, why Ahmed was not sufficiently agitated by the absence of Jess to send another runner. What was happening beyond this sound-proof door? Had they begun again without Jess?

It made no sense but she must concentrate for now on the code, on locating the buttons for 8698 without pressing the wrong ones. She believed she had found eight and was gingerly running her fingers upwards to five to go sideways to six when Helen heard the noise on the stairs.

It was very faint but enough to tell her that someone was there and that whoever it was wanted discovery no more than she. The slight sound was not repeated and Helen, motionless, trying not to breathe, peered into the velvety blackness, her ears straining to catch the smallest swish of clothing, the lightest tread of someone enfilading towards her through the dark.

The urge to scream and run was becoming overpowering but she remained still until what was left of her reason told her that if the unseen being was heading her way he could be seeking only the studio and that he too would try to feel for the code box. Very slowly, terrified of giving herself away by the tiniest of sounds, Helen crouched down against the wall until she was on the floor itself.

From a distance of inches a man cleared his throat, Helen gave a piercing shriek which seemed to bounce off the very walls in the same moment as the heavy studio door opened, crushing her against the wall, banging her head on its stony hardness and pitching her into the deeper darkness of unconsciousness.

When the lights went out the studio filled with voices as a babble of surprise and excitement came from the audience, Ahmed swore softly and the cameramen muttered in disbelief. When the darkness proved more than momentary agitated queries from the director in the gallery poured into Ahmed's earpiece. Into millions of homes the calm voice of an FBC announcer would be heard apologising for the hitch and saying the programme would be restored as soon as possible. The show was recorded as live and mistakes, even one of this order of magnitude, would be left in.

In the studio emergency lighting from the exit signs and floor strips began to penetrate the dark.

"Oops!" murmured Fred. "There'll be a court martial. Top brass will be furious."

Emily giggled and then yelped as Tatum trod heavily on her foot, her heel digging in with her full weight. Simultaneously Emily began to whimper and Tatum to call on the Almighty.

"Oh, my God! Who's that? Em? I'm just sooo sorry. Are you OK?"

Open the *door* for God's sake!" Ahmed, his voice dark with anger and chagrin, added an oath of his own. "And get us some light from the corridor."

"The Deity would appear to be much in demand," observed Fred.

"Shut up, Reverend, and open the damn door." Emily recognised the irate tones of the assistant producer who, rarely calm, was now giving an impression of being demented with fury.

"And the Devil too," whispered Fred but loudly enough for his victim to hear. Nevertheless he began to feel for the door.

It was Emily who suddenly located the handle just as Bruce tripped, propelling her, Tatum and Fred against the heavy structure, which flew open just as the lights came back on.

"Well, done, Sparks!" The relief in Fred's voice was echoed in a thousand exclamations from inside the studio where a freshly excited buzz now emanated from the audience.

"Right, let's get back into line. Is everyone all right? Em, was it you who yelled? Are you OK?" Ahmed's determinedly cheerful tones squashed the dramatic ones of the assistant producer then suddenly turned irritable as his eyes failed to locate Jess. He forced himself to professional calm.

"Still no Jess? Where's Helen?" He dispatched Ed to find out.

Five minutes later the director in the gallery learned through his earpiece that a contestant had been strangled with a flapper band in her dressing room and the work shadow was unconscious behind the studio door.

It was, he muttered drily, the kind of occasion on which the show did not go on. Half an hour later he found himself stammering to an incredulous detective that, no, he had not thought of keeping members of the audience in their places.

CHAPTER TWO

IN WHICH WE MEET THE REST OF THE DANCERS AND THE
DETECTIVES GET TO WORK.

"It probably doesn't matter that much," the detective sergeant
said to the detective inspector. "They were all either invited
or applied for tickets. Anyway if somebody got up and went out the
people beside him would have noticed."

Peter Frobisher nodded. Brendan Molloy was right but it
was frustrating all the same. Certainly the death had occurred
after the audience was seated and people had been discour-
aged from leaving the studio during the interval but it had
been dark.

"It's the lights," said Molloy unhappily.

"It's the lights," agreed Frobisher.

"It just can't happen." Those were the words of the lighting
engineer, the technical director of FBC and just about everybody
else, expert and layman alike. But it had happened.

"Anyway, what was the point of the lights going out? Lawrence
may not be able to give us the exact time of death yet, but it looks
as if it had certainly happened by the time they were all lined up
backstage. Whoever did this did it in a well-lit dressing room and
had plenty of time to escape. There was just no reason for the lights
to go out then."

Frobisher shook his head. "Any news of the girl?"

"Helen Brown?" Molloy glanced at a note in his hand to check
the name. "Badly concussed. May or may not be able to help us in
the morning."

"Well, let's assume the murderer caused the lights to go out and forget why for the moment and let's assume it wasn't some stranger who got past security but someone connected with the show. Let's start with the dancers."

"All accounted for from about ten minutes before the lights went out. Before that, scattered in separate dressing rooms. We should be able to plot pretty well who saw whom and when because the dressers, hairstylists and make-up artists were in and out of the rooms all the time."

"And that at least will help us with the time of death. Probably more than Lawrence can, given the small time frame. We just need the last one who called on Jess. What about all those artists?"

"Again all accounted for from ten minutes or so before lights-out. They were touching up the dancers back – stage. Before then as I said we should be able to work out who was where when. Same will probably apply to all stage hands but we aren't that far yet and people are getting tired. When do we let them go home?"

"Now," said Frobisher wearily thinking that he was also tired and would be forced to cancel an already overdue holiday. "We appear to have a cast of thousands."

Molloy grinned ruefully. "Well, dozens at any rate. Possibly scores. Unless we have to look at the audience too. I just hope there aren't dozens of motives as well."

"Well, it wouldn't be dancing," said Ahmed sadly when Molloy interviewed him the following afternoon. "Her celeb was averagely good but nothing like good enough to win and she reckoned he tried hard enough. This won't be jealousy."

"Any ill-feeling between any of them?"

Ahmed thought for a few seconds before shaking his head. "Trev upset most people but I can't remember him having a particular problem with Jess."

"Trev?"

"Trevor Langdon, the A.P."

"A.P.?"

"Sorry, assistant producer. He's good but horribly short tempered. Fortunately he seems to save it for the pros rather than the celebs or we'd have had to get rid of him in week one. He's particularly aggressive towards Fred. Calls him the Reverend."

"Why?"

"Fred's pretty devout. That's unusual in this game. He is also, of course, much older than your average pro and I think Trev reckons he's past it and belongs to another age. Maybe he does, but he's popular with the viewers and we just give him the older or less able dancers. He treats them like princesses and the audience roars. Getting rid of Fred wouldn't be a good move."

Molloy looked at his list. "He dances with Em? Emily Carstairs?"

"Yes. She plays Jane in *Mummy!*"

"How did she get on with Jess?"

"I can't say I ever noticed."

That, Molloy was to find, was Ahmed's reply to most of his questions about relations between various members of the cast but he answered frankly, if blushingly, when asked whether Jess were particularly close to anyone.

"I am afraid she had a bit of a crush on me but a, I am happily married and b, it just wasn't reciprocated. Apart from that I think she was divorced with two teenage children."

"Boyfriends?"

"Don't know." Ahmed's tone added an unspoken "and don't care."

Yes, he agreed, all the dancers and all the professionals were lined up in the studio a few minutes before the lights went out. Only Jess was missing. Was the rumour true, he asked Molloy, that all the electrics in the studio had been fiddled with?

"So we understand, sir," was the detective's careful answer.

"No doubt about it," said the expert Frobisher had brought in. The computer controlling the stage lighting also controlled the lighting in the wings and had been re-programmed. The corridor lighting worked in the ordinary way, with switches at either end. So Helen should have been able to see her way to Jess's room and back without difficulty. There were also switches at the bottom and top of the staircase where, for obvious reasons, they controlled both corridors. It was all utterly basic with a fuse box in the small kitchen next to the studio and there was no connection to the computer at all beyond the studio.

Molloy shook his head. "And we still don't know why the studio lighting should have been sabotaged. It wasn't to cover the murder because that had already happened."

"We should however be able to work out who had the opportunity to mess with the computer. And I suppose we must remain open to the possibility that the lights and the murder are not connected."

Molloy raised a disbelieving eyebrow.

"We have to at least allow for it," insisted his superior. "Assumptions are dangerous. Maybe someone had a grudge against the show or was playing a very risky practical joke or........."

"If all that was involved was flicking a switch, then, yes," interrupted Molloy without ceremony. "But we know that whoever did this had to re-programme a computer. He needed a damn good reason............."

"Which may not have been murder," was Frobisher's own interruption. "I agree it isn't very likely but at the moment we can't work out why the lights were switched off after the event."

"To enable someone to escape?"

"But the corridor was lit so that implies that whoever did it needed to escape through the studio. But if you are right then we have one murderer and one accomplice? That implies a shared motive."

"Talking of motive, any thoughts?"

Frobisher shook his head. "She appears to have stirred up no very strong feeling at all................"

He broke off as his mobile bleeped. "The Brown girl is OK'd for interview. Right Molloy, let's go."

Molloy glanced at his watch. His supper would be as cold as his wife's mood. From half a dozen paces in front of him Frobisher sensed rather than saw the glance. Alice Molloy was eight months pregnant with her third child.

As it was he might just as well have let Molloy go home to her for Helen Brown could tell them nothing. She could remember being sent to find Jess but after that all was blank. She could not say whether she had found Jess's dressing room or whether she had fainted as soon as she left the studio.

"I think we can help you there," observed Frobisher. "You have a nasty bump at the back of your head and another at the front. It looks as if the door got you when they opened it and knocked you into the wall."

Not to mention the blood on both door and wall, thought Molloy, admiring the other's tact. Helen smiled weakly but still remembered nothing. All the doctor could tell them afterwards was that the amnesia could be either temporary or permanent but that there was no means of predicting which would be the case.

"Helpful," muttered Frobisher as they left the hospital, then in a more hopeful tone added "Do you think Alice has gone to bed?"

This time Molloy didn't need to consult his watch and they both headed for the Pig and Pen.

They had discovered the pub with the incongruous name when they had visited the same hospital on a previous case. Its interior was delightfully rural too and the food was good.

"This is near enough to the FBC as well," observed Molloy, happily.

"Peter? It is Peter, isn't it?" Frobisher's smile faded slightly as he looked at the advancing galleon cleaving through the waters. Molloy, turning, saw a woman of middle age and statuesque proportions bearing down on them. He looked back at his boss who was wearing a puzzled expression. No, he thought, surely you wouldn't forget this giant once you had met her?

The woman also was now noticing the dawning bewilderment. "It's Laura," she faltered.

Frobisher recovered memory and self-possession simultaneously. "Of course! Too long, no see. How are you? Meet Brendan
Molloy. Can I get you a drink?"

He was babbling, thought Molloy.

Laura smiled and refused as Molloy tried not to stare. She turned
from him back to Frobisher. "I was just meeting some friends from
the FBC. All they can talk about is the murder. Is that why you are
here? Are you investigating it? I wonder what Fred makes of it all?
He's such an unworldly fellow in many ways. Or was. Oh, I must go,
Lizzy is signalling. Such a bore. Great to see you!" She flashed them
both a toothy smile and began to power her way through the drink-
ers towards her friend.

"Is she....." Molloy hesitated.

"Yes. When I last saw her, he was Laurence and just leaving the
army."

Molloy grimaced. "It doesn't look so very convincing."

"No, poor devil, it doesn't. Let's forget him. Or her. I want to
talk to you about the suspects or rather the potential suspects. Let's
begin with the dancers."

"O.K. Fred n Em first?"

"Yes. We know Em was close to the door during the darkness
and that Tatum was beside her because she trod on her foot. We
know that Fred was at first further back because he called out
to know if Em was all right but then got near the door and that
Cobb Grainger was right next to the door because when Em finally
opened it, he was the first one she saw. Ahmed also recalls bumping into him as the door flew open. Beautella was next to Hal and
Leonie and they were debating what the cause of the lights failure
might be. Matt was still asking where Jess might have got to and
both Belle and Bruce were making reassuring noises in response.
Only Ru was silent but we know he was there because when the
lights came on he pushed his way towards Tatum and several of the
others remember that."

"Why weren't they standing in order?"

"They had been. When the lights went out all became confusion. The important thing is they were all there and given that Jess was already missing we can presume she was dead. That means none of the dancers was relying on the lights failure to cover coming or going."

"But who was? All the dancers were in place but so is each member of the band accounted for, the make-up girls, the dressers, the....."

"I know. I know. Everyone was seen by somebody in the right place at the right time. But that is because the murder had already happened. We need to concentrate on where people were before they were called to stage and we need to go back in time to discover if anybody knew Jess before the competition began. The murder may be new but it doesn't follow that the motive is too."

Molloy yawned and Frobisher, taking the hint, called it a day.

Anton Caesar watched them leave. The younger one, he reflected wryly, was clearly more tired than the older though neither looked in particularly good condition. The one he had heard called Frobisher was a big, shambling man with still-thick curly grey hair and a mildly dishevelled appearance. Unpressed, thought the fastidious Caesar with a mental sniff. The younger one- what was he called?- Molloy, looked as if he could do with a few sessions at the gym. Caesar subconsciously tightened his own stomach muscles.

He felt the same reaction when facing them next day. Yes, he was Anton Caesar and, yes he had been with *Lively Toes* since the programme began. Yes, he and his uninspiring if perfectly pleas-ant partner had been eliminated the previous week and, yes, he was there because he was dancing with the other professionals in a special group dance. The fewer dancers left in the competition, the greater need for other events to fill up the time. No, he knew of no reason why anybody should want to murder Jess.

"How well do you know the other dancers? The professionals?"

"Everyone knows Fred. He's been on the dance scene for years. Bit parts in films about Fred Astaire or musicals or whatever. Began teaching on cruise ships before I was born. They say he was once a vicar".

"And his partner?"

"Em? Mad as a fish. The scattiness isn't part of the act: it's real. Fred says 'left foot, Em' and her right shoots forward but the viewers love her because they love her character in *Mummy!*"

"Beautella?"

"Gorgeous!"

Frobisher paused. Eventually he prompted "Anything else?"

Caesar came out of his reverie and grinned. "Sorry. No, what you see with Beaut is what you get. She's lovely. No malice, no jealousy, no tantrums and then she gets that brute Grainger to dance with."

Molloy looked at his list. "The politician?"

"The animal."

Frobisher paused again but this time did not need to nudge a response from Caesar, who made not the smallest attempt to control his anger.

"Anyone can see she's terrified of him. He rehearses one set of moves, then gets on the floor and tries all manner of daredevil stuff and she just has to take it. He doesn't seem to realise that it takes two to do those lifts, that if she isn't expecting a move she can't employ the right grip or distribute her weight properly. Or maybe he does realise it and doesn't care. He just wants the applause. She's flying on wires next week and completely against her will because she's got height phobia."

"Why do the producers let it happen?"

"Because she won't complain. She needs to win."

"Needs to?"

"Yes. She runs her own studio and it's in trouble with the recession."

Molloy grimaced. "Sounds a nice chap, this Grainger. How does he get on with the other dancers?"

"They hate him but he remains quite agreeable. Part of the act, I suppose. Only Em has ever got the better of him. She smacked his bottom."

"What?" the startled expression came from both detectives and Anton Caesar smiled reminiscently.

"Grainger pretended he was going to let Beautella fall during band call. You know about band call?"

Frobisher and Molloy shook their heads.

"Well, as you may realise by now we train the celebs at studios near wherever they happen to live so throughout the week we dance to CD music but, of course, come Friday the music is live. There is therefore a probability that there will be some slight difference in the way the music and vocals are delivered so before dress rehearsal everyone practises their dance with the live band.

"Anyway a couple of weeks ago there was a sequence in which Grainger carried Beautella on his shoulder for eight beats. He seemed to let her fall off backwards, head down. She actually screamed, damn him. Then of course he held on just in time.

"Fred n Em were waiting to go on next and as Grainger left the floor and passed her Em gave him an almighty wallop on the backside and told him to stop scaring little girls. He pretended to find it funny but he was scarlet with fury and the story went round like wildfire."

Frobisher smiled. "So, don't tell me. Let me guess. Is there any chance you think he's an arrogant, self-centred bastard?"

"And a lot else besides."

"He's popular enough with the public."

"Because he says whatever they want to hear."

"Could he do murder?"

"He could do anything if he thought it helped Cobb Grainger. The real mystery is why nobody has murdered him."

Later Frobisher was to recall that remark and wish he had paid it more attention. He glanced again at his list and decided to speak to Beautella next.

"There are three others scheduled ahead of her so she may not be here," he observed to Molloy who went to find out and returned triumphant.

Gorgeous was an understatement, he thought when his sergeant brought her in to the dressing room which had been allocated for their interviews. Beautella LaReine was of very average height but of exceptional everything else: immaculate figure, huge brown eyes fringed with long, thick lashes, a face regular enough in structure for a supermodel's, thick, lustrous hair, even, white teeth and a smile somehow tinged with sadness. The sort men slayed dragons for, Frobisher reflected, and wondered how many on the set were in love with her. Clever, too, running her own business. But what a damn silly name.

"Miss LaReine? I hope we haven't caused a problem with the change in schedule?"

Beautella smiled and shook her head. "No, no. Not at all."

"Perhaps we could just deal with the formalities? What is your full name?"

"You mean my real one? Amy Catherine Hobbs. But I have almost forgotten it. I began using Beautella LaReine when I was seventeen and changed to it by deed poll before I was twenty."

"How well did you know Jess Allward?"

"Quite well. She joined the show at the start and those of us who were about then are quite close because we were all involved in making the idea work. There are only three of us left now: just Fred, Anton and myself."

"Tell me all you know about her. Everything. Even if it seems irrelevant. Even if thoughts come to you at random. Just talk about her."

"She was actually one of Fred's pupils ages ago. He was teaching in a church hall and she went along. He had been a vicar or something. After a few lessons he told her she had the makings of a very good dancer. She said she had been through a bit of a bad time and thought a career change would do no harm, especially as she had a small legacy and could afford to take a risk so off she went to dance school and Fred's prediction proved spot on. She then began teaching and then put together her own dance troupe which broke up not long before *Lively Toes* was born. It was the first time she had seen Fred in years. She said she wouldn't be able to keep it up much longer, that she would return to teaching and coaching. After all most of us are in our twenties and early thirties while she was in her late forties. She was fed up with everyone saying that the only reason she and Fred were kept on was so nobody could accuse the FBC of ageism."

"Was that the reason?"

"No. Or maybe in Fred's case. Not in Jess's. Anyway they were both in the last six while young things like Anton have already been eliminated so they can hardly be past it."

"We know she was divorced. Boyfriends?"

"Plenty. None serious, at least not while I knew her. A lot of people thought she was keen on Rashid but I couldn't see her as a marriage-breaker. I think she just rather liked him and wanted to know him better."

Plenty. Molloy's heart sank. The cast of witnesses and potential suspects was big enough already. He tuned back into the conversation to hear Frobisher saying: "Any reason for somebody to hate her?" and watched the large brown eyes fill with tears.

Beautella shook her head. "No, none."

"Breakfast spread," muttered the detective sergeant as he closed the door behind her. "That's what that name reminds me of."

"She probably thought it romantic. She said she was seventeen when she chose it. Who's next?"

"Henry James Edwards. Hal, he calls himself."

Hal was a smallish, brown-haired man of about thirty, who had joined the cast that year because they needed someone to partner the short Leonie. He offered nothing new and nor did Leonie, who played a flirtatious secretary in a police drama but apparently in real life was demure and perhaps also shy, wearing a dark green, calf- length skirt and ice green top. Her sandy, straight hair sat loosely on her shoulders. Only her chunky jewellery proclaimed any individuality or interest in her appearance. One ankle was tightly bound and she walked with a slight limp. Molloy had overheard suggestions that the injury might be diplomatic but he thought not.

When she had gone Molloy expressed surprise at her appearance.

"Oh, I don't know, Brendan. We forget that what we see on stage and screen is just acting. Nothing more than that. Pleasant people play villains and nasty ones doddery vicars, so I suppose there is no reason why shy ones can't play show-offs or vice versa."

Belle, a tall, sinewy athlete who had won a gold medal in the last Olympics merely confirmed what everyone else had said as did her partner Bruce, the youngest among the professional dancers who looked like a character from *High School Musical* but who spoke so fast the detectives had difficulty following him.

"By the time you got a supplementary question in edgeways he was already four paragraphs further on," complained Frobisher. "Who's next?"

"The news reader."

Frobisher regarded the woman who entered the room with interest. Known as an ice cool news reader of both elegance and eloquence, her entry into the *Lively Toes* competition was greeted with surprise and, in some quarters, disdain which intensified when it was realised that her conversation was infantile and faux modern. It would be impossible ever to look at her in the same light again.

Tatum Isaacs was less good-looking in the flesh than on television with thick, blonde wavy hair and high cheekbones but dull skin and a tendency to almost anorexic thinness.

"They say the camera puts on twenty pounds", Molloy had enlightened him afterwards.

Her professional partner, Ru, looked at them through red eyes and spoke listlessly. Frobisher suspected he had spent the previous evening drowning his sorrows but, if the timings given by the hair and make-up artists were right then he was the last person to have seen Jess Allward alive.

"You left hair at the same time as Jess?"

Ru nodded. "Yes. It was just before ten past."

"And she went to her dressing room?"

"Yes. It's next to mine and we walked together. When we got to our rooms we stood outside chatting for a moment and then we went in."

"So by quarter past seven she was in her room? Did you hear anyone knock on her door or did you hear her speak to anyone?"

"No. I've asked myself nothing else since it happened, but no. Nothing. Stage call was at twenty five past. There were people coming and going all the time but the walls are paper thin and I'd have heard if she was talking to anyone."

"When you came out for stage call, who was coming and going?"

"Cobb and Em came out of their rooms. Cobb went straight up to the stage but Em turned back for something. Angela was coming out of Tatum's room. Claire from wardrobe was walking with Fred, brushing him down as they went. She was saying something about Trev being in a worse mood than ever and giving some member of the crew hell and wondering how Rashid put up with him. When we got to the stage everyone was there except Em and Jess."

"When did Em get there?"

"I don't know. All I know is she was in the line-up when we noticed Jess wasn't there."

"I got there with about ten seconds to spare," Em told them half an hour later. "I didn't pass anyone in the corridor."

"Why did you turn back?"

"Because I didn't want to walk with Cobb. So I pretended to have forgotten something but waited just long enough to be sure he would have got well ahead of me."

It was plausible, Molloy thought, particularly in view of the smacking incident. Frobisher was asking her about that now.

"Oh, I just lost it but I'm not sorry. He gives that kid hell every week. He's even persuaded her to fly but she's terrified of heights. When I asked her why she was doing it she said that at least while she was on the wires she wouldn't be at his mercy. He reminds me of one little horror in my nursery in *Mummy!* But I'm not allowed to smack him!"

"Did Mr. Grainger complain?"

"He would have looked too much of a fool. No, he just took it or pretended to. I have no doubt he'll get his own back in his own way in due course."

"Did you hear anything at all from Jess Allward's dressing room?"

"Not that I remember but I was concentrating on stage call and catching the others up."

Fred confirmed Em's reason for turning back. "She arrived backstage in the nick of time and I asked her what she had forgotten and she said 'how to be civil to that rat'. He heard, of course, but didn't react."

The dancer also confirmed Beautella's version of his and Jess's earlier relationship.

"I met her when I was filling in a bit of time running dance classes in the village I was staying in with my mother, while I tried to decide what to do with my life, which was at a bit of a crossroads. Mother had moved in there a couple of years earlier."

"Which village was that?"

"Christmas Pie." Fred's mouth twisted. "Yes, really. That's its name. It's between Guildford and Aldershot near Normandy."

"Normandy?" Molloy and Frobisher spoke with simultaneous incredulity.

"Not the French one. It's another village."

Frobisher blinked.

"Anyway, I think Jess grew up there. She was about eighteen, as far as I remember but I can't be sure. She had been planning to go up to University but she turned out to be such a good dancer that she decided to go to dance school instead. Her parents weren't pleased and blamed me. I asked Jess when we met on this lark if they had changed their minds and she said they seemed happy enough once it all took off but that her mum still worried about what would happen when Jess got past dancing. She used to point to Bruce Forsyth but I don't think they were convinced."

Fred smiled sadly and fell silent for a moment. Frobisher, who had seen the sudden moisture in his eyes, waited.

"After a few months I left Christmas Pie and began to make a living from dance. It kept body and soul together. Teaching. Bit parts. Nothing very exciting until *Lively Toes* came on the scene and there was Jess again, about thirty years older and still as enthusiastic as ever."

"You didn't see her at all in the interval?"

"No. At least not to speak to. I glimpsed her once at an awards ceremony and once at a premiere of a film about Fred Astaire but three years ago was the first time we had met since Christmas Pie. For a while she had dropped the odd line in a Christmas card about what she was doing and how grateful she was for my introducing her to dance but I was away a lot on cruise ships and we lost touch."

"You must have had some catching-up to do. Did she say anything about her life now?"

"She'd been married and divorced. Two kids: a boy and a girl. One is about thirteen and the other sixteen. She didn't say much about her ex but he obviously stays close to the children because occasionally Jess would refer to them as being at their father's for the weekend."

"Can you think of any reason for anybody to wish her harm?"

The detectives waited for the usual puzzled "none" but when it came Frobisher felt a shaft of unease. He could not have said why but his instinct fairly shouted at him that Fred was lying.

Of the dancers there was now only Matt to interview. As he had been rehearsing with Jess days at a time for seven weeks Frobisher hoped he might be able to offer greater insight than the others and he was not disappointed. Matt, a satirist known for his impersonations of the famous, automatically took a close interest in the people he met, wanting future material for his gags, possibly without even realising it.

"She was tense." His Australian vowels took Molloy by surprise, the accent so unlike anything he had heard from Matt's impersonations.

"In what way?" Frobisher frowned.

"Difficult to say exactly. But she was expecting something to happen. I'm sure of it."

"Something bad?"

"I don't think bad exactly," said Matt slowly. "Perhaps not bad but not good either. I don't really know how to describe it. If it was good she would have been excited and if it was bad then she would have been a bit frightened but it wasn't either. Just tense."

"How did she get on with the others?"

"OK. We all got along except there were issues around Cobb sometimes."

"Rashid Ahmed?"

Matt smiled. "She wasn't in love with him if that's what you mean but she liked him. He's a nice chap, particularly compared with that AP."

"Boyfriends?" This came from Molloy.

"Not that I know of but then I didn't know much. We rehearsed and then went off home or whatever but we didn't hang out."

"Not even the odd drink?"

Matt shook his head. "She had kids to think about. Anyway we hadn't much in common."

"Tense," mused Molloy later. "Nobody else said that."

Frobisher grimaced. "Probably didn't notice. Unlike Matt they weren't with her day after day but I think Fred knew more than he was telling us. Meanwhile it looks like a long haul. I've just found out that every single move of every single rehearsal of every single dancer is recorded every single day which should keep somebody occupied for a very long time. We had better get some extra help."

"What are we looking for specifically?"

"I wish I knew. Any evidence that Jess was tense. Any casual word which might indicate anyone less than enamoured with her. Anything. Meanwhile get off home to Alice. Tomorrow won't be easy."

No, thought Molloy. Seeing the relatives was never easy. WPC Angelus had told them that the children were "taking it especially hard". What else did anyone expect?

He was home before nine but Alice was already in bed and asleep. "Casserole in the oven" read the note on the kitchen table. Another by the phone informed him that his sister, Carmel, had rung at seven hoping for news of the baby. "Just because hers always come early!" Alice had added and Molloy smiled, hearing in his imagination the morose indignation. The last month was proving uncomfortable and wearisome and Carmel's breezy tones would not have been much solace. He recalled that his sister's last labour had been so short she had only just arrived at the hospital.

Faced with spending a couple of hours alone, Molloy sat down with his notes and a large pad of blank paper. Half an hour later it bore no more than: Em? Fred?

All Lawrence, the pathologist, had been able to tell them was that Jess had died between roughly seven and half past, which they themselves could narrow further to between quarter past when Ru saw her and about seven thirty five when Helen must be presumed to have found the body.

Em had turned back at the last minute and was alone on the corridor and she had a temper as proved by her assault on Grainger but there had been no sign of a struggle. Whoever had strangled Jess had struck from behind and performed the deed without much difficulty. Em was a biggish woman but Jess was a strong one with the fitness and muscular tone of the professional dancer.

Fred was on his list of two only because Frobisher was convinced that he had lied when saying that he knew of nobody with a grudge against Jess.

After a few seconds' earnest chewing of his biro top, he wrote "Ru – only his word that Jess was alive at 7.15." But he had claimed that he and Jess had stood chatting outside their adjacent rooms. In that case anybody in a nearby room would have heard. He suspected Ru would be off his list fairly quickly.

Leaning back in his chair, Brendan Molloy tried to envisage the scene. Jess was sitting at her dressing table, her back to the door, looking in the mirror. She would have seen the murderer enter, approach her with two quick steps and then....He jumped wildly as two arms wound round his neck.

"You're home early," said Alice delightedly.

Chapter Three

IN WHICH A FLAPPER BAND POSES A PROBLEM BUT A WHIP IS FORTHCOMING.

The Allwards lived in a small semi – detached house in a road of identical dwellings in a sleepy Warwickshire town. Frobisher wondered what changes had brought them here from Christmas Pie, recalling that Fred had said he thought Jess had grown up there, indicating a settled rather than peripatetic parental lifestyle. He had established that there were no siblings and knew that the elderly Allwards had lost their only child, feeling the old reluctance as he prepared to interview the grieving, having no faith that a life-time's experience would guarantee the right approach when questioning the bereaved teenage children.

The car came to a halt and he heard himself say with false heartiness "Right, Molloy. Let's get on with it."

The door opened at once when he rang and he realised the occupants must have been watching for the policemen's arrival. Mrs Allward, unlike her daughter, was a small woman. She preceded the detectives arthritically to the tiny front room where WPC Angelus, of the local force, was sitting with Jess's father. There was no sign of the children.

As the introductions were made Molloy observed the parents as unobtrusively as the cramped space allowed. Anne Allward was in her mid- eighties and her husband a few years older. Jess must have been a late baby for those days. Her mother's eyes were red-rimmed and her father's face drawn but they spoke quietly and answered with steady attention. He felt a rising anger on their behalf and, to take his attention from them while Frobisher began the questions, he looked around the room.

It was cluttered with ornaments and photographs seemingly on every surface. On the window ledge a preposterous pink pig nestled into a clutch of small, elaborately decorated pill boxes. From the centre of the mantelpiece a twelve year old Jess smiled back at them against a background of sand and sea. On either side was ranged a variety of photographs: an old black and white wedding portrait, a sepia snap of people who must have been Jess's grandparents, Jess clad in a shimmering ball gown and held high above the head of a fellow dancer, Jess receiving a certificate, Jess in a formal school photo, the other grandparents, the family at Christmas lunch, Jess as an infant, Jess in a white confirmation dress surrounded by others similarly clad standing either side of a Bishop resplendent with mitre and crook, Jess's own wedding.

A small table was devoted to photographs of the grandchildren as babies, infants and teenagers. On the coffee table a stack of women's magazines fought for space with an equally high pile of knitting patterns on top of which sat knitting needles and the recent work – in- progress, a man's pullover presumably for Henry Allward. In the corner a cake stand, symbol of a lost age, offered the only bare surfaces in the room, causing Molloy to suppose that it was used.

Such space as existed was clean and polished. The chairs and all three seats of the sofa sported immaculately- ironed antimacassars. The television was small and under it was curled a ginger cat which seemed unperturbed by the sudden invasion. A second such animal wandered in, surveyed the scene and wandered out.

Molloy noticed a pile of albums neatly stacked under the coffee table and, with a glance at Mrs Allward for permission, pulled one out and began to flick through the photos while trying also to concentrate on what was going on in the conversation between Frobisher and Jess's parents. The first album contained an assortment of family photographs taken at christenings and weddings, all in colour. The second was similar but from further back in time and the portraits were all in black and white. The third consisted largely of holiday snaps, many sun-ruined and poorly focussed, taken, Molloy guessed, with an instamatic. He had reached the fifth before he found what he wanted, an album devoted entirely to Jess, neatly ordered from her earliest days. The sixth continued the story, ending with her wedding, and he guessed the next would be devoted to the grandchildren.

Jess as a baby, Jess in a high chair, Jess crawling, Jess toddling, Jess walking, running in some race, swimming, dancing in ballet classes, acting in nativity plays, on a Sunday school outing, in the school play, on school trips, singing in a church choir, at a funfair, receiving confirmation, walking up the aisle and at every stage in between. A thought was beginning to occur to him but before he could catch it and explore it his concentration switched to Frobisher who had just asked, gently, if they remembered Fred.

Both policemen noticed the shadow of disapproval which crossed the faces of Jess's parents.

"Yes. We lived in Surrey at the time. He was living in the same village with his mother. He had been in the church, I think, but had left for some reason or other so he wasn't doing much." There was no doubt now of the censorious tone and Frobisher wondered if Mrs Allward was more disapproving of Fred's renouncing his vocation than of his introducing her daughter to dance.

"He was a nice chap," said Mr. Allward pacifically. "Started dancing lessons at the church hall. Apparently he'd been some sort of amateur champion. Our Jess went along because there wasn't much to do in Christmas Pie and she got hooked straight away."

"She'd done so well at A-level as well," lamented Mrs Allward. "Three As and in those days that was quite something. They didn't give those sorts of marks out like confetti then."

"Could have gone to Oxford," agreed her husband.

"Instead she decided to train as a dancer." Mrs Allward shook her head as if still unable to fathom such a choice. "Still, it all turned out right in the end."

"One of her friends says she was unhappy about this time?"

There was a hesitation so fractional it might not have occurred but Molloy knew it had just as Frobisher knew that the Allwards had been about to catch each other's eye and had thought better of it.

"Both her granddads died. Within a month of each other it was."

So that explained the legacy, thought Frobisher. Probably there were rows in the Allward household about the use to which she intended to put it, rows they didn't want to talk about now, rows that had made Jess unhappy. He hated himself for pressing the point but knew he must.

"You tried to persuade her not to give it all up for dancing?"

"Just for a while," Mr Allward sighed. "We said get your degree first. Dance in your spare time, then if ever anything goes wrong you've got something to fall back on. But she wouldn't listen and when we asked Fred to help he just said it was up to her."

"At least she did make a success of it," conceded his wife. "But it always worried us that she had nothing at the back of her. Even when she married she chose a pauper."

"But he's been a good dad," put in Henry Allward quietly. His voice caught suddenly and he began to fumble in his pocket. His wife leant forward with a box of tissues, then took one herself. Frobisher looked tactfully away.

At least it gave him an entry into asking about the children, Sarah Jessica Anne and David Henry Samuel. They were surprisingly traditional names for a showbiz star, Molloy had remarked on the way down in the car. Frobisher had smiled and asked if Molloy was expecting them to be called River and Cruz.

They were going to live with their father and stepmother, the Allwards told him. They thought it a good idea.

"We're too old now," observed Mrs Allward. "They'll still visit though. David promised us that."

"Your grandson?"

"No. I mean big David, his father. He said we mustn't worry about anything." She was crying again.

Frobisher looked at Molloy and the sergeant took over the next stage.

No, they shook their heads adamantly, Jess had no enemies. She wasn't the type. No, they knew of no occasion on which she had seriously fallen out with anybody. A few schoolgirl tiffs obviously, perhaps a bit of jealousy from other dancers occasionally but nothing dramatic. The divorce had been quite amicable. A few heartbroken boyfriends along the way but that was just life, wasn't it?

No, they said in answer to the next question, no current boyfriend. Nobody ditched and pining. Molloy, looking from one to the other, caught sight of the albums again and something tugged at his mind but eluded him before he could identify it.

"She used to talk about some Indian chap a lot," said Mr Allward.

"Rashid Ahmed?"

"That's the one."

Molloy saw no point in observing that Ahmed was born in Burnley to Pakistani parents.

"Was she in love with him?"

"Perhaps, but he was married and that wasn't our Jess's way."

"A friend suggests she may have just wanted to know him a bit better."

"Perhaps," repeated Mr Allward unhelpfully.

The children could throw no further light. Sarah, a tall redhead, sobbed through the entire interview while her grandmother held her close and her older brother, who looked very much like his mother, sat looking down at his twisting hands. No, there were no regular male visitors now. About a year ago a man called Graeme had been quite often on the scene but he disappeared. Before that there had been a Mike. Their mother told them both had since married. No, Jess had not argued with anybody that they knew of. Yes, they could assemble a list of her friends and close acquaintances. When was that required by?

"Grim," muttered Frobisher as they left. Glancing back he saw through the window Henry and Anne Allward embracing each other simultaneously with their grandchildren, a group hug of despair and loss.

Molloy murmured an expletive.

"We'll get him," said Frobisher in a hard voice.

"They seemed to think she could be in love with Rashid."

"Let's go over his movements again and check out his religion. If he's a practising Muslim the last thing he would need is that sort of scandal."

"Lapsed Catholic", reported Molloy a few hours later. "And his wife is from Wales, born Bronwen Morgan- Hughes. Shall I find out if she is Church or Chapel?"

Frobisher grinned reluctantly. "And I suppose his movements are all accounted for and witnessed by dozens?"

"By two dozen and rising."

"Let's go over all the movements we know about again. On Friday we'll re-enact the whole thing so make sure the room can be unsealed by then."

"Forensics are still at it but anything we find could have got there innocently. A fibre carried from one room to another on the shoe of somebody from wardrobe or make-up or hair. Even DNA on the body. In luvvie land they all embrace each other all the time. Only the strangulation itself could reveal anything significant and it hasn't. The flapper band shows traces of at least ten different DNAs and that's just what is separable and identifiable."

"Any more news of the flapper band?

"None. Unrecognised by wardrobe but clearly it has been about for a long time. They think it was in amongst a rather neglected case of spare bits and pieces. Someone has a vague recollection that it was designed for a Charleston which never happened."

"It matches Jess's dress."

"She was dancing the American Smooth."

"We had better DNA the whole box of these spare bits and pieces. Whoever took the flapper band may have rummaged a bit."

"Shouldn't we wait to see what comes up on the band itself? It may all be old hat. If there's nothing on the band there won't be anything on the rest of the stuff."

"I suppose that has to be right. What about the three bits of paper? The ones the judges got saying 'Jess'?"

"Nothing. Clean."

"The lighting computer?"

"Umpteen. We've taken samples from everyone but so what? Anybody could touch it innocently and whoever did it would have taken care not to leave dabs. In fact all anyone has to do in this inquiry is to say 'yes, I did touch that band stroke cable stroke door stroke switch' and nobody could say that means anything. People mill around all the time, brushing things, grabbing things, falling over things, nudging each other into things. I suppose if it was some obscure cable up in the rafters........"

"Is it being so cheerful as keeps you going?"

"My grandmother used to say that!" exclaimed Molloy delightedly. "I haven't heard it for years."

"Thanks. I would wager this re-enactment won't turn up much either. Meanwhile let's look a bit more closely at Cobb Grainger. It may not be a criminal offence to be disliked but he appears to have been cast as the pantomime baddie."

"Not a nice man," the party chief whip told them. Frobisher felt he was holding back a more robust form of expressing the sentiment.

"In what way?"

"He likes Cobb Grainger a bit too much."

"Is that unusual around here?"

The chief whip smiled wryly but Molloy could see that he was annoyed.

"Perhaps more unusual than the public or media realise. True, Westminster has no shortage of egotists but most people come here in order to make the country or the world a bit of a better place. They have causes or principles. They fight hand, tooth and nail for constituents. Some matters are so big that they will resign high office rather than go along with whatever it is that's so offended them. Cobb's cause is Cobb."

"But if he is so ambitious what is he doing in a minority party?"

"Oh, he doesn't want *responsibility*. Good heavens, no! That might mean being unpopular or working on endless piles of paper well into the night. He wouldn't want even to lead this party. He just spouts popular views, espouses popular policies regardless of any practical considerations, plonks his rear end on any television sofa that's offered, always has an excuse not to serve on committees and leaves the real grind to his constituency secretary."

Frobisher smiled. "Charming. Any serious enemies?"

"No. Most people give him a wide berth but there's no real nastiness that I know of."

"Close friends?"

"Not really. Not here. I can't speak for his life away from this place."

"Ever hear him talk about somebody called Jess Allward?"

"The murdered woman? No. Most of his colleagues didn't approve of his doing the programme so he didn't talk a lot about it."

"Have you met his wife and children?"

"Yes. Jane's a lovely woman. Heaven knows what she sees in Cobb. I was expecting a trophy wife but she's plain and homely and very kind. Probably does wonders for him in the constituency. I haven't seen the kids much lately because they're grown up with their own families and don't often come to party political dos. I used to see quite a lot of the boy when he helped out at elections in his teens. Alastair, I think he's called."

"Is he a bully? Cobb, I mean."

"Odd that you ask that. I've never had any complaints here and his staff seem to last but years ago, when he was first elected, I got talking to some fellow who had known him and said he was someone to avoid at school."

A bell began clanging, filling the room with din.

"Sorry, division," said the chief whip and disappeared at speed.

On their way out they passed Grainger as he was moving quickly across the central lobby on his way to the vote. He greeted them in passing and Frobisher could see he was startled and, noted Molloy thoughtfully, perhaps worried.

"I'm not sure I know why but I think we should track down some of his school chums." Frobisher was staring after his retreating back but Grainger passed from view without turning round.

"If everyone who was a bully at school turned into a murderer you and I wouldn't be able to keep up with the corpses," observed Molloy. "But I've got the same instinct, sir."

Twenty four hours later he was more sceptical. Three classmates emphatically denied that Cobb Grainger had bullied anybody. One vaguely recalled trouble at prep school. Nobody liked Grainger but as Frobisher had already pointed out being disliked was not a criminal offence.

"We had better start looking at Em," decided Frobisher. "She was the only one on the corridor after the others had reached the stage. Not that it means anything. We don't know that Jess was still alive then. Arguably we should have looked at Em first given that there is nothing which points at Grainger."

"Most things seem to point away from any of the celebs. We need someone who could move around freely and at odd hours to fiddle the blackout and someone who had access to the judges' papers. I think we should be focussing on the crew and stagehands."

"None of whom were on the dressing room corridor during the vital fifteen minutes. Apart from the singers, presenters, judges and dancers only hair, make-up and wardrobe were wandering about there."

"Is that all?" replied Molloy so gloomily that his superior gave a loud guffaw.

"Cheer up! We can eliminate the singers because they were there together and nobody left. Likewise the judges. The presenter, Venetia Whatshername, was alternately on the phone or calling out to her co-presenter in the next room. He testifies that neither left before it was time to head for the stage."

"Suppose Jess was genuinely delayed? Then the murder could have happened *after* seven thirty. After they had all gone to the stage. Between then and when Helen Brown found her. For that matter, Helen might have walked in on the very act. We're all assuming the door caused her amnesia but may be it was shock."

"If Helen had witnessed murder she wouldn't be alive now."

"But maybe she fled and he had to finish off Jess and then he went after her but when he heard the studio door fly open he knew he'd lost her and must get away himself."

"If we believe that really is possible then we should put a guard over young Helen. Where is she?"

"Gone home to Mum and Dad. But it isn't very likely to have happened that way, is it, sir?"

"No. If the murderer was surprised and couldn't catch Helen then it is a cast iron certainty that he would have fled. He couldn't have known that Helen was about to be concussed and would have assumed he was to be denounced. There is no record of anyone not being where he should have been once the door was opened. However, your opening premise is pretty sound, Brendan. We have been assuming Jess was dead by half past seven but we don't know that. All we know is she didn't turn up for stage call. If she was killed after the others had gone then we can eliminate everyone but Em, which brings me back to where I came in. We must concentrate on her. But after the re-enactment."

For the re-enactment the detectives had hijacked the time normally spent recording the programme. Their instructions were, he thought, simple: all the participants were to wear what they had been wearing the previous week and to carry out the routine they had adopted then at exactly the same time. The hair and make-up artists were to visit in the same order, to construct the same styles and everybody must try to hold the same conversations, make the same phone calls and carry out the same casual errands. Once they had reached the stage where Jess's body was discovered the scenario would stop and they could be re-dressed and coiffed for the genuine recording which would indeed now be much later. Helen was still too ill to take part so a runner was filling in and, Frobisher suspected, enjoying the drama.

Soon Frobisher found there was nothing simple about it at all.

The dresses were said to be a problem. Forensics still had most of them but two had been returned and were now half way to the United States where the costumes were sold. One of the hairpieces required some special equipment which the stylist had borrowed and she did not know if she could get an equivalent in the time available. The producer made some comments about the logistics of keeping the audience out until the re-enactment was over. The head of programming was close to apoplexy as the first half of the show would now start long after the time normally allocated to the second half.

"Tell them to calm down," snapped Frobisher in exasperation. "The hairpiece need not be exact and those dresses don't matter because we had already eliminated the wearers, which is why Forensics returned them in the first place. They were for a couple of the professional dancers who had already been voted off and were back for the group dance. They were together in a group dressing room, just like the singers. Those two didn't so much as go to the lavatory in the relevant time frame.

"As for rescheduling, they must just get on with it. It is vital we do this within exactly the same time frame and they can bring the audience in when it's over because there will be plenty of time while they all get into this week's costumes and have their hair and makeup done to match. "

"What about the Honeycats? They've gone to New Zealand." The celebrity booker sounded close to panic.

"Where they are welcome to stay. They don't come into this, dammit. They were together and on a completely different floor. We must try to keep things simple."

"Simple!" roared Trevor with an oath not normally associated with family television. "There's nothing simple about messing up a record-as-live show this way."

Only Ahmed seemed unfazed.

"I want everyone to do just what they were doing from about six fifty. We will have a WPC to play the role of Jess," Frobisher told him and he nodded serenely.

Yet, recalled Molloy, he had cursed aloud when trying to get someone to open the door while the lights were out. Was his calm now real or enforced?

"What will you and DS Molloy be doing?" inquired Anton.

"Floating between the various scenes," replied Frobisher, noting that Caesar alone had asked.

"I'll start in Jess's dressing room," he told Molloy. "You take Ru's and we'll test out his proposition that the walls being paper thin he would have heard anybody come in. I'll talk to WPC Leroy and then you tell me what you hear."

"OK."

At ten minutes before seven o'clock, he was wondering how anybody could hear anything at all. Ru's observation that there was "coming and going" on the corridor was an understatement. Doors opened and shut, people called casual greetings, Angela from hair and make-up and Claire from wardrobe compared progress. Jayne from hair only conscientiously dropped a box of rollers and a can of spray right outside Jess's door as she had done by accident the previous week.

Frobisher immediately opened the door. "Did Jess look out to see what had happened?"

"Yes. She asked if I was all right. Then Ru appeared and helped me pick it all up," she added as the dancer materialised, on cue, from the next room.

At seven exactly WPC Leroy walked along the corridor to hair, past four other dressing rooms. Frobisher, walking with her, noted the order: Em's room was next to Ru's, then came the singers' and the last this side of hair was Matt's.

The room set aside for hairdressing was on the opposite side of the corridor, facing Cobb's room. Frobisher walked in and immediately found himself inhaling hairspray. In between coughs he greeted Ru and Anton.

"I'm surprised you don't all get lung disease."

Ru grinned. "You are taking us off script."

WPC Leroy consulted the papers in her hand. "Hi, all! Thanks for helping Jayne, Ru. My nails were still wet."

The policewoman sat down in a chair marked with a piece of white tape.

"No, she didn't face the mirror, immediately," said Anton. "She swivelled round and talked to us."

Not for the first time Frobisher noted the dancer's keen powers of observation and decided to question him again. He might prove a useful witness if he had such recall.

Ru's memory was less certain. "Sorry, we must have talked at this point but I can't remember what about," he confessed as he walked side by side with the WPC back to their dressing rooms.

Arriving at the door, where he had informed them he and Jess had stood chatting, his brow cleared and he recollected that they had discussed the edit of Jess's music.

"Production had been awkward about a pause she wanted inserted. Said it was adding to the piece and therefore in breach of copyright. Jess was cursing them all for a bunch of jobsworths."

Frobisher looked round and saw an empty corridor.

"Nobody passed you?"

At that moment Em put her head round the door of her room and called out "Anyone seen Jayne?"

Ru called back: "No, we've just come from hair and she wasn't about so she must be still doing the rounds."

Em retreated into her room.

"No," said Ru. "Nobody was on the corridor at this point. Em saw us standing here but she would have been the only one."

Could she have been checking if the coast was clear? Had she chosen that moment to slip along to Jess's room and been thwarted?

"Is the corridor usually so quiet?"

"No." Ru shook his head. "Jess, Anton and I were the last in hair. Jayne must have been about somewhere going in and out of dressing rooms. The dressers were probably fussing round the dancers in the group number further along because they were first on. Angela would have been checking their make-up. So if you are asking if someone could have relied on moving about unobserved the answer is that this *could* have been a good moment but the risk would have been huge. There is simply no set pattern of movement."

"Thanks." Frobisher thought that what the young man lacked in memory was compensated by his intelligence.

The detective glanced at his watch which showed fifteen min- utes past the hour- the last time anyone claimed to have seen Jess alive. He sat with WPC Leroy in the late dancer's dressing room and was wondering for what he was now waiting when the room was filled with a loud "weewo, weewoo, weewo" in an ascending octave and then immediately again in a descending one. The sound died away and was at once repeated.

In the short silence which followed he heard Ru saying to Molloy in an agonised tone "......believe it. Oh, dear God........" before the scales began again.

Frobisher jumped up and almost cannoned into Molloy outside the door as both detectives had the same idea.

"Did you hear me open my door?" each demanded simultaneously.

Frobisher shook his head. "No and I didn't hear what Ru said to you while the singer was in full flight. Anybody could have come and gone unheard and Jess could have uttered any sound bar a full scream and not been heard either."

Ru joined them in the corridor. "Sorry, I don't know how I for- got the singers."

"Never mind, this alone may have made the whole reconstruc- tion worthwhile. Do they always do it at the same time?"

"Approximately, yes. They do it just before stage call which is a bit ahead of ours because they have to be in their places with the band by the time we enter."

Frobisher glanced at his watch. 7.19pm.

"I think we may have just narrowed the time of death. Now the question is where everybody was *now*. Let's check every room and see who was with whom where. Later we can ask everyone if they can remember what they were doing when the singers began practising scales, but not now. For now, just look - don't get in the way of the reconstruction."

At this moment, thought Frobisher, someone was sitting in a dressing room recalling how he or she had just returned from committing a murder.

CHAPTER FOUR

IN WHICH THE ASSISTANT COMMISSIONER IS DISSATISFIED
AND OUR DETECTIVES STUCK

The rest of the reconstruction yielded a great deal of confusion but little enlightenment. From the moment the lights went out the actors in the drama were sunk in muddle and then giggling. Nobody could get in the same place as before.

"Can't see a thing," Fred stated the blindingly obvious to explain why Em did not manage to be next to Tatum nor to locate the door handle on this occasion. Cobb was not the first person everyone saw when the lights suddenly came back on as the door flew open, because lights and doors failed to synchronise and all that was illuminated was a scene which bore little resemblance to the original.

"Never mind," soothed Molloy. "It hasn't been a waste of time."

And, for the discovery of the singing alone, it hadn't, commented Frobisher as he and Molloy made an unerring path to the Pig and Pen.

"It happens all the time," he said when Molloy wondered how everybody had managed to forget anything so intrusively loud. "The first law of detective work. What is utterly familiar you do not notice. Poor old Ru! He couldn't believe he had told us the walls were paper thin but then forgot that racket."

"Nevertheless apart from possibly narrowing down the time of the murder, I'm not sure we are any further forward." Molloy sounded almost morose.

"It also confirms that the murder was done by somebody from the show and somebody on that corridor which is what we've been assuming but for which we have not much proof. Whoever did it knew there was a moment when any sound would be drowned out and chose that moment to strike. At least that is now the strongest possible likelihood."

"It would still have been a hell of a risk, sir. That corridor is a beehive of activity. What if he – or I suppose she – had come out of the room just as someone was passing? How many seconds elapse with that corridor empty?"

"Sometimes a few as we saw tonight, when we asked Ru if it was usually that quiet. But I agree nobody could have relied on that. Whoever took that risk was desperate. The only other option must be that it was spontaneous and not premeditated but then where did the flapper band come from?"

"Or the motive? Where did that come from?"

"Or, as you say, the motive. Somewhere there is something between a member of our cast and Jess that nobody else knew about."

"So how do we find it? What next?"

"Next, Brendan, we grind. And grind. We look at all the transcripts from the tapes of all the dancers in training. We go back over all the statements and all the interview records. We investigate private lives. We live in that corridor every Friday night."

The Assistant Commissioner looked less than impressed when Frobisher repeated this intention the following morning.

"Peter, have you *seen* the press?"

He had scarcely been able to avoid it, reflected Frobisher bitterly. The terrible punning headlines "Deadly Toes", "Death Dance"; the predictable cry after a mere two days "Did police miss vital clues?" and, after three, "The Trail goes cold". Meanwhile the photographs of Jess stared at him from the front pages and of her family from the inside pages. Two days were given up to speculating what the reconstruction might reveal while reporters clamoured to know who would play the role of Jess. Then Helen became news and her parents complained bitterly about the press pack at the gates, first to the local force and then to the Yard.

"Yes, sir, and I have no doubt it will get worse. They have already found out whose dressing room is next to whose and Ru has his phone on answer all the time."

"Who is this Lisa Verrelli they are all writing about today?"

"The pro who has taken over from Jess and is dancing with Matt. She was one of the pros who were eliminated earlier in the competition. Bruce and Belle went out last night."

An expression of pain crossed the AC's forehead. "Never heard of any of them but I gather this is a popular programme?"

Frobisher repressed a grin. He had often thought the AC would fulfil wonderfully the role of an out of touch judge listening, baffled, to a witness talking street culture. He also knew the AC's brain was sharper than any judge's.

"A flagship programme, sir. Biggest thing FBC has in the autumn. Gets around twelve million viewers."

"Well, never mind that. What do I tell the press?"

"That the investigation is making progress."

The AC looked at him without speaking.

"Tell them we are analysing seven weeks of daily training for twelve dancers. Then all they will want to know is how many extra personnel we have drafted in, how many sheets of paper they will be dealing with and what the resource implications are."

"Hmm. You should have been a politician. Where's Molloy?"

"At home, sir. His wife is about to give birth any moment."

"Literally?"

"In the next few weeks. There are two other children under five."

The AC grimaced. His own arrangements had been more orderly, with seven years between his firstborn and the next. When the next turned out to be twins he spent more time in the office.

More time in the office was what Frobisher knew he needed now but it was Saturday and he had promised his elder son that he would take him to a football match. Barbara had reminded him when he left the house before eight o'clock that day, with a note of warning in her voice.

"It *is* a murder enquiry, love ," he protested when he arrived home with five minutes to spare.

"And it *is* your son," she retorted. "Jonathan. Remember him?"

Frobisher ignored the challenge. "What are you doing this afternoon?"

"Zoe needs a new skirt. We're going to Oxford Street."

He doubted if his daughter needed anything new in the wardrobe department unless it was another wardrobe itself to house her vast collection of clothes. She was fifteen, rebellious, lazy at school and moody at home. He thought her spoiled while Barbara thought her neglected. If he asked his wife whether Zoe would be required to finish her homework before the proposed shopping expedition, there would be a row and he did not want an atmosphere before taking Jonathan to the Spurs match.

His son was already by the front door, clad in the blue and white which were the club's home colours. Frobisher looked at his watch with a sinking feeling, mentally calculating the time it would take to reach White Hart Lane but when the door shut behind them Jonathan looked at his father with a grin.

"I'd rather just have a burger."

"Mum will want to hear about the match."

"No. When you were late and she was getting worried, I told her I was going off football."

"What did she say?"

" 'Your father will be pleased.'"

Frobisher grimaced. "OK, but you can't spend every Saturday in McDonald's. What else would you like to do?"

"Movies?"

"How about swimming?"

"All Zoe does is shop till she drops. Why do I have to do the healthy stuff?"

"Zoe does a lot of sport at school. You don't."

"So what, Dad? She likes it. I don't. She likes acting too but I don't and I like physics but she doesn't. Then I like debating but she doesn't........"

"OK, I get it. Which movie?"

"The King's Speech."

Frobisher slowed his steps and stared at his son.

"There's a James Bond........"

"And probably a Harry Potter too but I want to see The King's Speech."

"Right. George the Fifth it is."

"George the *Sixth*," corrected Jonathan gently. Suddenly he grinned. "Surely you remember him?"

Frobisher laughed. "Cheek! But your grandparents will, of course."

"Granny does. She told me about the day he died and how everybody was upset and the Queen was up a tree."

"Perhaps not quite up a tree but................"

"Dad, that was a joke."

Frobisher smiled absently, trying to remember what had interested him at fourteen. Whatever it had been it was not the speech impediment of a long dead monarch. But it wasn't football either. Girls? No, he thought them irksome then, especially as he had two older sisters who were interminably bossy. Pop music? Films? What *had* he liked? Disconcertingly he searched his memory in vain. All he could recollect was hanging out with his mates but what did they actually *do*?

"I used to ask you that all the time," said his mother when he spoke to her on the telephone the next day. "Your stock reply was 'nothing'. Jonathan is rather more serious as you and Barbara must surely realise by now. He will probably turn out to be a bit of a boffin."

"As long as he doesn't become a nerd," was Frobisher's observation to his wife.

"As long as he's happy he can be what he likes," came the retort and, as was so often the case with Barbara's pronouncements, he could not gainsay it.

"He talked a lot about the film," Barbara went on. "While you were working and Zoe was getting ready to go out he was engaging me in a conversation about overcoming limitations. He said what a terrible handicap a stammer would be if you had to make speeches. Then he went on to Beethoven composing while deaf and Milton writing descriptive verse and Evelyn Glennie......"

"Who?"

"The percussionist. Deaf as a post. Then he moved to Stephen Hawking."

"What does he know about Milton? I didn't think they did that sort of stuff at that age these days."

"Try looking in his room. You'll find Paradise Lost."

Later, as he was trying to sleep, she spoke into the darkness. "We may not be able to leave him where he is. He's talking about learning Latin, Greek and Hebrew."

"What?"

"To 'see if the Bible is true'."

"Leave it, for pity's sake. It could be just a phase and it looks as if the school is doing more than OK by him. Whoever does Hebrew nowadays?"

"Clever people. Historians, Theologians, Linguists."

He remembered Jess's mother sniffing that A grades were showered about like confetti in the modern education system and realised that, without consciously recognising it, he had been making the same assumption. Jonathan's excellent marks had always been a source of quiet satisfaction rather than growing excitement. He was not at all sure that he was excited now. Supposing Jonathan grew to look on the rest of the family as dullards?

When he confided the thought to Barbara he felt the bed shake with her laughter. "Well, there will always be Zoe."

As if on cue, their daughter came out of her bedroom, switched on the landing lights, went downstairs with a heavy tread, opened and closed the fridge loudly and stomped back up the stairs without sparing anybody who might be trying to sleep.

As his wife drifted into slumber Frobisher stared up at the pattern the street lamp was making on the ceiling and pondered that it might be more reassuring if his son would, for a couple more years anyway, act in the same thoughtless fashion.

"You're scared," his thoughts accused him. "Scared that your own kid might be about to take you right outside your nice, cosy comfort zone."

As the alarm clock announced another Monday morning he thought it would be a relief to get back to murder.

"Good weekend?" asked Molloy cheerfully. "Any inspirations?"

"Sort of and no. You?"

"Not bad. Alice can't do much now but her parents took us out to lunch. Alas, no inspiration. The report is in from Forensics. I spoke to them just now and they confirm what we already guessed. DNA, dabs, fibres and dirt everywhere. Lawrence has taken another look but says he was thorough the first time and has nothing to add. She was strangled with the flapper band which was found round her neck. The murderer was strong and in his words "expert" and there was no sign that she put up a fight against what was almost instant death. Nothing under fingernails, no unexpected position of the body. She wasn't doped so whoever did it knew exactly what he was doing. Contents of stomach the curry they all had from the FBC canteen. In short, nothing new under the sun and the Allwards are asking when we will release the body."

"Anything from the training tapes?"

"Transcripts making good progress. The AC has given us all the extra help we need. I looked at three tapes over the weekend, all of Matt and Jess, but couldn't see anything, not that I really know what I'm looking for anyway. I have interviews today set up with Matt and Beautella at their homes and with Fred for this evening. Helen Brown is expected to be back at work by Friday's show."

"Good work," acknowledged Frobisher, wishing his own weekend had been as productive. "We need to focus on motive which is like a needle in a haystack but somebody had one so strong and so pressing that he took an almighty risk. If I were planning a murder

I wouldn't choose the next best thing to a public thoroughfare to do it in."

"Definitely a 'he'? And definitely planned?"

"Probably both. No sound of a row and nobody saw the flapper band before the murder. If it had been spontaneous there would surely have been an argument and the killer would have picked up the first handy thing lying about. There were tights, for example. But it looks as if he took the band with him deliberately. Then don't forget the lights. If that was connected to the murder then it was certainly planned. And, yes, unless you can find me a seriously strong woman then it was a man. However, if you take Lawrence's evidence literally we may well be looking for a trained killer. Expert. That was what he said and I suppose in the twenty first century that could be a woman. Or a woman could have attacked Jess and broken her windpipe immediately by accident. Or a weak man. But I don't think any of it was an accident."

"So, for now, we look for a strong man. That rules out Fred. He's got a touch of arthritis in his hands."

"Yet he still lifts weights like Em? She's got to be eleven stone at least. And I'm sure he was lying to me on one occasion. No, we don't rule out Fred. We don't rule out anyone. We need to get back to that corridor and start seeing how the timings would work if the murder was committed during the scales practice. If it was Cobb he had to walk in front of hair where the door is always open, past Matt's dressing room and then Ru's, do the deed and walk the same journey in reverse. Matt would have had a shorter journey and did not have to pass hair and would have had more reason than most to visit Jess, being her partner in the dance. If he had been spotted he could have said she was alive when he left. Ru was nearest of all and I suppose it is possible that he omitted telling us about the singing deliberately and his chagrin was all an act. Also he would have heard hair, make-up and wardrobe coming and going and would know when it was safe to attack without one of them suddenly wandering in."

"So the further away we get from Jess's room the more prob-
lematic it would have been for the murderer. On the other side of
it there is not much beyond stores and things of that sort. We must
however allow that a murderer could have concealed himself there,
come out, killed and then hidden again until they had all gone up
to the stage. That would mean it needn't be those with dressing
rooms on that floor at all."

Frobisher looked at his sergeant balefully. "You aren't by any
chance auditioning for the role of Job's comforter, are you? Such
a man would have needed a pretty good nerve. If Jess was found
before stage call then the alarm would have been raised and his
presence would most certainly have been discovered as soon as our
chaps arrived if not before. If he wasn't meant to be there he would
be the number one suspect."

"OK, let's say he hid, killed and moved off. But nobody gave
him a second glance. It's a bit like Ru and the singers. He forgot
them because he took their singing as given and nothing unusual.
So let's say the murderer was so often about that seeing him was
nothing out of the ordinary so they have all forgotten."

"Which was what the reconstruction was supposed to test."

"But the singers sang during the reconstruction which is why Ru
suddenly remembered them but the murderer didn't walk during
the reconstruction so no recall was prompted."

Frobisher looked mutinous. "You realise you have just enlarged
the cast of suspects by dozens at the very least?"

"I think, sir, that all we have to do is to go back and ask them
all again who they often see on the corridor. We needn't confine
their observations to the night of the murder, just ask who would
normally be about. But meanwhile we are due at Beautella's flat in
an hour."

The flat turned out to be a small, one –bedroom apartment in
a new block but what Beautella lacked in space she had made up in
taste. The tiny rooms had cream walls, beige carpets and wooden
venetian blinds. The bathroom was brightened with red accesso-
ries giving a warmth to the gleaming white of the suite. The rug

on its floor was of rag in red and white. The kitchen boasted half-size washing machine, tumble dryer and dishwasher and its only extravagance was a huge Kenwood mixer which seemed to take up most of the limited working surface. It was the home of somebody on a strict budget who was not defeated by necessity.

Three people seemed to fill the sitting room. The detectives took the two armchairs, which they suspected were worn and threadbare beneath the throws which covered them, while Beautella insisted on sitting on a floor cushion. She looked up at them expectantly.

"How's the show going?" Frobisher held the mug of coffee she had produced and realised he had nowhere to set it down.

His hostess read his thoughts. "You can rest it on the floor. It's OK. Cobb could actually win it."

"I thought you were flying on Friday?"

"This Friday. You guys were everywhere last week and we couldn't get the equipment in."

"I'm told you don't like the idea."

"You're told wrong," the tone was unexpectedly sharp. "It's true I have height phobia but it's all ultra - safe and I won't be going at all high. I think it's a great idea and will certainly get us through next week."

Molloy knew he was listening to nonsense. An amateur daring to fly would take them through to the next round possibly but nobody would see anything remarkable about a professional a few feet up in the air. She was flying for no better reason than that Grainger was insisting but why should she let him? The professional must surely always have the final say?

"Are you afraid of him?" Frobisher had obviously been making the same analysis.

She was ready for that. "No. He takes too many risks and I get annoyed but that's all."

"And if you don't fly he'll do something unexpected?"

Beautella kept her cool. "I want to fly. I've told you it's a great idea."

"That's not what other dancers have told us." Molloy knew his own tone had become sharp.

"Perhaps they're just jealous. Cobb thought of it first."

"What sort of a man is Grainger?"

Frobisher, expecting to find himself up against the same blank wall as he had throughout was surprised by the answer.

"Ghastly."

"In what way?"

She hesitated. "How confidential is this conversation?"

"Unless it turns out to be relevant to the murder, it is wholly between the three people in this room."

"And some note transcriber and your boss among others".

She isn't stupid, thought Molloy. Childlike, perhaps, stubborn certainly but a very long way from stupid. Frobisher's tone was patient.

"Miss LaReine, we are talking to everyone. We are looking at all the training tapes, we have more DNA than I have ever seen, we have notes of the reconstruction, notes of the corridor layout, notes of the electrical systems, notes of the cause of death, notes, in short, of everything and the very last thing my superior wants is to read them all. It is our job to determine what is relevant and that is all anybody else will see. Anyway, a woman has died and you have a duty to be frank - an inescapable duty, Miss LaReine."

"You have already repeated to me what other dancers are supposed to have told you about my being scared of Cobb. You will challenge Cobb and if he thinks I have been blabbing to you he will........."

Beautella stopped suddenly.

"Quite." This time the detective inspector's tone was less patient. "You have just as good as told us that you are afraid of him. Why?"

"As I said he takes the most awful risks but, of course, he won't let anything go wrong because he wants us to win and he does get away with it. However he is not a professional and one day he will simply make a misjudgement and if I'm afraid it is because I never know when that day will come."

"But why not just rehearse all the moves?"

"We do. It's just that he always changes the routine. He's got a good ear and anything he improvises fits the music perfectly so only I know it wasn't meant to happen like that. At first he would just make daft excuses like 'I just couldn't resist it' or 'I just got carried away' or 'it seemed too good an inspiration to resist.' Now he doesn't even do that. He winks and thinks it all a huge joke."

"How does he get on with the other dancers?"

"I can't say I've really noticed. I keep away from him. Some of the others have worked out what is going on and don't like him much but I don't think there has been a quarrel or anything like that."

"How did he get on with Jess?"

"She couldn't stand him. She didn't like the way he treated me and as she was older than me she felt protective. But she didn't interfere. She was too professional for that."

"Did Jess have a problem with anybody else?"

Predictably the dancer shook her head, forbearing to add that she had told them that in the previous interview.

As they left, Molloy commented that they had learned little, to which Frobisher replied that they had learned nothing.

"We are going to need a large slice of luck with this one," he added as he pressed the button which opened the door of the block to the street.

From a distance of a yard flashbulbs exploded and a babble of voices broke out.

"Have you been interviewing Beautella?"

"Do you have a suspect?"

"Can you tell us if there is any progress?"

"When can we expect an arrest?"

The police driver was clearing a path but as they got into the car cameras were pushed against the windows.

"They don't make things any easier," sighed Frobisher. "You know, Molloy, I am beginning to think this is one of those cases where if the murderer never strikes again the trail will go cold."

"I would like to think there was any trail at all, sir. Just a faint indentation on the path would help. Usually we complain that we haven't enough evidence but this time we have a cast of what feels like thousands who could have done it and good enough reason for any of them to have been anywhere at almost any time. Everyone seems to have trampled the crime scene before if not after the event and I've been meaning to tell you that I found out something else over the weekend."

Frobisher looked unenthusiastic. "Do I want to hear?"

"No, sir. It seems that the dressing rooms were not fixed. The celebrities had the same throughout but the professionals began by sharing and then as celebs were eliminated they took over from them and shared less. It was done on seniority according to who had been on the show the longest so Fred, Jess, Beautella and Anton had first shout but Anton went out early. Beautella should have had Ru's room but she didn't want to be so close to Grainger so she gave way to him and took one much further away when it became vacant."

Frobisher began calculating aloud. "We began with twelve couples and by the week of the murder we were down to six. That means six celebs had already been eliminated leaving room for the six professionals still in the race to have their own rooms. Fred, Jess, Beautella and Anton had priority but Anton went out himself. Three of them moved in then the other three week by week."

"Translate it into weeks, sir. On week one all professionals shared. Jess moved in on week two, Fred on week three, then Anton on week four but only for that week because he went out. Beautella should have moved in on week five but instead Ru did. So Ru and Jess were next door to each other for two weeks, including the week of the murder."

"And?"

"He hadn't that much time to get used to the singers. It's not as though he had heard them for six weeks but yet he took that huge noise so much for granted that he didn't even remember it?"

"Clutching at straws," grumbled Frobisher. "All I can see coming out of this is a lot more confusion for forensics, if that's possible."

"I found something else out too, sir."

"Something more helpful?"

Molloy shook his head. "Apparently the programme bosses don't allow anyone from outside backstage until after the show but make the very occasional exception. They made one that week but forgot to tell us. Rashid Ahmed's wife."

"Well, there's half a motive in her case but something tells me there is an anti-climax coming?"

"Yes. She's in a wheelchair following an operation. Or she was that week. She couldn't have done it. She stayed behind the scenes but only upstairs before the show and went to the bar with Ahmed himself afterwards. In between times she just sat in the audience. She couldn't have got downstairs."

"You've checked?"

"I will check," parried Molloy. "There hasn't been enough time."

"Good. Check lifts. Then time the journey from the audience to Jess's room and back and see if it could have happened while the lights were out."

"Sir, if Jess had been delayed she would have been running to the stage by then, not sitting in her dressing room waiting to be murdered."

"Nevertheless check it on the assumption that it could have happened that way. Ahmed, more than anybody, could move about without exciting comment. See if his training included computer lighting."

This time it was Molloy's turn to recall the cliché of clutching at straws but, unlike his superior, he kept the thought to himself.

CHAPTER FIVE

IN WHICH OUR DETECTIVES VISIT A DESOLATE PLACE

The rest of the day's interviews were no less frustrating. Matt lived in South London, sharing a house on Fentiman Road with three actors, two of whom were also Australian and one American. It was untidy and the decoration badly needed renewing but it was none the less obvious that the inhabitants were not unsuccessful. There was a great deal of expensive technology trailing leads, over which miraculously nobody appeared to trip. Only one of the cars outside was more than three years old and the shoes, carelessly discarded along the hall were of good make.

Matt could only repeat previous information. Jess was increasingly tense but he did not know why. He knew of no falling-out between her and any of the others on the show. He had not seen any evidence that she was trying her luck with Ahmed and as far as he knew she had no close friendships with any of the others and knew them only in the context of *Lively Toes*. Naturally those who had been in the show from the start were closer to each other but he did not think they associated much off set.

So he didn't know about Jess's old acquaintance with Fred. That, thought Molloy, was odd as he saw his puzzlement reflected in Frobisher's eyes. Matt had been dancing with Jess for two weeks of rehearsals and then six of the show and yet she had never mentioned knowing Fred when she was a girl.

"What did you talk about while training?"

"Dancing mainly and, of course, we kept speculating on who might win. We certainly weren't going to but Jess thought we might get another couple of weeks if we were lucky. Jos has been much tougher on Leonie and even poor old Em. Probably Cobb will do it if he doesn't kill Beautella in the process."

"Did she ever talk about her children?"

"Yes, all the time. It seems to have been an amicable divorce and the kids move about between the parents with no hassle."

No hassle anywhere, lamented Molloy afterwards. They needed hassles. Murder resulted from hassle not calm. Frobisher grinned but did not disagree. Nevertheless he was becoming irritated and it began to show in his interview with Fred.

The dancer lived alone in a large apartment overlooking the Thames in Battersea. The block was fashionable but Fred's flat looked as if he had little interest in his surroundings but much in his books and music, with floor to ceiling shelving crammed with his collection. Stuffing oozed from the battered, faded chairs and the carpet was threadbare. On a windowsill a dead plant hung from its withered stem. One of the photographs in a collection on a side table sported a large crack in its glass and all the furniture was old and chipped. With surprise Molloy commented on the absence of a television set.

"It isn't necessary. Most of the entertainment is tawdry. If the jokes aren't coarse TV bosses don't think they're funny. Half the schedules appear to consist of soaps with people shouting at each other in Estuary English and news bulletins which prefer melo-drama to boring old truth. Give me Radio 4 any day." Fred smiled. "I know. I'm Luddite."

"Do you think *Lively Toes* tawdry?"

If Fred was surprised by the aggression of Frobisher's response to his explanation he did not show it.

"No. Merely vacuous. I do it for the money, Inspector."

"You were once in a loftier calling. Why didn't you stay with that if you despise showbiz?"

Fred raised his eyebrows and Molloy shifted uncomfortably. Frobisher was not being intimidating as such but his approach was better suited to a suspect than a mere witness.

"Have you had a bad day, Inspector?"

Molloy half- expected his superior to relax with a smile but instead he snapped "answer the question."

"If it is any of your business, Inspector, I fell out with the Anglican church and did not fancy the celibacy which the Roman church would have imposed on me."

"So you turned to dancing?"

"Initially I saw it as a stop gap while I worked out something better to do with my life........"

"Such as?"

Fred did not seem put out by the interruption and Molloy realised that he was consciously trying not to show any annoyance. Bad move, sir, he thought sadly. We need him open to emotion not in a state of heightened control.

"Such as teaching R.I. in schools or theology at university or working on one of the religious newspapers or for one of the big charities. I even thought of helping out in an overseas mission. But the longer I delayed making a decision the more I drifted into dancing and I cannot say it has been uncongenial even if it hasn't changed the world or saved any souls."

"Did you marry?"

"Twice. My first wife died of septicaemia following a very standard operation and my second of lung cancer despite not smoking."

"I'm sorry," Frobisher grimaced.

"I expect you already knew all that, Inspector. Indeed by now you probably know more about us than we know about ourselves."

"I only wish that were true," Frobisher seemed to relax for the first time in the course of the interview. "Unfortunately it isn't. Something in Jess's life was big enough to warrant a murder and we have not the slightest idea what it was."

Fred did not let down his guard. "If I could help you, Inspector, I would."

Liar, thought Frobisher but he had no idea why.

"I was watching him closely and couldn't see anything to suggest a lie," was Molloy's comment when the inspector voiced his doubts later.

"Yet he was lying. I would stake my life on it."

"Tomorrow we have the joys of Cobb Grainger and I suppose it will take us all day to get to Devon and back. The AC is going to want more than we are producing."

"Tell me about it but at least he understands what this sort of work is like. The press doesn't. It would take the assassination of the monarch to get us off the front pages at the moment."

Molloy reminded him of this prophecy when the next day's papers devoted their headlines to an expenses-fiddling MP.

"Nothing till page 5 today, sir. Our contact in Devon is a Detective Sergeant Gardiner. He says mind the animals on the moor because it won't look good if a police car kills one of the ponies and he reckons Grainger's house is pretty difficult to find. If we get lost we won't be able to phone him because the area doesn't have reception."

"What are sat navs for?"

"Misleading trusting tourists according to Gardiner."

Frobisher grinned. "Into the jaws of the Hound of the Baskervilles, I suppose? Right, Molloy. Let's get there. With any luck, we can be out of town before the rush."

"It's not just the Hound of the Baskervilles," observed Molloy as he drove along Westway towards the M4. "There are also the hairy hands."

"The what?"

"Hairy hands, sir. They grab the steering wheels or a bike's handlebars and cause you to crash."

"Let's stick with reality, shall we? In this case the unpleasant reality of Cobb Grainger. He'll be at home because Parliament is prorogued before the Queen's speech. Any more luck with his schooldays? Or with Fred's vicar days? Though I can't believe it will help us much. Even if Grainger bullied half the class or Fred was unfrocked, there can't be any connection with Jess."

"Still trying on both fronts. Also I'm trying to take a good look at Ru after that business with the singing."

"And Em, who alone turned back."

"What about Ahmed and his missus? There could have been half a motive there."

"If she was indeed in love with him but pretty well everyone says not."

"It could have been a person unknown, hiding in the store room, who escaped when everybody had gone to stage call."

It could be anyone, brooded Frobisher as the traffic slowed near Reading and his mood was not improved by a long hold-up near Bath.

"Stop at Gordano's," he said when the row of cars in front began to move. "It's not long after Bristol."

Molloy, grateful for the air and the chance to stretch his legs, wandered to the far end of the car park while Frobisher took a call on his mobile. His own phone rang as he was about to turn back and the diffident voice of Caesar greeted him.

"I hope it's all right to call you, Sergeant."

"Of course, Mr. Caesar."

"Anton, please."

Caesar was one of the few they did not suspect, reflected Molloy.

"Anton," he agreed.

"I've had a thought but it's a bit of a cheek really."

"Not at all, sir. Anything that can help is welcome."

"I'm not sure it will help and you're bound to have thought of it."

"Try me."

"Well, it's like this....."

Two minutes later Molloy was thanking him profusely and telling him that if ever he decided to give up dancing there could be a big future in detective work. He fairly ran back to where Frobisher was waiting by the car.

" Something up with Alice?" asked the Inspector.

"No, sir. That was Caesar on the phone. He seems to have spotted something that might have eluded us."

Caesar, explained Molloy, had been at a lunch party on Sunday where one of the guests was a trainee barrister, full of enthusiasm about his first appearance in court. He had been examining an elderly lady who said she had witnessed a traffic accident. She was an impeccable witness, a former school teacher, member of the church choir and leading light in the local Women's Institute and she was adamant that it was the red car's fault. The barrister who was representing the driver of the red car asked her if she had seen the accident happen and the answer was a confident yes.

" ' you were looking that way?' he persisted.

" 'yes,' replied the old lady. 'I heard the bang and the red car had hit the blue one.'

"Our barrister pounced. 'You *heard* the bang? But did you see it? Which came first: the bang or your seeing the two cars?'

"And so on, until the old lady admitted, in tones of great shock, that she could not be sure whether she had heard the bang first or seen the cars. It was damning because if her attention was focussed only as a result of hearing the bang then beyond peradventure she had not seen the accident. The barrister was cock a hoop."

"I take it that also beyond peradventure this is leading somewhere?" Frobisher was making no attempt to conceal his impatience.

"Caesar has pointed out," continued Molloy in unruffled tones. "That the lights came back on simultaneously with Em forcing the door open and that the first person she saw was Cobb Grainger. We all assumed that meant he was by the door but perhaps in that split second she was wrong and that the reason she saw Grainger was because he was on the other side of the door. It was all happening at the same time: the lights, the door, people tumbling through it."

As Frobisher seemed lost in thought, Molloy went on with mounting excitement. "Nobody heard Grainger before the door was open. He didn't speak. People heard Tatum, Em and Fred for example but I can't recall anyone mentioning Cobb."

"But we do know he joined the line-up, so if he left, then he did so as the lights went out. It wouldn't give him much time to do murder but when you next encounter our dancing detective, buy him a drink."

"How did we miss it, sir?" wondered Molloy as he turned the car out of the service station and back on to the M5.

"I don't know but tomorrow we start asking each and every person in that line-up and anybody else within hearing distance if Cobb spoke out of the darkness or if anyone remembers bumping into him in the confusion *before* the door was opened. And in an hour or two we can ask the man himself."

It proved an optimistic forecast as shortly after leaving the A38 they found themselves enshrouded in mist. Molloy slowed to a crawl.

"We need Bovey Tracey," he muttered peering through the gloom. "Then Haytor or Widecombe-in-the-moor."

"Bovey straight on," pronounced Frobisher triumphantly as he glimpsed a sign.

"Buvvey, sir, not Bohvey. Gardiner was most particular."

"Arrr!"

"Arr is Cornish, sir, not Devonian."

Frobisher grunted. He was fairly certain the expression was from Somerset but his mind was still working out the implications of Caesar's brainwave. Cobb and Jess. What could be the connection?

"Well, it can't be anything to do with the show," pointed out Molloy. "He and the beautiful Beautella were streets ahead of Jess and Matt. Nobody has suggested that they had much to do with each other off camera or had any particular argument."

"Anyway, we mustn't get ahead of ourselves. Someone may yet remember Cobb being there before the door opened and even if they can't there is no proof that he was on the other side when it opened. Even so, we need to test Em's recall again. She said she found the handle just as Bruce tripped and she was flung against the door with Tatum and Fred, who up till then had been further back. But does she remember actually opening the door or could it have been already opening as she found the handle? With everyone bumping into everyone else it was pretty confused. Could she, like Caesar's old lady, have a false memory? I'm afraid that we are going to have to get them to go through that scene again, but at least this time we needn't hold up the show."

A sudden rattle caused Molloy to start slightly.

Frobisher grinned. "Cattle grid. Not that you would know in this mist. We appear to be climbing pretty steeply."

"Did you see what that sign said?"

"Yes. 'Take moor care.'"

"What?" Molloy sounded offended.

"Moor as in M.O.O.R., not more. That plus the grid presumably means look out for the ponies Gardiner mentioned."

"He says the worst time is when it's dark. They suddenly come from nowhere, cows as well."

"It couldn't be much worse than this. We'll be lucky to find......"

The inspector's words trailed into silence, lost in the gasp of admiration from his sergeant as, ahead of them and above the swirling mist, a large black pile of rock dominated the horizon, dark, brooding, menacing.

"It's a tor," pronounced Molloy, not thinking Frobisher needed the information but wanting to say something, anything that might restore an air of normality to an atmosphere suddenly tinged with night.

"I bet it used to give our ancestors a fright if they came upon it unawares."

"It gave me one, sir. Gardiner says folklore has it the Devil rides out with a pack of spectral hounds. No wonder Conan Doyle got his inspiration here."

"Brendan, it's a pile of old rock. That's all. There's even someone standing on top of it. Look, there he is."

"Yes, sir. We need signs to Postbridge or to try the sat. nav. This damned mist is getting worse every second."

"We can ask a native if we can find one," suggested Frobisher as he tapped in the postcode. "Beware this thing taking us up cart tracks."

They sought directions at an inn, from two different dog-walkers and from a man on a horse whose mud-spattered riding mac suggested a healthy gallop, having abandoned the sat. nav. when they reached a farm gate instead of a cross roads.

"Back to the stone age," muttered Frobisher as he took a map from the glove compartment. Molloy had pulled into a passing place in a narrow lane and the detectives bent their heads over the mass of tiny roads indicated on the ordnance survey. This, thought the sergeant, is why ambulances get lost, the drivers despatched by some central control room miles away and then someone dies and there's a scandal.

He looked up and jumped with shock as Grainger's grinning features appeared out of the mist, pressed against the driver's window.

"If you want to know the way, ask a politician." He made no attempt to hide his amusement. "Two hundred yards further and turn left. Look for a camellia on one side of the gate and a rhododendron on the other if the mist lets you."

"Can we give you a lift?"

"Thanks, but the walk will do me good. Jane will take care of you."

Jane Grainger was as the chief whip had described her. Molloy knew she was five years younger than her husband but the years had been less kind. Her grey hair was only loosely styled and her make-up minimal but she had a kind face that had once been beautiful, a welcoming smile and, seeming somehow incongruous, the figure of a model.

"Cobb has gone out to look for you. Most people get lost and this mist isn't helping."

"We met him. He's on the way." Frobisher refused the bathroom, saying they had stopped at the inn, but accepted tea which he vaguely expected to be served in china cups in a chintzy lounge but found himself instead installed in the kitchen with a mug "made at the local pottery".

As his superior made idle conversation with their hostess Molloy glanced around the room. The fridge was covered with children's drawings kept in place by magnets. The grandchildren, he thought. On the old-fashioned pine dresser Delia Smith nestled next to Jamie Oliver and Mrs Beeton, the last badly stained and well used. A Rayburn, which had seen better days, was valiantly trying to dry a rack of clothes, including thick hiking socks and jumpers. Clearly Grainger made the most of his time out of London.

As if on cue, the object of his thoughts called out from the hall before appearing at the kitchen door looking windswept and healthy. He sank down at the table, bending to unlace his mud-caked boots before holding one foot up to Jane who seized the boot and tugged theatrically until it came off. As she tackled the other, rather more stubborn one, both detectives arrived at the same conclusion.

There had been nothing subservient in the action, nothing reluctant, nothing suggesting Cobb expected her to pull off his boots as his due. It had been a simple act of companionship, a familiar unresented ritual, which, to an outsider emphasised the closeness of the participants. They had a good marriage, this nice woman and this ghastly man.

The reflection caused Frobisher to feel almost gloomy. He did not want to link the brute who bullied Beautella with the comfortable, motherly soul who was re-filling the teapot. When he had drained his second mug he decided it time for business and Cobb led the way to his study.

Only a computer belied the old –fashioned style of Grainger's sanctuary, with its mahogany desk, brown leather armchairs and rows of black and white photographs on the walls. Frobisher glanced at them and, as Grainger took up position behind the desk and the Inspector sank into a rather too comfortable chair, Molloy began a close-up examination. He sensed rather than saw Grainger look at him before beginning to answer the questions.

The first six or so were school photos with his host at the centre of each: captain of cricket, surrounded by his team at prep school; victor ludorum being hailed by a group of formally-posed boys waving boaters in the air at the same school; head boy of a major public school; captain of rugby; lead role in the school play. The theme of Grainger as leader, victor or star diminished only when the next row turned out to be a chronologically-ordered series of Oxford Union Standing Committee photos charting his progress in that august society's *cursus honorum* from ordinary committee member to secretary, treasurer and then, predictably, president.

Molloy wandered along looking at the other photos and then returned to look at Cobb Grainger, aged twenty and president of the Oxford Union, flanked by three of the top politicians of the day and a famous television presenter. All had long since passed from public life but men of Molloy's age had still heard of them.

Molloy had seen the pictures in the press of those arrogant young men of the Bullingdon Club looking out disdainfully at a world they assumed to be their footstool but this photograph did not conjure up the same image. These students were confident, determined, ambitious but their expressions were not those of people who took the future for granted as if it lay ready-made before them. Cobb Grainger gazed steadily at the camera, a young man ready to take on any opponent, any setback, any pitfall in the cause of Cobb Grainger.

He glanced once more at the school photos and then took the vacant chair as a persistent note crept into the tone of Frobisher's questions.

"Did you say absolutely nothing, sir? Were you really quiet for the whole time the studio was plunged into darkness? What about when it first happened?"

"I can't remember. I expect I gasped."

"You were next to Beautella?"

"Of course."

"What did she say?"

"She gave a little scream and then began giggling." Grainger was not quite successful at repressing the scorn his dancing partner's reaction had provoked in him, although whether it was for the scream or the giggling Molloy could not be sure.

Jane of course would neither have screamed nor giggled. She would have exclaimed and wondered and then speculated on the cause. That, it seemed to Frobisher, might help to account for the man's attitude towards Beautella: he was irritated not charmed by her.

"Did you reassure her?"

"There was no need. Matt began telling her it was OK. Then we all started milling about and I don't know what she did next because it was dark."

The last words were tinged with exasperation, as if Grainger resented being obliged to state the obvious.

"Did you move about, sir?"

"We all did. Then the emergency strip lighting came on and all I could see were feet but at least it told us which way the door was and at that stage we all presumed there would be light on the other side."

Molloy felt a sudden surge of excitement but Frobisher let the comment pass, taking Grainger painstakingly through the initial line-up and the milling about. What had he heard? Who had said what? Did he so much as mutter a comment? To the detectives' disappointment his account tallied with those of the other dancers.

The phone rang but their host ignored it. He was saying that the A.P. was a loose cannon when Jane put her head round the door.

"Sorry, darling but it's important."

Grainger rose and left the room. His wife had not specified the nature of the call but whatever it was he was clearly unwilling to pick up the extension in the study. Molloy looked at the instrument with longing.

Frobisher read his thoughts. "Almost certainly nothing to do with us."

"Did you notice when he said…"

Frobisher raised a warning finger to his lips. Molloy, understanding him, repressed the impulse to play spot the recording device. Instead he began to speculate how long it might take them to get back to London.

Grainger returned smiling. "That, believe it or not, was Anton. He is visiting some aunt at Manaton and suddenly realised how close he was to me. Jane has invited him to tea. I hope you'll join us."

"That's very kind, sir, but we shall have to be on our way soon. Just a few more questions and we'll be gone. Had you ever met Jess Allward before *Lively Toes*?"

"No. At least not as far as I know. People are always coming up to me asking if I remember giving them a certificate at speech day fifteen years ago."

Frobisher smiled. "Did you have much to do with her on the programme?"

Grainger shook his head. "No. I didn't have much to do with any of them except Beautella. I chatted to Anton a bit before some of the shows and during supper break because he was intensely interested in what went on at the House of Commons. It wasn't the politics he was interested in but the way of life, the procedures. Silly things like why did MPs stand up all the time during Prime Minister's Questions and what was meant by a division lobby. Did we drink with our opponents? That sort of stuff. Mops it up like a sponge."

"Do you like Beautella?"

The forthrightness of the reply startled them and it was only with conscious effort that the policemen avoided exchanging glances.

"Not much. She's a pretty little thing but lightweight. Lightweight upstairs, that is. No brain."

"Wrong," thought Frobisher.

"Some of the others suggest she may feel a bit bullied," ventured Molloy.

"By *me*, sergeant? Nonsense."

"She is scared of heights but you are making her fly."

Grainger sat back in his chair and looked at the detective as he might have looked at a not very bright constituent who was urging him to an unconstitutional course of action.

"Gentlemen, I cannot *make* Beautella do anything. She is the professional. She does the choreography. Of course I make the odd suggestion here and there and I did indeed suggest flying but she has the final say."

"Does it bother you that she is scared of it?"

"I repeat *she* is the professional. She must gauge her own abilities. She does not have to fly if she doesn't want to and all she is doing is coming down from the lowest tier not the highest. I doubt if it will be any great trauma on Friday."

They were all to remember that prediction but it was an earlier part of the conversation which pre-occupied Molloy as they sat in the Old Inn at Widecombe-in-the-moor.

Frobisher would have preferred to make straight for home but, although they had left London before the morning rush hour, being held up by traffic, losing the way and the length of the interview had meant they did not leave Grainger's house until nearly four. Other than Jane's home- made biscuits which accompanied the tea, they had eaten nothing all day and it was now vital that they refresh themselves and have a quick meal before facing the long return journey.

"He said they had all "presumed" there was light on the other side of the door. But there was no suggestion that the corridor was in darkness as well when they managed to open the door, so what did he mean? Only Helen was on the other side and she can't remember anything."

"It could have just been a careless way of saying that they were trying to get the door open to find some light but that it came back on anyway. But I agree. It didn't sound like that. If Helen ever remembers what happened and she says it was dark, then that remark takes on significance."

Molloy looked mutinous. "I still reckon he was on the other side of that door."

"Caesar's old lady again. Talking of which, what do you make of his sudden visit?"

"You don't believe in the aunt at Manaton?"

"Do you? He obviously also has a hunch about friend Cobb."

"But what could he achieve by dropping in for tea?"

"I don't know but I expect he'll tell us."

"Could he become a nuisance?"

"Possibly but given that so far he has produced the only bright idea in the investigation, I'm prepared to wait and see. By the way when I brief the AC, I shan't mention that the idea of the split-second timing being reversible occurred to one of the dancers first. There is no need to weary him with tales of barristers, red cars and respectable members of the WI."

"Of course not, sir," agreed the dutiful Molloy.

They emerged into the November evening to find the mist replaced by driving rain and had to run to the car, their feet sending up sprays of mud as they hastened through the car park which was half field and half very uneven concrete full of puddles. By the car next to theirs a group of hikers, their faces ruddy from the wind, laughed as they discarded muddy boots and rain-soaked fleeces.

As Frobisher drove up the steep hill outside the village, Molloy's phone bleeped.

"It's Gardiner texting to say hope all was well and do we need anything more today?"

"Thank him and say no."

Molloy was already doing so. A final text in response read simply "Mind the Moor."

"Thinking of the ponies again," muttered Frobisher but he fell silent as they drove through the deserted, dark landscape, peering through rain which was reducing the visibility from his headlights to feet rather than yards. He braked, seeing the hazard at the same time as hearing Molloy cry an urgent warning.

Wonderingly he stared at the profile of the figure which had loomed in front of them, a tall robed individual with hooded head who walked calmly on across the road as if he had not just brought himself within danger of death. Molloy gasped as he was immediately succeeded by another and then four or five more who did not so much as glance in their direction. It was the last who stopped in the middle of the road, turned to face them and bowed as if in thanks before being swallowed up in the gloom as he joined his companions.

The two men in the car looked at each other in disbelief.

It was Molloy who found his voice first. "What on earth was that?"

"Almost certainly a coven."

"Witches? Ought we to stop them?"

"It's not against the law, you know."

"Nearly causing an accident and holding up the traffic are", protested Molloy as his superior drove on. "What on earth are they doing? Looking for a sheep to sacrifice in one of those stone circle thingies?"

"You've obviously been watching films long after bedtime. That or Gardiner's talk has got to you. Let's get back to our case."

They talked of nothing else throughout the entire three and a half hours it took to reach Hammersmith but arrived no further forward than when they had left. Frobisher insisted Fred had been lying and Molloy that Cobb was on the other side of the door when it had been opened but neither had a shred of evidence to support either conclusion. Next day they would spend going through the statements again, on Thursday they would go over the c.v. of each dancer and each celebrity and on Friday they would once more attend the recording of the show and haunt the dressing room corridor. First, however, they would ask everyone present on the fateful Friday to reprise yet again the minutes after the lights went out.

"Not that anything much is likely to come of it," opined Frobisher with the gloom of defeat in his voice. "Normal service will probably be resumed."

Later he was glad that only Molloy had heard that hopelessly false prophecy.

CHAPTER SIX

IN WHICH A DANCE BECOMES A DRAMA

"**I** tell you it's *safe,* perfectly *safe.* I would be out of business if it wasn't."

It seemed to Buzz Roberts that it might be easier were he dealing with an amateur. This dancer was supposed to be a professional and had been nothing but trouble from the start, squawking with terror in the practice harness when it was a mere eight feet from the ground, then standing rigid with fear on the balcony and refusing to take off. Now she was having a fit of the vapours because he had let slip that the wires were controlled by computer rather than human hand. He did not much like Cobb Grainger but he was certainly beginning to share his impatience.

"Perhaps I should be doing the flying," sneered the object of his reflections.

Beautella ignored him. "I do wish a little man were operating it. What happens if the computer gets it wrong? If you were doing it you could change it immediately but a computer won't."

"Yes it will because we can override it."

"And do it manually?"

"And tap another button. Don't *worry.*"

On the other side of London, Helen Brown's mother was uttering the same exhortation.

"Don't *worry,* darling. I'll be around for a few days and everything will be all right. Just enjoy the play."

The FBC had been good to her, thought Helen, keeping open her job even though it was merely an unpaid shadow of one, but she did not want to stretch its patience and the doctor had said she could come back to work as soon as the headaches and that dreadful feeling of weakness had gone. She would not admit to her mother that her uppermost fear was fear itself, knowing she had witnessed the aftermath of a murder but without any memory of it. Helen was certain that one day the gap in her memory would close when she least expected it and that terrible images would dance unbidden in front of her. That she had not the slightest notion when this was likely to occur only fuelled her terror. Please, she prayed, let it not happen at night when I am alone.

The doctors at the hospital had told her it might never happen: that not all memories were retrieved. She did not believe them, her doubts fuelled both by the fear of recollection suddenly besetting her and by a contrary hope that her memory would be made whole thus removing any suggestion of permanent brain damage. When her memory was recovered she could believe she also had recovered.

Her parents had persuaded her to return to work slowly rather than re-entering the fray at a gallop. "Trot for a while," her father suggested, grinning as he recalled her childhood adoration of her pony.

So Helen had decided she would return to London but instead of resuming work today as she had intended, would relax over this weekend, work a few hours on Monday and Tuesday and then start full time on Wednesday. Tonight she was due to go to a play with two other girls while her mother met an old friend for dinner. If all went well over the weekend her mother would then return home.

Predictably Mrs Brown was now sending her on her way with her father's favourite *don't panic, Captain Mainwaring*. Helen caught the tube and completed the journey without any sudden visitation from lost memories and as she arrived at the pizza restaurant and the safety of her friends' company she began to believe that she might enjoy the evening after all.

Nothing and nobody could persuade Beautella that she was going to enjoy the show, at least not until her own dance was over. Inwardly cursing Cobb Grainger, she found herself looking at the clock every few minutes longing for the moment when her feet would feel the studio floor and her ordeal would be over. Even then she would have to endure the uncertainty of whatever Grainger might be planning to spring on her this time. Perhaps next year she would give *Lively Toes* a miss and if she couldn't find anything to fill the gap that would leave in her finances then she would close down Studio LaReine.

"Happy?" Angela was referring to her hair but Beautella could think only of her dance.

"Good luck," said Ru cheerfully as he took her place in Angela's chair.

Beautella smiled at him. "Thanks. You too."

"We need it. They won't eliminate their darling Fred and Em, You're flying so you and Cobb will go through for a cert, Matt will have a huge sympathy vote after what happened to Jess so it's between us and Hal and Leonie."

"Flying won't give us any edge. I'm a professional so nobody will find it remarkable but I dare say Cobb will come up with something just as he always does. I only wish I knew what it will be."

Ru smiled. "Belle is here. Those detective chaps are insisting that anyone who was here on the night of the murder must lurk around in case something suddenly jogs their memories. It's all right for Bruce because he's part of the professionals' dance but Belle looks like a thundercloud. She doesn't even have a dressing room so she's just wandering about like a Bedouin in the desert but without the latter's sense of purpose."

"Ru, do they really think it was one of us?"

"Well, it is a bit difficult to see how anybody else could have been around, unless he or she was lurking in the store cupboard. I would think it has to be someone from the show, wouldn't you?"

"Poor Jess. What had she ever done to anybody?"

"Clearly something. And something pretty big."

"I don't believe it."

"You look amazing! Uh- may - zzing!" Em materialised from the corridor clad in a towelling dressing gown, her head full of large mauve curlers.

"Thanks," Beautella tried to inject some enthusiasm into the word. In other circumstances she would have rejoiced in the long, pale green, sequin-studded ball gown and the cascade of curls which fell from the bun Angela had contrived.

Em shot her a curious glance. "Is it flying or him?" she asked shrewdly.

"Mainly him, but I'll be glad when the flying is over."

"Don't let the creep bug you. It's all over in ninety seconds."

"I know but right now I just wish I were somewhere else."

"I wish I were in the studio," sighed Helen as she settled in her seat at the Pizza Parlour. Normally they would have eaten after the performance but Helen's mother had asserted it much too late when Helen was still recovering her strength and, somewhat to her own uneasy surprise, Helen agreed. She *did* feel a bit weak.

"You will be soon," Josie's tone was unnaturally quiet, designed to soothe an invalid and Helen quelled the resentment which rose inside her, knowing her friend, with whom she had been at school, was trying only to be kind. They were all in and out of make-up now, getting into all those complicated clothes and then deciding they needed the loo, driving the dressers to distraction. Em would be muttering about how it took so long to get the glitter off her eyelids, while piling it on more than anyone else.

Helen smiled. Em was enjoying every second of the glamorous life.

She thought of Beautella. Flying! Helen sympathised because she was also scared of heights but there was nothing she would not have dared if she had but a fraction of Beautella's ability. Nothing. She would have flown to the rafters.

The restaurant was filling up with pre-theatre diners. Some looked harassed and carried briefcases, while others were freshly coiffed and made-up as if there had been a leisurely preparation. All looked at their watches as they greeted companions and picked up menus. All focused, thought Helen, all successful, all knowing where they were going.

Helen glanced at her own companions. Josie had found employment with an insurance company in the City and in just that first year had developed a confidence, a snappier style of clothes, a greater casualness with money. Sara had qualified as a secretary and was talking about how one day she would have her own agency. What, she wondered, did they think of her now? An unpaid "intern" with no certain prospects?

The conversation was no more reassuring as they brought each other up to date with news of their schoolfriends, who had variously gone to University or become bank tellers or were learning to be hairdressers or cooks. Everybody seemed set on some safe and certain course while Helen drifted, buoyed only by hope and the same sense of futile anticipation with which her parents bought lottery tickets. Drifting and dreaming, thought Helen, living on her parents, while everyone else was forging an independent life. Depressed, she began an earnest debate with herself about the merits of pepperoni versus ham and pineapple.

A few minutes later she was undecided. "You choose", she said to Josie and was taken aback by the irritability in her own voice.

Why did Sara's nails have to be so immaculate? Why was that ridiculous little dog dangling so ostentatiously on Josie's bag? Just to tell everyone it was a Radley, supposed Helen. Oh, stop it, stop it, she begged herself. Think of anything else. Think of the show. Any minute now they will be lining up for the start.

⚜ ⚜ ⚜

The first piece was a professional dance with Anton and a dancer named Alice, an old –fashioned number, *We're A Couple of Swells*. As all the competitors were now gathered in the pod at the other end of the floor Frobisher had come to watch the show from the wings. Molloy was still prowling the dressing –room corridor, walking between various points and the studio, meticulously noting down timings.

When the competition began Ru and Tatum took the floor first, performing a Charleston. Tatum's blonde hair was held back in a headband which matched her bright yellow, 1920s style dress, while Ru sported a boater and spotty bow tie. The tune was from the ragtime era and Tatum gave the dance her all, her feet executing the steps seemingly without effort, her thin figure ideal for the boyishness of Ru's interpretation. One almost sensed that the war was well and truly over and a new era promised fun and abandon. Ru spun, performed with a walking cane, threw away his boater and finished the dance by lifting Tatum almost to his shoulder as the audience came to its feet with enthusiastic cheers.

As the judges began to deliver their comments, Molloy arrived at his elbow.

"No Beautella yet?"

"She's on fourth. Hal and Leonie next. Then Fred and Em. Then some pop group, then our unlovely Cobb. Come back in time for Fred and Em."

"OK. Why? What will I be looking for?"

"I don't know. But I am still sure Fred is hiding something and I just want to watch him, that's all."

Molloy disappeared and Frobisher turned back in time to see a dinner-jacketed Hal sweep a white-gowned Leonie into his arms for a waltz. Her ankle had obviously fully recovered, mused the detective. She danced confidently but even Frobisher could tell that she had muddled a step.

"A double whisk," muttered Anton, who appeared beside him, now normally dressed and smelling of soap.

"Ambitious?"

"Not at this stage of the competition. Oops there goes a right instead of a left foot. Did you see Ru and Tatum?"

"Yes. It looked good to me, but I'm hardly an expert."

"Oops again. Hal's trying so hard not to look despairing." The sympathetic words were belied by an ironic grin and Frobisher found himself responding with one of his own.

"Did you have a good visit to Dartmoor? Grainger said you were going to drop in on them."

"I'm not sure. There's something I want to check out before I start any hares. Did he receive you in the study?"

Frobisher tried to conceal his astonishment. "Yes. And you?"

"Also the study. I think he may have been a little careless."

"Would you care to share your thoughts, sir?"

"Anton. Not here, Inspector! I may be barking up the wrong tree but I'll soon know."

He could have pressed him but Frobisher had a keen scent for how far a witness could be bullied or cajoled and he was anxious to keep Caesar on side.

"All right, sir, but please be careful. Somewhere in all of this is a murderer."

"Who will be wary of you, not me."

"You can't be sure... Oh, here comes Fred."

Molloy joined them. "A polka, I'm told."

Em, resplendent in turquoise chiffon, descended a staircase towards Fred, who, clad in the uniform of an Austrian officer of a century earlier, waited for her on one knee, glowing red rose in hand.

"Well, that's taken up some time," observed Anton cheerfully. "Dear heaven, they've even sprayed the damn rose with glitter."

The policemen laughed but their eyes never left Fred, who successfully re-created the atmosphere of a bygone age despite the awkwardness of his partner who looked no more convincing than a child trying too hard at a fancy –dress competition. Undeterred, the audience gave them a standing ovation.

"And you have gleaned what exactly?" murmured Anton.

"Nothing," said Molloy with gloomy certainty.

Frobisher was less forthcoming, although he could not have said what, if anything, he had observed.

"Would you care to share your thoughts, sir?" asked Anton and was rewarded with a smile.

While the pop group performed they went to the makeshift canteen, stationed in a nearby studio, for coffee. "I think I should not be seen too much around thee," murmured Anton as he melted away. The policemen looked at each other.

"It's OK. That one is likely to be able to take care of himself and he is not doing anything to hinder us. Yet."

Molloy looked doubtful but it was of Beautella not Anton that he spoke. "I wonder how she's feeling now, sir?"

"Scared but it's OK. Flying is nothing out of the ordinary and I am told she is coming from a very low height. For a certainty nobody will know she's afraid. She's too much of a pro to let anybody at home see."

As the last notes of the guitars died away and applause shook the studio, the dancers began to re-assemble in the wings and the judges to take their places on their dais.

Jos Lewison heard a gasp from Serena and something akin to a moan from Liz at the same moment as he too turned over his papers and saw the name staring up at him from the plain white card: Beautella.

Frantically he rose in his chair but the shout died in his throat. A few seconds earlier, Beautella had appeared on the balcony which was still in darkness as the technicians strapped her into the harness. Thirteen feet below her Cobb Grainger had edged towards his place in the spotlight, preparing to look up in supplication and mime an entreaty to come to him. As the judges rose to their feet, lights and music swung simultaneously into action, Beautella felt herself lifted from the vine-swathed balcony and holding out her hands to Cobb prepared to descend gently into his arms now outstretched towards her.

"Aaah," breathed the sentimental audience, a susurration entirely drowned out by Beautella's scream which seemed to trail behind her as, instead of descending languorously, she flew at speed towards the ceiling.

Ahmed tried in vain to keep everybody calm.

"Can you hear me, Fabulous Flying?" he demanded of the technicians and was relieved to hear a calm response in his earpiece.

"Yes. We don't know what has happened."

"Can you override the computer?"

"We're trying."

With a supreme effort of self-control Ahmed did not tell them to hurry: it would have been a most unnecessary instruction. Suddenly the music started again and to his amazement he saw Cobb Grainger giving a solo performance, spinning, tapping, gyrating, anything to keep the audience looking at him rather than at the petrified figure seventy feet above them, towards whom the politician sent the occasional worried glance. Just to remind them what he's doing thought Ahmed bitterly.

They did not need reminding. Most of them were held not by Grainger's performance but by the lonely figure dangling a few feet below the ceiling.

This, thought Beautella, was the worst possible nightmare come true, the ultimate horror, the horror beyond which there was no horror, the nightmare from which there was no waking. Hell itself could hold no greater fear. She kept her eyes resolutely closed, some residue of her professional duty reminding her that nobody could see for she was well above the upper tier of the audience. Don't look down, Beautella, she told herself, don't look down. Any minute now you will feel yourself being lowered to safety and you can smile and wave as you pass the audience and look as if it was all planned really.

Perhaps it might be better to look up at the ceiling. That would be solid, friendly, reassuring, full of apparatus. There might even be something she could touch, some dear, firm object. No, don't open your eyes, silly girl, they will be drawn towards the void.

She became aware of the wire cutting into her hands. She was holding on too tightly but it was the harness not the wires either side which held her in position. The certain knowledge that this was so was powerless to loosen her grasp, to stop the pain of the thin, merciless wires. She continued to grasp them as if they were all that stood between her and that terrible plummet towards death. Was it really only two weeks since she had woken, terrified by the thought of falling merely from Grainger's shoulders?

If only she could faint. She would be utterly safe in the harness which was designed for people to lean forward as they simulated angels and fairies flying. Then she would know nothing until they got her back to the floor. Blessed, sweet oblivion! Please God, let me faint. Please.

Sara looked at her watch. "Pud, anyone? We've plenty of time."

Josie shuddered as if she could see the fat, which surely such indulgence must produce, wobbling before her very eyes. It was, reflected Helen, one of the great benefits of her non-career that she could eat as carelessly as she chose. Not for nothing were she and her colleagues called "runners". They rarely sat down and the corridors at the FBC studios sometimes felt like marathon courses as she sped along them on some quest which could not wait.

"Vanilla ice cream. What about you?"

"Same but on top of some apple pie," grinned Sara. "Sure we can't tempt you, Josie?"

Her friend shook her head. She was already calculating the extra time she would have to spend on the treadmill tomorrow.

As Sara began signalling to a waitress, Helen, unable to deny the increasing fatigue which was manifesting itself in her still recovering body, wondered if she should not change her mind. The extra food might make her feel more tired and leaden and she could not prevent herself worrying. Surely with her youth and vitality she shouldn't be feeling the effects of concussion a fortnight later? Yet she was tired, irritable and depressed and her mother would have been unlikely to insist on accompanying her if she had been confident that Helen's recovery was complete. What were they not telling her?

"What's the matter?" asked Josie. "You look like a wet Sunday."

"Nothing. Just wishing I were well enough to work tonight. They must be coming up to the last dance now. The next bit's always chaotic: everyone goes out while the votes are counted and hair and makeup go mad getting them ready for the final results and judging."

"Isn't that when…" Josie broke off.

"The murder? Yes."

The other girls looked uncomfortable, not knowing if Helen wanted them to turn the conversation.

"I just wish I could remember what everyone thinks I must have seen."

"Maybe better not," offered Sara.

"One ice cream, one apple tart and ice cream," interrupted the cheerful tones of the waitress as she put the dishes down. "Will there be anything else, love?"

"Coffee and the bill please."

The exchange over, Josie turned back to Helen but this time she did change the subject, beginning to discuss the reviews the play had received, and her friends conscientiously concealed their disappointment.

"Half an hour?" The director's tone was incredulous.

Ahmed sighed. "They can't unfreeze the computer. We can simply progress with the rest of the show and try and get this sorted in the interval. With any other pro I would do that quite happily, particularly as lighting say they can black her out, but with her it's a big, big risk. We can't communicate with her except by yelling and we can hardly do that if the audience is still with us. Nonetheless I suggest we do black her out, carry on with Matt and Lisa, then clear the audience out for the interval while we sort it. Meanwhile I'll get

Em to go up to the top tier to talk up to Beautella and re-assure her if it comes to that. That way there is at least some chance that the show can be rescued. My real fear is she'll panic up there."

"Can she panic herself out of the harness?"

"No. Or so they say but they also said the computer couldn't go wrong."

"What are the police doing?"

"Watching. Just watching. Like hawks."

"OK, we try your plan."

A minute later the studio filled with music and a bejewelled Lisa started tangoing with Matt. It took a while for the other sound to penetrate the consciousness of those watching the dancers but it was there, faint, almost drowned out by the music. It was Molloy who noticed some sitting on the top tier begin to look up and point. As he nudged Frobisher, they began to scream.

As the music swelled climatically before dying away and Matt held Lisa in a romantic clinch the screams filled the studio, while Trevor Langdon surpassed all known records at the Family Broadcasting Corporation for profanity.

"Get the audience out," roared the director into Ahmed's earpiece.

"Should we be doing something?" asked Molloy. "Don't they have safety nets?"

"It's a dance show not a circus," observed Anton in mild tones as he appeared beside them. "But I think I'll go up and give Em a hand......*Crikey!*"

The exclamation was one of many as the lights came on to reveal the struggling, shrieking figure near the ceiling. The last of the audience was still leaving and runners were urging them out, as high above them Beautella, hysterical, was throwing herself about in an effort to rid herself of the harness and plunge into the void.

When she had first found herself suspended over the sheer drop she believed it could only be for a few seconds, possibly minutes before they rescued her, before a small tap of some button on the computer brought her down. All she had to do, she persuaded herself, was not to panic for just that short space of time, not to look down, to try and faint if possible but when the music heralded Matt's dance her frightened brain registered the only possible explanation: something was seriously wrong, they could not get her down and were now carrying on until the end of the show.

Startled by the music, she looked down and seeing the immensity of the drop in the same moment as understanding the reason they had abandoned her, Beautella felt the small thread of reason, to which she had been clinging as resolutely as to the wires, snap. It would be easier to fall than to endure this. Letting go of the wires, she began to struggle wildly. The harness, constructed to allow the wearer to simulate a bird in flight, obligingly let her lean forward until her body was almost horizontal with the floor. Screaming with fear, she tried to become upright again but the harness did not respond to her unco-ordinated, crazed movements.

Beautella kicked, screamed and struggled, finding relief in yielding to irrationality. The music stopped and the studio flooded with light. Through the roar of terror in her ear drums she heard somebody trying to speak to her, someone not standing down on the floor where faces peered up at her and a stream of people flowed into the studio clutching cushions and sacks of clothes from wardrobe.

"Anything", Langdon was shouting. "Hats, coats, towels, sofa cushions, *anything.*"

"They won't break a fall that big," muttered Frobisher as Molloy passed him bearing their overcoats, but as the pile grew bigger, obliging stagehands to stand on the first tier in order to build it up, he felt more optimistic. She was still likely to be terribly injured but Beautella might just live.

"Does this mean the flying guys think she could come out of that harness after all?" he asked Ahmed.

"They are not sure with the way she's carrying on but if she can get a grip they say it's as safe as houses."

From the top tier Anton and Em tried to reinforce the message. They had stationed themselves toward the back of the rows so that

Beautella would have to look across at them rather than straight down.

"It'll be OK if you cool it a bit," Em was advising.

"It won't be long. Just look at us instead of them," tried Anton.

Beautella's anguished sobs were the only reply but, to the relief of those standing far below, she seemed to struggle less.

"Well done," said Em but Anton began to give instructions with no more emphasis than he might employ over a difficult step on the dance floor.

"Raise your arms above you and push your bottom down but don't kick. Let your legs dangle."

Beautella, with a sudden determination, obeyed him and found herself gradually returning upright. She grasped the wires again with hands still bloodied from her earlier encounter with them. She felt an overpowering urge to look down, to depart again into an abandonment of reason, to kick and scream, yearning to lose the consciousness which allowed her to know what was happening.

"It's completely frozen. I can't do a thing. We'll need to solve this some other way." Buzz Roberts was forcing himself to speak calmly.

"Oh, for Pete's sake! You're supposed to be the flaming experts round here!" snapped Langdon in another rush of anger even as Rashid Ahmed, in a rare loss of control, banged his fist down on the keyboard.

"What the hell...." Began the third technician Fabulous Flying had called to the scene in the last half hour. His words trailed away as lights appeared on the computer and his colleague hastily began the procedure to lower the harness with its weeping cargo towards the studio floor. Anton and Em cheered as it passed the top tier only to find their rejoicing drowned by groans as it stopped level with the first tier.

"It's OK," said Mike from sound who had just added two more sacks of clothes from another programme's wardrobe to the growing mountain. "If you fall now, all you'll do is roll about in old clothes."

He watched her eyes travel upwards and knew she feared a return trip to the rafters but slowly the wire moved again and she disappeared downwards.

The soft pile now impeded her way and two dozen pairs of hands began to pull the makeshift mountain apart. Beautella hung on to Ahmed as Fabulous Flying removed her harness and then, at last, she did faint, sliding into merciful oblivion at the producer's feet.

As Helen slid into her seat for the first act she wondered if she would fall asleep as soon as the theatre darkened. She rather hoped she might, providing of course that she did not snore. A woman climbed over her feet and Helen retrieved her handbag from the floor, trying to hold both it and her theatre programme in her lap with one hand at the same time as switching off her mobile phone with the other. Beside her Sara looked round for Josie who had stayed behind in the bar to order drinks for the interval.

Helen looked at her watch. 7.25 pm. She tried not to invest it with any significance, like midnight in horror stories or 3.00 am in *The Exorcism of Emily Rose.*, but she knew that it would be a long time before she ceased to associate it with the stage call and murder.

Josie took her seat on the other side of her and presently the lights dimmed. The audience began coughing, knowing that such relief must soon be pent up. The curtain began to rise and the man immediately behind Helen cleared his throat. In the light of the stage an actor froze and in the surrounding gloom hundreds of scandalised faces turned towards her as, the memories searing her mind with the ice of terror, Helen sent a scream of naked fear bouncing from the walls and pitched forward in a dead faint to land on the head and shoulders of the grey-haired lady in front.

"All in all it appears to have been quite a night for screaming and fainting," observed Frobisher wearily as he put down the phone in the dressing room Ahmed had procured for him. "That was Mrs. Brown. Apparently Helen brought a West End play to a halt before it had even started by screaming fit to wake the dead and fainting all over the row in front. An elderly woman had her neck hurt and has been taken to hospital. So has Helen, just to be on the safe side."

Molloy felt his jaw drop. "What brought that on?"

"According to Mrs Brown, Helen has remembered everything and I said we would be round first thing tomorrow morning by which time Helen should be back home and had a night's sleep."

Molloy groaned inwardly. Another Saturday on duty when the kids would be home and Alice getting less and less able to summon up the energy to deal with them.

Frobisher read his thoughts. "I know. My family won't be ecstatic either but since when was policing nine to five?"

"Frankly, sir, we have enough to do here now. There's a near mutiny that we won't let anyone go home. They are all expecting the series to be pulled as a result of this and they have no programme in the can for tomorrow. Cobb and Beautella couldn't compete, Matt and Lisa were at a distinct disadvantage and the audience has gone without voting. They will have to show an old film instead."

"That is the least of our worries."

"But not of theirs. This is their living. All they want to do is go home and think. After all, this time nobody is dead, everybody is feeling pretty impatient with poor old Beautella and nobody understands what we expect to gain by keeping them here to describe what they all know we saw in glorious technicolour for ourselves."

"Right, Molloy." said Frobisher heavily. "But they can *not* leave without giving statements. Who had access to the computer? Was anybody seen near the computer or fiddling with the judges' papers? You know what we need so let's set about getting it. Then they can go. But you can give them the bad news that we start interviewing them tomorrow afternoon and no messing so we need to know where they will be and their contact numbers. And if anyone objects just remind him that what we saw tonight could have been a damn good attempt at another murder and that it might be any of them next."

CHAPTER SEVEN

IN WHICH AN OUTING GIVES MOLLOY A BRAINWAVE

Helen was up, dressed and had finished her breakfast when the detectives arrived at 8 o'clock the next morning. Her mother was pleased to see that she had taken the trouble to apply make- up but there was no concealing the dark circles under her daughter's eyes, eyes which stared into the distance as they replayed a scene which would take a long time to fade into the background.

Looking at her as she sat nervously on the battered sofa, which Molloy suspected was a cast-off of a flatmate's parent, the detectives reached the same conclusion: here was a damaged girl, damaged but determined.

"I'm sorry to have to ask these questions, Miss Brown," began Frobisher with genuine pity.

"Helen. Unless of course that contravenes some procedure?"

Articulate and composed, thought Molloy. Good. He might get a few hours with Alice today after all.

Helen recounted her movements from being sent to find Jess until hearing a man clear his throat in the darkness but the moments in which the door flew open and concussed her were still lost and would probably now always be so. She could not remember seeing any light return or the door opening. So there was no means of putting Anton's theory to the test.

Her account was thorough. She even recalled how she had at first panicked when she could not immediately locate Jess's room - another runner had always looked after Jess- drawing a small smile from her mother when she told them how she had used the *Dad's Army* catchphrase.

"And you are utterly certain you passed nobody? By that I mean might you have noticed a door closing? Any sensation of anybody in the vicinity before the lights went out? Any small sound?"

"No, I'd have been terrified. All I wanted was the safety of lots of people."

"As would anybody. Are you quite sure the sound you heard was from the stairs? Could it have been from further along the corridor? Or from the top of the stairs?"

Helen closed her eyes in an effort of memory. "If you hadn't asked me that question, I'd have sworn it on the Bible. But now......... I don't know."

"It doesn't matter. Let's think about the throat clearing. Was it certainly a man?"

Helen blinked. "Clear your throat."

Frobisher obliged and Helen turned to her mother. "Now you."

Mrs. Brown conscientiously made a sound as near to Frobisher's as she could. Helen smiled.

"Definitely, definitely a man, Inspector."

"Thanks. We shall check this next bit out for ourselves but can you tell us if the rooms on the corridor that leads to the studio are locked? Could this man have fled when you screamed and hidden in a nearby room just in time before the door opened?"

" Easily, if he had time. The room just before the studio is a small kitchen where those without fridges in their dressing rooms can store milk and snacks. Not everyone likes the canteen or wants to socialise in breaks."

"Thank you," Frobisher's glance took in both the girl and her mother. "We may be back in touch but if not we'll see you at the next show."

"If there is a next show, Inspector."

Molloy heard the misery in her voice and searched in vain for something comforting to say but he had still not thought of anything when the door closed behind them.

"We appear to be back to square one," observed Frobisher in tones which were almost cheerful. "We have been assuming Jess was dead before stage call and that one of the dancers did it. But in this scenario someone else did because all the dancers were there and visible to each other when Helen was sent to find Jess. The lights did not go out until she was pretty well back at the studio door and the murderer was then only just coming up the stairs or along the corridor or whatever. At least that is if we assume the man moving about in the dark and terrifying Helen out of her wits was the murderer. And it dents your theory about Grainger being on the other side of the door because Helen would have seen him as she ran towards it."

"But it does raise the question of that odd statement of his about *presuming* the corridor lights were on. We now know that they were off immediately before the door opened and then on when everybody tumbled out but how did he know that it was ever dark out there?"

"And I suppose we must assume the man who cleared his throat *is* the murderer. But why was he trying to get back to the studio? That implies he worked there but we know for a certainty that all stage hands, dancers etc are accounted for. And could it have been innocent? Somebody with a perfect right to be there who heard Helen running and came out to see what was happening? Some assistant making his way to the kitchen? I know Helen says he was creeping about but he could just as easily have been moving cautiously in the darkness and had no idea Helen was there."

"Yes, but we questioned everyone on that corridor with a right to be there," pointed out Molloy as they climbed into the back seat of the car. He told the driver to head for the office, dearly hoping the Inspector would contradict him and let him have the next three or four hours with his family.

"Yes, everyone with a right to be there before stage call. But supposing somebody was moving about quite legitimately later on?"

"Whoever it was would have stayed around when Helen screamed and told us what he had seen and heard."

"Or he might have had another reason for concealment. It might be worth finding out if there has been any theft or anything like that."

"Or fiddling with the electrics?" Molloy sat suddenly very still. "He could have caused the blackout from somewhere or other and then started coming back to wherever he should be without arousing suspicion."

"And now we have another computer fiddle as well. Suppose whoever it was had sent a signal to the computer from some distant point? And then he was making his way back? Why not? We also know because everything was OK at band call and dress rehearsal that it needed an actual activation to cause the blackout. It wasn't done hours before."

Frobisher shook his head at his own proposal.

"That works if the Fabulous Flying computer was kept in the studio but we may find it lived in their own offices. They are nothing to do with FBC. And anyway, why? We've been assuming that the lights had something to do with the murder and were perhaps mis-timed but what does the Beautella incident have to do with any of it? Without her name on the judges' cards we might well be assuming it was an accident and that the computer just went wrong. So somebody wanted to make sure we knew it was deliberate. Why?"

"And was the Beautella incident just designed to give her a fright or was it really an attempt at murder? Could someone have banked on her panicking and falling out of the harness?"

Frobisher looked askance at his sergeant. "I don't know but for a certainty that is what all the papers will be asking tomorrow. Today they have reported it as a sensational accident because they didn't have much time to theorise but the Sundays......"

He let his voice trail off in gloomy speculation as Molloy answered his own question. "I suppose nobody could have *banked* on it but they might have *hoped*."

"In which case one must suppose it did not matter whether she died or not so what was the motive? What I would give for a *motive*. If only this were one of those cases you read about in books where the detectives have half a dozen motives to choose between. All we've got is the faintest possibility that Bronwen Ahmed was angry or jealous."

"And she could just have done it if all we look at is the timing. When I was on that corridor last night I timed it from the lift to Jess's room and back. She could have got there after the others had gone to stage call and disappeared before Helen got there but that suggests she knew Jess would still be there. It also makes no allowance for the difficulties she would have encountered in a wheelchair and even if she stood up to do murder she would have been in no physical condition to strangle someone as strong as Jess. Furthermore and crucially the lift is deactivated once stage call is under way to protect the security of the dressing rooms."

"Em might have been strong enough and we know she alone was on that floor after the others had gone to stage call. But if it was premeditated she could not have relied upon Jess also being there and if it wasn't one would have expected some face to face confrontation, not strangling from behind."

"There is always that little thing called opportunity," murmured Molloy. "She suddenly realised that Jess was still around and nobody else was."

"Motive?" Frobisher's voice was leaden.

"Yet to be established, which is what we would have to say in every case except Bronwen's. Meanwhile, if there is any possibility that someone really tried to do Beautella in we need to find some connection between her and Jess."

The car slowed in heavy traffic and Molloy summoned up his courage.

"Sir, we've got a bit of time before we start the interviews. Could I just look in on Alice? Just for an hour?"

In his dreams the Inspector said "I'll see you at FBC just before we talk to Ahmed." In his dreams he managed a snatched lunch and cooked sausages for his children. In his dreams Alice's face lit up when he walked through the door.

"Sorry, Brendan. We need to go over quite a lot before we start the afternoon's interviews."

Not even the "Brendan" softened his bitterness as his dreams swam away like clouds over the horizon. It was a very different expression he could see on Alice's face now. Nor would it have comforted him much had he known that Frobisher was picturing the disappointment on his son's face and the ire on his wife's.

For the rest of the morning they worked again and again on the timings but, other than a decision to focus next on Ru and Em, they reached no conclusions. The AC rang in, predictably unhappy with the press reports and the lack of progress which Frobisher made no attempt to dress up as anything else. They had sandwiches brought in for lunch and then set off for the FBC studios, where they were due to see the director, Ahmed and Langdon.

All three were listless, with none of the self-importance that often characterises a witness in a murder inquiry. There was, thought Molloy, an almost tangible pall of black depression hanging over the studios.

"Doomed," said Ahmed, with a face that might have presaged a world war. "They'll have to pull the show."

"No choice," confirmed the director later. "We lose one show to a murder, mess the audience about with reconstructions at the next so that some of them go off without voting and then lose the next to a computer cock-up that sends a dancer who should know better into hysteria and frightens everyone in the upper tier. The bosses won't wear it and you can't blame 'em. 'Thank God it's not live' is all anyone up there can say."

"We were going to go live." Langdon seemed close to tears. "This run was going to be the test. If we could go live then all the viewers could vote as well as the audience and it would be one in the eye for *Je Ne Sais Quoi*."

Molloy suppressed a smile as he imagined explaining that to the AC, who had almost certainly never watched the rival channel's talent show which had for some years used viewers' votes in determining winners.

"All we had to do," lamented Langdon, "was to keep exactly to time for each programme, which we have always managed anyway in the past, and to increase our ratings which we have done week on week, year on year without any trouble. Nothing else. Just what we had always done and now look at the mess. It's unbelievable."

Frobisher's tone was surprisingly mild. "Mr. Langdon, I can appreciate your disappointment but one woman has been murdered and another has come within an inch of same."

Langdon gave no sign of understanding he had been rebuked. "Perhaps someone from *Je Ne Sais Quoi* did it."

There was a short silence.

"I've heard of ratings wars," said the inspector and this time not even Langdon could have missed the ice in his tone. "But never of somebody actually dying in one."

"Well, at least Beautella didn't die."

Were there no limits to this man's insensitivity? wondered Molloy so angrily that he briefly thought he might have given voice to the question. Langdon, however, was looking not at him but at Frobisher. The A.P. alone had not asked after Beautella, whereas her well-being had been the first question of both Ahmed and his director.

"If the silly cow hadn't had hysterics, we could have finished the show and given her and Cobb automatic entry to the next round. The audience would have put them through anyway after Cobb's impromptu solo. Instead she's wrecked everything. Professional, indeed! Bloody amateur, if you ask me."

"I've just discovered someone I dislike more than Cobb Grainger," observed Molloy as the interview finished and Langdon closed the door.

Frobisher shook his head. "No. He can't help it. He's just nasty whereas our Mr Grainger chooses so to be. Indeed he strives after the very perfection of nastiness, refining it with each attempt."

Frobisher had adopted a thespian tone for his last sentence and Molloy smiled but did not disagree. His heart rose as his superior looked at his watch only to sink as the chief inspector declared triumphantly "time for one at the Pig and Pen," which Molloy knew meant several hours of brainstorming.

Alice was in bed and asleep when he finally arrived home but there was no trace of protest when Molloy carelessly tripped and, falling on the bed, woke her up. He expected her to ask the time but instead she told him, in urgent tones, that she could not get over what had happened to Beautella. There had been amateur footage taken by some of the audience on mobile phones which had been played throughout the day on all the news bulletins. Some ardent fan had thrown a brick through the windows of Fabulous Flying.

"That poor, poor girl! They were saying tonight that it could have been attempted murder."

"What took them so long? You didn't seem so upset about Jess."

"This is worse. Oh, I know she's not dead, but to think of her all the way up there and helpless. One of her friends told the news that she hated even the top of a double-decker bus. Have you seen her today?"

"No. The doctor was very clear that she was not up to it. They've kept her in all day and were going to discharge her tonight but then changed their minds. The medic Frobisher spoke to said she was still in deep shock."

"They won't section her, will they?"

"They can't. She won't be remotely a danger to anyone including herself. She is going home to her parents and fortunately they live in London, so she can stay there as long as she likes and still try to get back to work, eventually. We will try to see her on Monday."

"And tomorrow?" Alice could not keep her voice entirely tremor-free.

"Home all day," grinned Molloy and his heart rose at her delighted reaction.

"Let's go for a drive out to Kew. The children can run round in the fresh air."

Molloy grunted assent as he began to drift towards sleep. Just before consciousness departed he heard Alice murmur "Home all day" and her contentment led him into a dreamless night of deep, deep rest.

"Home all day," Jonathan repeated. "That's great, Dad."

Zoe appeared less convinced. "Well, I hope nobody is going to suggest a walk. I promised Alex I'd go into town with her."

"Zoe, you see Alex every day at school." Barbara's tone was sharp.

"So? I see Dad every day."

Frobisher knew he should tell her not to be rude to her mother but he did not want the day marred by bickering.

"But it would be fun to go out all together, wouldn't it?" he tried.

"Not if it's a walk. It's too bloody cold."

Frobisher warned Barbara with a glance not to take the bait of the profanity.

"Well, what do you suggest?" he asked.

"Ice- skating."

Jonathan choked on his toast.

"Well, what then, nerd-head?" challenged his sister.

Their parents waited. Some wretched museum, predicted Frobisher. Some obscure gallery, thought Barbara. Jonathan cheerfully confounded both prophecies.

"There's a Doctor Who exhibition at White City."

Frobisher watched amused as Zoe struggled with her inner child. The inner child won.

"Well done, Jonathan," he grinned, repressing the feeling that he could do without any more behind- the-scenes glimpses of flagship television programmes and caught the thought reflected in Barbara's worried glance.

"It's OK," he told her when the teenagers had gone upstairs to get ready. "As you know, I rather like Doctor Who myself. I just hope it won't be too crowded."

A forlorn hope, he reflected ruefully when they found themselves standing in a long queue in the November rain. He toyed with the idea of suggesting that the youngsters go to Westfield and find a Starbucks, while their parents kept their places in the crocodile that was moving as slowly as a keenly- watched clock, but knew that Zoe might be too distracted by the shops.

So they endured the wait, stamping their feet and banging gloved hands together in the intervals when they were not holding aloft umbrellas. When at last they reached the head of the queue and warmth was no longer quite so distant a prospect, Frobisher braced himself for a large crowd in a confined space but was pleasantly surprised to find plenty of room.

A jostling group of children had gathered around K-9 and there was a queue for the "Tardis Experience" but otherwise circulation was easy. Some of the "companions" were there in person and Tom Baker himself was at the controls in the centre of one room. Zoe was examining a showcase of the clothes worn by Sarah-Jane Smith while Jonathan was peering intently at a Dalek, as if trying to fathom out its inner workings.

"It's odd," remarked his son when they all joined up a little later. "You would have thought they would have thought of teleporting, but that only came along with *Blake's Seven* ."

Blake's Seven? Surely that had been well before his son's time? Repeats, perhaps? Or had Jonathan studied the history of TV science fiction as seriously as he studied the curriculum at school? Or perhaps one of his friends was a fan and they had watched DVDs from boxed sets in their bedrooms? Frobisher felt saddened that he did not know.

"Of course," Jonathan was saying, "*Blake's Seven* was surprising in that the main character loses out to a subsidiary one. You can't imagine the Doctor playing second fiddle to, say, a companion. But then he usually travels with only one companion so I suppose there's an absence of competition......""Oh, put a sock in it," broke in Zoe rudely. "You sound as if you come from another age yourself. Actually another planet might be...."

"Zoe!" remonstrated both parents simultaneously.

"Oh, I know. He can't help it."

Jonathan grabbed her scarf and pretended to strangle her.

"Stop it or you'll get us thrown out," said Barbara, relieved that her children, now growing into such different people, could still demonstrate the affection of play-fighting. Jonathan rarely took offence but her concern was for Zoe, fearing that her daughter's scorn and insults proceeded from a sense of inferiority rather than from exasperation.

"From both, probably," said Frobisher when his wife confided the thought to him later over a glass of white wine for her and a Stella Artois for him. "Anyway, here's to a successful day!"

"Have you had any further thoughts about Jonathan's schooling?" asked Barbara and immediately the feeling of happy relaxation drained out of him. He did not want to face such a question tonight. He did not want to decide anything more exacting than the time Zoe should be in bed or the tie he should wear tomorrow.

Barbara opened her mouth to pursue the topic and then changed her mind. He was tired and she was more likely to prevail if he wasn't. She must let him get further with this *Lively Toes* case first. Frobisher gauged her thoughts accurately and felt a fleeting relief but, his mood destroyed, he found his mind engage once more with Jess's murder and Beautella's ordeal. He wondered if Molloy had managed to switch off.

"Just switch off," advised Alice as three- year-old Immie and four-year-old Conor fought in their child seats in the rear of the Ford Focus. "If you ignore them they'll stop."

"I haven't noticed that work yet."

"It will."

"Before we get to Kew?"

"Before we get half way to Kew. Trust me. I'm their mother."

"Shall we bet?"

"Bad example."

Molloy smiled as did Alice when her prediction was fulfilled five minutes later and both children fell asleep.

The roads were fairly clear after the fashion of a Sunday morning, the traffic slowing only occasionally. Pedestrians ambled with children in tow or dogs on leads where normally the pavements were busy with people hurrying to work clutching briefcases or smart handbags, fumbling in their pockets for season tickets as they approached the tube stations. Cars glided lawfully along bus lanes, church bells rang out their summons, children played in tiny front gardens despite the cold and rain, lights shone from windows which on weekdays were dark with absence while large office buildings were dark instead of illuminated on every floor. As they passed one such block, Molloy saw a solitary light on a high floor.

Alice followed his glance. "Someone trying to impress the managing director."

"Or trying to get some work done in peace and quiet. No telephones ringing or secretaries coming in every five minutes."

"Or escaping the nagging wife and screaming children at home."

"Probably none of the above. He just forgot to switch the light off ."

Alice cut off a laugh, afraid of waking the children before she could give them the freedom of space, fun and play.

"I know! Why not go through Richmond and see the deer?" said Molloy suddenly.

"You'll have to wake them up to look, but go for it! They'll love it."

"Deers!" yelled Conor waking unprompted at just the right moment. Molloy slowed down.

"Deer," said Alice. "It's one of those funny ones like sheep. One deer and lots of deer."

"Reindeers! Rudolph!" shrieked Immie, woken by Conor's shout.

"Rein*deer*," corrected Conor loftily.

"Where's his red nose?" demanded Immie. "Mummy, his nose isn't red."

Molloy, almost deafened in the confines of the small car, felt the tension of the last two days drain from him.

"That one isn't Rudolph. That's why," said Conor in the tone of one who knew that Rudolph did not exist but deigned to indulge those less well-informed.

"Mummy, which one is Rudolph?" Immie's tone combined urgent inquiry with a small seed of doubt.

"Ask Daddy," answered Alice wickedly. "He's the detective."

"Thanks, Mummy. I don't know, Immie. I shall have to study their hoof prints."

"You don't need hoof things," retorted his daughter with inarguable logic. "You just need a red nose."

"Touché," murmured Alice.

"Let's all look for him," said Molloy hastily and the game lasted till they were out of the park.

"We didn't see him," wailed Immie.

"Of course not," retorted her brother. "It isn't Christmas yet."

"Out of the mouths of babes and sucklings," grinned Molloy. "Talking of which, that looks like a christening."

They had come to a halt in a queue at some traffic lights and to their left was a church on the steps of which stood a group of people smiling at a photographer. In the centre stood a man holding a baby. Some of the older women wore hats and one or two younger ones sported fascinators. The men were in suits.

"They're making quite an event of it," observed Alice.

Surprised by her husband's silence, she turned to look at him and saw him staring into the distance with a surprised look on his face. The lights changed but he made no attempt to drive on until irritably blaring horns brought him back to reality with almost a physical start.

"Sorry," he said as he took his foot from the brake and let in the clutch.

"What is it?"

"I've just realised what was missing."

"You've lost me."

"No. I'm right here and I'm not going to phone Frobisher. In fact I'm so not going to phone Frobisher that I'm giving you my mobile." He began to fumble in his pocket, located the device and passed it to his bemused wife.

At intervals throughout the day, Molloy's distracted look returned. Alice said nothing until they were home when she gave her husband his mobile, while also picking up the handset of the landline and handing it to him.

"I am going to put the children to bed. You are going to phone Frobisher."

"But………"

"I am not going to spend the evening with a man looking into space. Get dialling."

Molloy watched her helping Immie upstairs and then went into the dining room into which the sounds of Conor's children's pro-gramme occasionally drifted. Both Frobisher's mobile and landline answered with a message service. He left one on each and sent both a text and an email to Frobisher's mobile. He could do no more and had no real need to do even that. It could wait till the morn-ing and meanwhile he should concentrate on Alice, offer to do the cooking, put her first for once.

Ten minutes later he was focussing with urgency on his wife as she leaned over the bannisters and called down in calm tones that she had just had a contraction. Two hours later her parents had arrived to look after the children and her mother was telling him not to hang round any longer.

"Never mind timing the contractions. Third babies can be very quick. Get her to hospital now."

They had been gone less than half an hour when Frobisher rang. Alice's mother told them where her son- in- law was and Frobisher decided that no, this was not the moment to pursue his sergeant on his mobile. He could only hope, probably in vain, that speculation as to what Molloy might have wanted to tell him would not keep him awake during the night.

He finally soothed himself with the reflection that third babies were quick to arrive, there was still the whole night ahead, Alice's mother was there to cope with the children and so there was no reason why Molloy should not appear in the office in the morning.

He made the mistake of revealing these thoughts to Barbara whose hollow laugh apprised him of the error of his ways.

CHAPTER EIGHT

IN WHICH MOLLOY MAKES A BREAKTHROUGH

Molloy appeared after lunch, his eyes ringed with shadow and his hair slightly awry. Frobisher looked up in surprise and relief as he entered the room, having already learned by text that his sergeant was now the proud father of a baby girl, Kathleen Fenella.

"Kathleen should make her stand out these days," observed Frobisher to the AC. "It's all Kylies and Chantelles but I haven't heard of a Fenella in years."

"There was someone once called Fenella Fielding." The AC was delighted to reveal some knowledge of trends even if half a century out of date. "What is rather more important is whether Molloy wants this paternity leave nonsense."

Frobisher now put the question, using the AC's own words and, perhaps somewhat disrespectfully, in a passable rendering of his superior's cadences.

Molloy gave a wry grimace. "Perhaps not just yet, sir. Alice's mother, who by the way is the original Kathleen, has taken over and Alice says there are too many of us in the house. I have been politely asked to leave."

He was lucky in Alice, thought Frobisher, undeceived by the light tone, who accepted the life of a policeman's wife more readily than did Barbara. He doubted Molloy would want much time off, despite the circumstances. Indeed the sergeant was now engaging with the task to hand as if he had not spent the night in hospital watching the birth and first hours of life of his new daughter.

"I was trying to phone you before it all happened. I've suddenly realised what it was that was nagging at me when I was looking at those albums at Jess's parents'. There were no christening snaps."

Frobisher, baffled, raised his eyebrows. "You've lost me."

"Her parents are religious. Remember Mrs Allward's tone when she remarked upon Fred leaving the church? Those albums were full of family christenings and one of the photos on the mantel-piece - you remember? - was of Jess and a Bishop in a confirmation group. Jess's album had umpteen shots of her in nativity plays, singing in a church choir, having fun on a Sunday School outing, all very standard C of E stuff, but no christening shots at all."

"Perhaps something went wrong with the camera. What are you getting at?"

"Sir, both of us noticed that Jess didn't look like either of her parents and that she must have been a late baby and there are no siblings."

Frobisher caught the other's excitement. "You're saying Jess could have been adopted?"

"Yes, sir. It fits and we've always said that the motive in this case must lie outside the show. I know it's an outside chance but maybe Jess's background holds the clue."

"The victim's background usually does. The birth certificate must be in our files."

"We'd need it for the coroner. Surely we'd have noticed if it had been an adoption certificate? Or if it had been the original birth record with a different name?"

"We should have but we've been working backward through her life, expecting to find more recent clues and connections with some of the other actors in this drama. The AC won't be pleased. Better check before yesterday."

It did not take long. The Allwards had supplied an adoption certificate for the coroner and a trace unearthed the original birth record. Jessica Allward had been born Tracey Jane Woods in 1966 at a hospital in Aldershot. Her mother was Margaret Anne Woods but no father was named.

The detectives drove to Warwickshire the next day. It was no good, thought Frobisher, asking why they had not mentioned the adoption when they had handed over the certificate. They would presume the police already knew and it was, grimaced Molloy, only too reasonable an assumption. Yet had he not had that chance sighting of the christening group on Sunday, it could have been a while before they realised. He had found through first class detective work what was simply lying about waiting to be discovered and the excitement of his deductions had metamorphosed into embarrassment.

"We are not infallible," Frobisher had soothed him but Molloy knew that it was thoroughness not infallibility, which was in question. Hell! How could he have missed something so obvious? Something that was just staring up at him from a file? The inspector had been kind about it, commenting on the mass of paper and large number of files they were dealing with but it was an elementary mistake, *his* mistake and both knew it.

"It isn't the only mistake you'll ever make and it could be a lot worse. *I've* made worse in my time. It's only in detective novels that the clues are always obscure and the sleuths never forget a damn thing. And in the end this may all lead nowhere, anyway. Indeed the odds are that it probably will."

It was not, Frobisher was later to reflect, his most successful prediction.

The Allwards seemed to have aged in the space of less than three weeks. Mrs Allward's eyes were no longer red but the lines on her face looked somehow deeper and Jess's father was visibly more stooped. The house was dustier, the windows duller, the antimacassars creased. Even the tea, poured by Mrs Allward with a trembling hand, tasted blander. The light and purpose of the elderly couple's life were extinguished. As before, there was no sign of Jess's children. Probably they had already gone to their father.

The social pleasantries over, Frobisher came straight to the point.

"Mrs Allward, we know that you adopted Jess when she was less than two months old. Do you know anything about the birth mother?"

"No. We didn't want to. We chose Jess from several babies in a home. That was what you did then. All we asked about was if there was any serious mental history or major genetic illness or anything like that, but they didn't really know and quite honestly having your own doesn't prevent that, does it? We just had to take our chance. I think the mother was young and single but that may have just been a general impression, because it was what most of them were, poor things."

"Did you know her name?"

"Oh, yes. There was paper work. It was Margaret Woods but that was all we knew. I never heard anything about the father."

"When did you tell Jess she was adopted?"

"From the start. I didn't want it to come as a shock later. We told her that her real mother was too poor to keep her and loved her so much that she gave her to us to have a lovely, safe home. Obviously over the years she began to put two and two together and worked out that Margaret was an unmarried mother."

"Did you tell her Margaret's name?"

"Yes, but not until she was sixteen. We had always hoped that we wouldn't have to but when she was nine the law changed and allowed adopted children to trace their birth parents once they became of age. It wasn't like that when we chose her or I think we might have gone into her mother's background more thoroughly, just so that we could be prepared for anything she might find out later."

"She didn't show much interest until she was about fifteen or sixteen," put in Henry Allward. "Seemed happy enough just to accept things but then she began asking questions. Natural enough, I suppose."

"And when she was eighteen?"

"She said she wanted to trace her birth mother. Told us we would always be Mum and Dad but she wanted to find her roots,"

Anne Allward's voice caught but she went on. "We couldn't tell her anything and she had to do this counselling stuff but then she found out and managed to track Margaret Woods down."

There was a silence, which to Molloy's tautened nerves was shocking as he guessed how it would be broken. He was already looking round to see if a box of tissues was to hand when Mrs Allward broke down, her shoulders heaving as the sobs dragged themselves from her stomach, tore her lungs with a rasping sound and erupted from her frail being in an explosion of helpless grief. She began to rock and keen and her husband struggled from his chair to comfort her.

Frobisher, his face white, felt nothing but icy anger. They would catch the murderer who had brought this misery to an elderly couple. They must. It was becoming personal. He glanced at Molloy who was in turn watching the Allwards, wondering how best to intervene. It was a situation from which one should creep tactfully away but they couldn't because they were policemen.

They waited until Anne Allward's sobs died but it was Henry Allward who supplied the explanation.

"She didn't want to know," his face was contorted with anger and disbelief. "She wouldn't even talk to her. Just said it was a long time ago and she hoped Jess had been happy but it was best they shouldn't have anything to do with each other and all but put the phone down. Until then we thought the worst that could happen would be to us. That Jess would turn to this woman as her mother and Anne didn't know how she'd bear it but it turned out much worse than that. Jess felt rejected. Of course we'd warned Jess that could happen but when it did it was terrible. I don't reckon she ever got over it."

"If Jess was eighteen, that must have been 1984?"

"Yes. It was all happening when she was coming up to A levels. We suggested she wait until they were over. After all there was also the heartache of her grandfathers' dying"

"When we were last here you talked of how Jess was a bit unhappy at that time and you thought she was making a mistake to reject university but you didn't mention any of this. Why?"

Mrs Allward looked startled. "I suppose we were just concentrating on what she talked about at that time, which was her granddads and her career options."

Frobisher remembered the glance that passed between them and was unconvinced. "Mrs Allward, we realise that this is a horribly painful time for you both and for the children but we are investigating your daughter's *murder* and if you withhold information, we may not do that successfully. Now, why didn't you tell us?"

Mrs Allward looked down in her lap but did not reply. Then Henry said quietly but fiercely.

"Because she was *ours*. I don't care what the law says. She was *ours*. Not hers. We didn't want all that stuff in the newspapers. Whose business is it after all this time? And what does it tell you anyway? You don't think the birth mother killed her, do you? It was someone from that show and that's where you should be asking questions, not here, not......"

His voice broke off in a sob and Anne Allward put her hand over his.

"We'll go," said Frobisher gently, "but before we do I have no choice but to ask whether you or Jess kept any of the information about Margaret Woods which enabled Jess to trace her."

"We never had it in the first place. I don't know whether Jess kept anything but you've searched her house in London, haven't you?"

"Can we see her old room here?"

"PC Angelus did that," objected Henry.

"Yes, but now we know what we are looking for, we may find something."

"Oh, get on with it," wailed Anne. "Just get on with it."

"Are the children in the house?"

"No, they've gone to their Dad."

Jess's room yielded several ragged bears, a dilapidated box of fuzzy felts, an old childish jewel case which played music when opened and nothing else. Clearly she had taken everything to London. There were no papers or address books, no notebooks, no clothes except a fraying dressing gown in the wardrobe. The drawers were full of spare blankets and household linen. This had not been Jess's room for many years. Molloy conscientiously looked under the mattress and felt a fool.

"Nothing," said Frobisher glumly. "We'll have to look through her house again and make sure the children haven't taken anything. And then we will need to talk to her ex-husband. He has a cast iron alibi, gave us a full statement and we've largely left him alone but now we'll have to see what Jess told him about her origins. Meanwhile we must look again at any scribbled notes she had in the house with numbers on and re-trawl the address books."

"And trace Margaret Woods."

"And don't forget Ru and Em. They are the only ones to offer any lead at all. Ru because of the singers and Em because she was alone on that floor with Jess. And find out who was creeping about in the dark clearing his throat and who had the knowledge and opportunity to fix the lighting and flying computers and who could have had access to the judges' papers. Then we can tell the AC we have it all sewn up."

Perhaps, reflected Molloy, he should have elected paternity leave after all.

The Allwards had recovered themselves, at least superficially, when the detectives arrived downstairs. Declining an offer of more tea, they got gratefully into the car, drained by the interview, frustrated by being as far as ever from the solution.

This time they were being driven and Molloy felt the tiredness of the previous night begin to overtake him. He began to nod.

"But what has any of it to do with Beautella?" Frobisher was asking.

Molloy did not answer. Perhaps if he drifted off, the inspector would leave him to sleep. Blessed, deep slumber. He waited for a dig in the ribs but it never came and he woke two hours later as the car was crawling towards the Yard.

He turned to apologise to Frobisher, only to see the inspector also asleep, mouth open, snoring gently. As the car stopped his superior woke up with a start already talking.

"Of course we will not be looking for a Margaret Woods in all likelihood. She may have married. More than once for that matter. If so, electoral rolls won't take us far. And it is hardly an unusual name anyway. Could be anywhere in the whole country. Hell of a job. Better start by seeing if that home is still around and if they have any records."

It wasn't. St. John the Baptist Church of England Children's Home had been closed for more than twenty years said the efficient looking clerk at Surrey County Council. Certainly in all normal circumstances there would have been records either with the Church of England or with the Council but she remembered a scandal in which a disgruntled employee had tried to set fire to the home when it was closing. There were no children there at the time and the fire was put out fairly quickly but not before it had destroyed the administrative offices in the attics.

"Just our luck," groaned Molloy.

"Were you looking for something in particular?"

"Yes. We need to trace a particular woman who put up her child for adoption in 1966."

"That's a long time ago but there was a nun, a nursing sister, who used to work there, although I couldn't be sure when. I remember her well enough because she actually fought the man who was trying to burn the place down. It was a huge story. You should be able to trace her through her order, which was a Catholic one, all part of the ecumenical movement which was gaining momentum at that time. I was about ten when it happened and remember the drama which was big round here."

"Do you remember her name?"

The clerk ran an elegant hand through her grey- white hair. "It'll come to me in a moment…. Aloysius. That was it. Sister something or other Aloysius."

"Thanks," grinned Molloy.

"My pleasure, good luck, good morning, sir, can I help you?" said the clerk in one pleasant, energetic sentence.

"Sister Aloysius? Yes, she left the order after Vatican two," and Molloy hated the cheerfulness in the priest's tones now coming across the telephone wires. "Her order might be able to tell you more but I do know she became Pauline O'Malley in real life. We all remember her well."

As indeed they should, thought Molloy who had spent a couple of hours locating the press at the time of the fire. One very small nun had fought off one very strong arsonist and had prevailed.

"Oh, that was nothing," she told him the following afternoon when he had run her to ground, so much more quickly than he expected, via another ex-nun, a junior nurse and a children's charity. "Poor old Ned. Wasn't he the unlucky one, now? His mother died when he was very small and then his father when he was not much older and there wasn't any family. And wasn't he the slow one? Couldn't learn, poor lamb, couldn't do the apprenticeship, but he could do anything with his hands and the home kept him on as a caretaker. And then they were closing it and he didn't understand. To be sure, I didn't have to fight him and didn't the newspapers talk rubbish. He was crying like a baby. Said he would have no home.

"The church wouldn't prosecute and so the insurance wouldn't pay and it was a grand old muddle but it wasn't Ned's fault."

Pauline O'Malley paused for breath and Molloy seized his opportunity. "Sister, were you working at the home in 1966?"

"I'm not Sister these days. I left the order. No, I didn't get there till 1973."

Molloy's heart sank. "Do you know anybody who was there then?"

"The matron, but she died. The old priest, but he died. Oh, yes one of the Anglican nuns. Sister Mary."

"Do you know what happened to Sister Mary?" Molloy felt his patience hanging by a thread.

"Yes, we all knew that. She went as a missionary to Africa and there was a coup and wasn't she the brave one? Stayed on with the children she was looking after. She came back a couple of years ago but she's old and ill in a church nursing home."

Molloy sighed. It seemed to be his fate to embark on a trail of elderly nuns while Frobisher was interviewing the delectable Beautella, an interview postponed until today to allow them to make the unexpected journey to Jess's parents.

The November day had darkened into a drizzly evening when he finally spoke to Sister Mary, somewhat reassured by the matron's statement that the nun was still mentally alert, often talked about the past and would certainly be up to answering questions. As he waited for her to be brought to the phone he believed he had wasted his day and seemed to receive confirmation of this almost immediately when she told him that she had started work at the home in 1967.

No, she had never heard of Tracey Jane Woods but then so many babies had come and gone. Margaret Anne Woods? No, sorry. She was sorry she could not help. Goodnight, Sergeant........*wait.*

Molloy jumped at the sudden excited emphasis. He waited.

"You don't mean *Maggie* Woods do you?"

"I suppose I might," Molloy felt the familiar fluttering sensation in his stomach as he sensed a breakthrough.

"If it's Maggie Woods we're talking about, then there'll be no shortage of people who'll remember. They were still talking about it when I arrived a year later and her name was always cropping up amongst the older sisters. It was such a scandal."

A scandal, mused Molloy, as he waited for her to recover from a fit of coughing, listening to the sounds of concerned murmurs and a glass of water being sought. Single mothers would scarcely have been a scandal for a children's home in the mid- sixties, even if it was run by the church. Had the father been famous? Was Maggie Woods then a twelve- year-old? Was she arrested on the premises of some back street abortionist?

Molloy's imagination ran riot but then he heard Sister Mary gulping water and presently she was talking to him in a voice now slightly croaky.

✤ ✤ ✤

115

It seemed to Frobisher that Beautella had aged ten years. Her large brown eyes seemed to have grown too big for her now pinched, pale face. She wore no make-up and the once thick, shiny hair was lifeless and dull. She lay on her parents' sofa, wrapped in a duvet, looking back at the detective without interest.

"Miss LaReine," he began "I won't......."

"You might as well say Miss Hobbs. Beautella LaReine has gone. Her show has gone. Her studio will follow and she'll be lucky not to be murdered."

Her tone was listless rather than self-pitying and Frobisher felt a flash of irritation. Helen Brown, with none of this girl's advantages, was fighting back. Why couldn't Beautella? Behind her, Gillian Hobbs shook her head sadly and he felt ashamed.

"You think somebody tried to kill you? That it was not just a computer error?"

"You weren't up there, were you? If you had been you wouldn't think it was all some silly mistake. I wanted to get out of that harness, I wanted to end it."

Frobisher decided to play along. "All right. But who would know that you would react that way?"

Beautella flicked her bandaged hand dismissively. "Anybody who knew anything about height phobia. Throw yourself into the void, get it over. Everybody knows real acrophobics react like that. You don't need a degree in psychiatry."

"How was Cobb Grainger behaving beforehand?"

"Oh, loving it. Just loving it. He knew I was dreading it."

"The dance he did when you were trapped near the ceiling. Was it part of the routine you had practised?"

Frobisher saw a flash of anger give life to her eyes.

"You don't suppose I was looking down watching?"

He had anticipated the answer if not the terms in which it was couched and withdrew an envelope from his briefcase.

"Miss LaReine, I have here a DVD recording of that dance. It does not feature what was going on up in the gods. I should like to play it to you and I would be grateful if you could tell me if you recognise any part of the dance."

"Then you must play it without the music. I never want to hear that music again. It was when I knew they couldn't get me down."

Frobisher obliged and watched Beautella watching the brief film. She did so conscientiously.

"It isn't any one particular dance. Lots of steps that don't go together but, apart from the tap, yes, I taught him all of them at one time or another. It looks as if he was doing whatever came into his head to keep the audience engaged. He would. As for those glances up at me, he didn't give a damn. It was all pure play-acting."

Beautella added a curse, vicious and profane, which took Frobisher by surprise. He glanced at her mother, who was observing her daughter anxiously.

"So, as far as you can tell, there is no evidence that he rehearsed this dance? He must have just made it up on the spot?"

"Yes. I see where you are going, Inspector, and I wish I could say otherwise but there is nothing in that dance which suggests he knew he was going to have to do it. Also it was clever of him not to do the one we were scheduled to perform because if I had come down, he would have had to do it all over again and it would have lost its freshness, so it looks as if he still thought I might come back and carry on."

"Or wanted us to think that," was Frobisher's mental reservation.

Gillian Hobbs said she could hear the kettle and tea was ready. Frobisher had promised not to question Beautella without her present so they waited while she headed for the kitchen, her daughter making no attempt at small talk while she was gone.

Frobisher found his thoughts wandering to Molloy and hoped he was having better luck. Unbeknown to him, his sergeant was at that very moment, hearing the words that would eventually set them on the right trail.

"You will have heard what it was like in those days, Sergeant? There was no abortion unless you wanted to take a huge risk in the backstreets or could afford Harley Street. If a girl became pregnant she had the baby and if she was young and couldn't look after it she had it adopted. A small number resorted to extreme stratagems, having the babies secretly and then leaving them on the steps of hospitals or Doctor Barnardo's or some such place. Quite a few were sent away by their parents and came back without the babies, who were taken from them often before they had even held them. Others were helped through it in an era of changing attitudes.

"Maggie was a grammar school girl. A sixth –former to be sure, but for a girl still at school to be having a baby was very shocking then. She had to leave but she had younger siblings still at the school and rather than have them endure the gossip and taunts, her parents sent her to a relative while they worked out what to do once the baby was born. I can't remember anything about the relative or where she lived but it must have been somewhere near our home.

"Anyway, there must have been discussions and I suppose Maggie must have decided that she wasn't going to keep the baby. So far nothing very remarkable, Sergeant, just a tale of the sixties. It was what happened next that shook everybody. Maggie didn't wait for the usual formalities. She just bundled up the child one day and dumped her.'

"At the door of your children's home?"

"Oh, no, sergeant. At the gates of a local dogs' home."

CHAPTER NINE

IN WHICH ANTON SPOTS A CONNECTION

Hearing Molloy's shocked exclamation, Sister Mary paused.
"It gets worse. There was a note, hidden in the child's clothing. I am afraid it said something like 'my name is Tracey Jane - or Tracey Sue or Tracey something- but it might as well be Spot or Rover or Fido because I am as much unwanted as they are.' So much bitterness, sergeant, I can hardly bear to think about it."

"Poor girl," murmured Molloy, thinking of his own new baby, cosseted, loved, coo-ed over by doting parents, grandparents and siblings.

"If you mean Maggie Woods, there are those who will tell you to think again. But if you mean Tracey whatever it was then, yes. I hope she had a good life, Sergeant."

"It was Tracey Jane. She was adopted by a couple who loved her and she married and had children of her own." It did not seem necessary to mention the divorce but he paused before the next bit. The nun was there before him.

"You said you were investigating the *Lively Toes* murder?"

"Yes. I'm afraid Jess Allward was Tracey Jane Woods, although I would be grateful if you kept that quiet for a while. It may have no relevance to the case and the Allwards have been through enough already."

"Of course, Sergeant. Do you want to hear the rest of the story?"

"I think I should."

"Well two children of I think seven or so were walking to school and found her. The dogs' home was not yet open for the day and they did not know what to do. Of course there must have been staff there but they were too young to work that out and, bless them, they knew they mustn't leave the baby so they carried her off, meaning to take her to school but she got too heavy after a while so they went into a church. Churches were often kept open in those days. There they left the baby by the altar believing God would keep her safe and ran off to school where they were very late.

"The story goes that the little boy got the ruler for telling lies but eventually they persuaded somebody to listen and the school rang up the vicar. On the way over from the vicarage he met a scandalised flower-arranger who told him there was a baby by the altar. Now, here was the oddest thing of all, Sergeant...."

Could it get any odder? wondered Molloy, as he waited for the final revelation in the terrible story.

"...The baby never once woke. She was dumped in a strange place, outdoors with dogs barking nearby. She was carried clumsily by two children, left alone in another unfamiliar place and finally rescued but she slept through it all. It came to light that Maggie had crushed up some sleeping pills in Tracey's milk. A tiny baby! She must have known the risk."

Molloy briefly closed his eyes. Poor, scared, desperate Maggie.

The nun's next words caused him to sit suddenly upright, eyes wide open. "You must talk to my niece. She was the secretary cum administrator cum assistant everything to the Matron. She told me she had been sent to interview Maggie when they admitted poor little Tracey. I have her number."

"And her address?" This was one for a visit.

"It's not that far away from where the home used to be," he told Frobisher later. "Even so tracing Maggie Woods won't be easy. We have no records from the home which would have been available when Jess was looking for her mother so we're going to have to start by contacting the Council and the main tracing agencies, to see if there is anything in their records about Jess. And if we strike gold there, it was still 30 years ago. Maggie Woods could have moved a dozen times or, as we've already thought, changed her name through marriage. It's just possible there's a parent still alive and somebody might eventually stumble on the name of the relative who took her in and we can see if there are any alumni records at the school, if it still exists, for the siblings. Then there's the parental will if they are both dead which may mention her, but it will be a long, hard slog. I'll get DC Forbes on to it."

"And get her some help. The AC will be champing at the bit again soon."

"Yes. But at the moment we don't even know where she came from. It was the relative who lived near the children's home, not the family itself. We will find out, but it will take time. I just hope the niece remembers something significant."

"When are you seeing her?"

"Tomorrow morning. It shouldn't take long to get there. Will you come?"

"No. This is your show. I shan't be in the office either. I am going to sit in my garden shed with a wet towel round my head and go over all we have. There must be something somewhere we haven't seen."

Molloy grinned. He had seen the garden shed, which in reality was a small annexe on the back of Frobisher's house. He envied his superior the ability to work at home, which the presence of small children made impossible for him.

"Meanwhile," continued Frobisher. "We shall look over today's findings at the Pig and Pen and then you can get back to Alice."

Molloy blinked. "The Pig and Pen is out near the FBC studios. Why not go nearer? We could go to....."

"You never know who else might be in the Pig and Pen. It's worth the trip."

Reluctantly Molloy began to gather up his work. As if sensing his mood Frobisher said. "Anton often goes there and at the moment he is playing his cards too close to his chest. We might persuade him to swap notes."

"We can always ring him and tell him he's blooming well got to."

The Inspector closed his eyes after the manner of a maiden aunt in whose presence some gross impropriety has just been uttered.

"Ever the diplomat, Molloy. Ever the diplomat."

As soon as they entered the Pig and Pen, Molloy saw Anton and, seeing also that he was alone, made his way between the tables towards him. The dancer's eyes slid past him to Frobisher.

"Hallo, Inspector. I thought you might come here. What are you having?"

It was Molloy who went to the bar, while Frobisher settled in the chair opposite Caesar, who immediately leaned across and, lowering his voice, said.

"I have a favour to ask, Inspector. When you next interview Fred please will you do it at his flat and let me know when?"

Frobisher raised his eyebrows. "What makes you think we shall be interviewing Fred any time soon?"

"Well, unless you have had a sudden breakthrough, you must surely start looking more closely at the cast of suspects and Fred is the only one who had any connection with Jess outside the show or from the past. So I reasoned you would want to talk to him again. If I know when you are going, I will find an excuse to call and then while you are talking to him I shall find an excuse to rummage round."

"And the result of all these excuses will be what, sir?"

"Perhaps nothing but if I'm right I will have something for you."

"Something about Fred and Jess?"

"No. Something about Cobb and Fred."

"They knew each other before *Lively Toes*?"

"Maybe. Possibly not. How are your own investigations going?"

Molloy returned at that moment and set down the drinks, a pint each for him and Frobisher and a fizzy water for Anton, whose glance seemed briefly to rest on their waistlines. It gave the Inspector a precious few seconds in which to make up his mind and answer a question he had been asking himself on their way here. To his sergeant's astonishment he briefed Anton fully, knowing that he was breaking half the rules in the book. Molloy stirred uneasily.

"Needless to say, if you breathe a word of this to anyone I lose my job."

Anton hardly heard him. He appeared to be staring into the middle distance. Eventually he muttered "It would make sense if it was her rather than the aunt or cousin or whatever."

Frobisher looked at him quizzically but did not ask him to expound.

"I suppose," said Anton suddenly with excitement in his eyes. "Fred could be Jess's father."

"Er…. that's quite a leap," demurred Molloy. "And why would anyone murder Jess because of that?"

"Perhaps she was going to expose him."

"You know showbiz better than we do, but somehow I can't see why it would matter. Wouldn't it be one of those long lost child reunions ? The sort of scenario that makes people say 'aaw' rather than 'tch, tch'? Even if anybody was censorious it was too long ago to get worked up about now."

If Frobisher was expecting Anton Caesar to look deflated at this demolition of his case, he was disappointed.

"Really? This was a vicar, don't forget. He may even have been already married."

"He was," confirmed Molloy. "Jess was born in June 1966. According to our records Fred married his first wife in 1965 by which time he was twenty one and a curate. So if he was Jess's father we have an adulterous curate who seduced and impregnated a sixth former and abandoned her so thoroughly that she dumped her child at a dogs' home. Anton could be right, sir, that could be blackmail territory. Fred has built a reputation as a courtly, old-fashioned gentleman. A revelation like that would blow it apart and destroy that career of his."

"And Jess would have been pretty bitter," mused Frobisher. "She traces her mother who doesn't want to know and then somehow or other finds out that her father is that nice ex-vicar who gave her dancing lessons and career advice when she was eighteen."

"So she says she'll tell the world." Anton's eyes sparkled.

"And Matt did say she was tense. He said she didn't seem frightened or hopeful, just tense. Well, if she was planning to denounce Fred she would be." Molloy was becoming as eager as Anton.

"Perhaps she even planned to do it on air." Suggested Frobisher, catching their mood. "But, no, that doesn't work. It's not yet a live show."

"Never will be now," observed Anton. "And I don't see her wrecking a show that was so central to her career but she would have plenty of other opportunities to give it air time and, to be blunt, she could have been axed anytime. She was forty-eight. She might not have cared about the repercussions on any future participation."

"So she tells Fred in order to make him stew. And he decides he can't take the risk. It's got to be worth thinking about seriously." Molloy looked at his superior for confirmation.

Anton's voice took on a cautionary tone. "But how would he know that she hadn't told anyone else or left a note in her house or with her lawyers?"

"If she was blackmailing him, then yes, that would be a standard precaution but if she merely threatened to denounce him and if Fred had any reason to think the outburst not premeditated........."

"Brendan, that's all very well but we appear to be getting completely carried away here. Will someone please give me the smallest reason to believe that Fred was Jess's father? Jess bore no resemblance to him at all."

Frobisher's comment was received in silence. Then he said. "We could do a DNA. We took everybody's as a matter of routine when we were trying to decode the flapper band. I can't help feeling someone would have noticed before this if they were similar."

"They were concentrating on comparisons with the band, sir, not with each other and there were an awful lot. Probably more than one person was doing it." Molloy sounded depressed.

Frobisher smiled. "Anyway, Anton, let's go back to where all this speculation started. Why pick on Fred as the father?"

"Well, if – and I acknowledge it is still if – Jess's background is the key then Fred is the only one old enough to have been involved."

"Or Cobb?" suggested Molloy.

Caesar looked genuinely shocked. "He would have been a schoolboy himself."

"It has been known," murmured Frobisher drily.

"And it would be a scandal for our squeaky clean politician." Molloy's depression seemed suddenly to have lifted. "Let's hope it's not too long before we find Maggie Woods. Who knows? Sister Mary's niece may yet have something to tell us."

"When will you be interviewing Fred?" Anton returned to his original theme.

Frobisher gazed blandly at the dancer. "It isn't fixed yet."

Anton pulled a face but did not pursue the subject. Molloy, who had not heard the earlier exchange, looked from one to the other.

"All right," relented Frobisher. "We'll try for the day after tomorrow. Nobody's training after all. I gather FBC have suspended the show. But tomorrow I am in my shed and the sergeant here is interviewing the only person we yet have who spoke to Maggie Woods. And before you ask, sir, no, you are not welcome in either place."

"No problem, Inspector, I have my own plans for tomorrow. And before you ask, no I shall not be giving you a pre-view."

The detectives laughed and shortly afterwards Frobisher broke up the gathering and let Molloy go home, where he was informed that both mother and child were fast asleep. He tiptoed into the tiny box room they called the nursery where Alice had painted Ratty and Moly on the walls. They both knew that Kathy would never come to appreciate it because once she was in a proper bed she would have to share the bigger room with Immie while Conor would be moved in here. They needed a bigger house but Alice never complained, determined not to work until the youngest child was at senior school and therefore resistant to any extra expenditure. She had made it

125

clear that she did not want to stop the family at the third child. "Bunk beds will do" had become almost a mantra.

For a while Molloy watched the sleeping baby, half-hoping she would wake so that he could lift her up and hold her close but knowing that his pleasure would be bought at the expense of Alice's well-earned rest.

When he finally crept out he found his mother-in-law on the landing with her finger to her lips. In whispers she suggested he sleep downstairs to avoid waking Alice and, reluctantly, he made his way to the sitting room where he discovered a bed already made up for him on the floor.

He awoke, surprised to find that he had slept soundly and comfortably. Alice was in the kitchen with the baby and his other children were impatient to gain access to his sleeping quarters. He rolled from the mattress, already wondering whether today might bring progress in a case that felt as sticky as treacle.

Sister Mary's niece was called June Kerswell. If she had worked in the home in the 1960s she was certainly at least in her seventies by now and Molloy expected a neat pensioner to answer the chimes, which rang in her semi when he pressed the bell. He was both amused and disconcerted when the door opened to reveal a bottle blonde in jeans, t-shirt and trainers who greeted him in the gravelly voice of a heavy smoker.

The small front room into which he was shown was immaculate, the coffee freshly brewed with a choice of hot or cold milk and a plate of home-baked biscuits smelled oven-fresh. In the corner was a small pen with four well-fed, neatly- groomed, inquisitive guinea-pigs, which had been provided with a small wooden house with *Chez Nous* painted over its door. He was absorbing the contrast when June Kerswell, following his glance, interrupted his thoughts.

"They're for the grandchildren."

Molloy smiled, mentioned his own new arrival and allowed a couple of minutes' social chatter before getting down to the purpose of his visit.

"Remember Maggie Woods? I shouldn't think anybody would ever forget her. She became part of the folklore of SJB." Her voice was a blend of reminiscent wonder and disgust.

"SJB? Oh, of course. St John the Baptist."

"A bit of a mouthful, Sergeant."

Molloy smiled. "Tell me all you remember. Everything. Even if it seems too trivial to bother with."

"Two children found little Tracey Jane outside a dogs' home. She was well cared-for and well-wrapped up but there was a very bitter note tucked in her clothes – my aunt told you about that? – and at first I thought this was bitterness on behalf of the child. Anyway the children parked the baby in a church and finally managed to persuade a teacher to take their story seriously and the vicar rushed over but a member of the Mothers' Union had already been in and found her.

"Our home was very nearby and the Vicar said to take her there while he called the police. By the time they came we had found the note. That evening a sergeant rang to say they had found a record of a child named Tracey Jane born in Aldershot at about the right time and next day another policeman rang to say that a woman had rung in to report both mother and child missing. It seems Maggie tried to run away as soon as she had left Tracey-Jane. The woman was, I think, an aunt. She was certainly a widow but I'm getting ahead of myself."

Molloy was having difficulty keeping up with his notes and Mrs Kerswell paused in her narrative to fill his cup. He looked up.

"Do you remember her name?"

"I thought I couldn't but then last night it suddenly came to me. Funny how those things happen, isn't it? It was Forest. I recalled it because there was some joke at the time about how it would be nice if Woods could grow into a Forest. Sorry, it sounds awful but Maggie *was* awful and the aunt or godmother or whatever was so nice.

"Anyway they found her and made her go back to Mrs Forest. She was only seventeen and in those days you had to be twenty one to do as you pleased. She was there when I went round to see her.

I had to check that she knew the baby would be put up for adoption and that she was happy to go along with that. Otherwise we would have needed a court order.

"Sergeant, that interview was the most shocking I ever had. Most times I just came away feeling drained. The girls came from all sorts of backgrounds but the one thing most of them had in common was that they hated giving up the babies. Some of them had no idea what they were doing when they conceived and didn't even realise they were pregnant until it began to show and their mothers started asking questions. Others certainly knew what they were about but didn't know anything like enough to avoid the consequences. If you have some notion of the sixties as the age of sexual liberation, Sergeant, think again. They were innocents abroad.

"But not Maggie Woods. It was still a time when a pregnant schoolgirl was a shocking phenomenon and I went along expecting to find a distraught girl but what I found was a defiant, heartless young woman. The older staff at the home called her a "brazen hussy" and the most common description of her was "bold as brass" and, believe me, sergeant, they weren't being prissy. They had seen it all before and weren't easily thrown but none of us quite got over Maggie Woods.

"I explained to her who I was and why I was there. Mrs Forest was in the room throughout.

" 'Well, of course you're going to palm it off on some silly cow, mooing because she can't have her own. What has it to do with me? I dumped her, didn't I?' That's pretty well verbatim after all these years. Of course at first I thought it was just a defence mechanism but as the conversation progressed it became clear that she genuinely cared nothing for the baby at all. Or for anybody else.

"Mrs Forest's son was a thalidomide baby and the wretched girl actually taunted her, saying that whoever else got the baby she didn't want it to be her because she wouldn't know how to look after a normal child. Then when I asked her if she was prepared to name the father she laughed in my face and said it 'could have been anyone'. Poor Mrs Forest didn't react at all, although she was scarlet and could not look at me. She obviously already knew what Maggie was like."

June Kerswell paused again, aware of the sergeant's furious scribbling. He glanced at the recorder and turned the tape over.

"I asked her what she wanted to do with her life and she told me to mind my own business but as I was going she stood at the gate and bawled after me: 'and don't ever let that brat know who her mother was. As far as I'm concerned she never existed and she can think I'm dead. Spin her some yarn with the violins in the background about how I died bringing her into the world.'

"She ran away again and this time I don't think anybody looked very hard for her."

There was a short silence before a shaken Molloy began his questions but each time he came to a dead end. Mrs Kerswell could not remember exactly where the aunt lived but that at least would be traceable from old records. Nor could she remember where Maggie came from originally. She did remember that she was a grammar school girl but not where. But Maggie had a "received English" accent and was probably from the Home Counties.

"Although of course that doesn't follow," she observed after a pause.

No, she had not kept in touch with anybody else who worked at the home except obviously Sister Mary. No, she could not remember the adoptive parents although she recalled them as very nice but then most of them were. She was sorry she could not be more helpful.

She asked no questions in return. Sister Mary had told her it was a murder investigation but she made no inquiries about his interest in Maggie Woods. The habit of discretion appeared to have followed her into retirement or perhaps Sister Mary had told her more than she should and she was protecting her.

When he at last closed his notebook and got up to leave Molloy felt the only progress he had made was to have a rather nasty picture of Jess's birth mother but he could not see that he was any nearer to finding a lead to her murderer. He wondered what Anton was doing and if Frobisher's wet towel had produced any fresh thoughts.

The sergeant had parked a short distance from the house and was glad of the brief walk in the early afternoon air. What had happened to Maggie Woods and even if they did find her what could she tell them? She did however appear to be spiteful and, if the years had not changed her, was it too fanciful to imagine her telling Jess who the father was? Just to throw a spanner into the works if he had a wife and family or to upset Jess if he was disreputable? In prison or something like that? It was the kind of unpleasantness with which Cobb Grainger might amuse himself so why should not Maggie Woods?

Frobisher would have told him he was letting his imagination run away with him but he had been right about the adoption even though he should have known it anyway. Reaching his car, he took off his jacket and put it in the back where his coat was already folded. Then he slid in to the driver's seat and placed his mobile in its cradle. He had just put the car in reverse when DC Forbes rang.

"Just leaving. Will be on the A3 in a little while," he told her when she had asked where he was.

"Then please turn the other way when you get to the A3 and make for Southampton. We've traced one of Maggie Woods's siblings, David Woods. She went to Priory Grammar School near Bath and so did he."

"Smart work!" congratulated Molloy but the interview caused him nothing but disappointment. David Woods was a bank manager with a wife and children but as far he was concerned no sister. She simply disappeared without trace when he was about twelve. Yes, she was living with their auntie Marjorie at the time. Yes, he would have that address somewhere because he never threw away an address book but Auntie Marjorie had died a while back and her husband long before that. There was a cousin, a thalidomide victim, but sadly he was killed in a car crash. Thank God Auntie Marjorie didn't live to see that. She had worshipped him.

Yes, he had a brother, Jack, who had also gone to Priory Grammar and was nearer in age to Maggie but he too had heard nothing. She was wild and the rumour was that she had gone to London but who knew? She had broken their parents' hearts. No, he had no idea who her boyfriends were. He vaguely recalled seeing her entwined about various boys in Bath on Saturdays and he remembered more than one occasion when there had been enormous rows because she had stayed out all night but no, he didn't know any names and could not recall faces. Yes, of course he had photographs of Maggie as a child and teenager.

He went off to fetch one and Molloy found himself staring down at a younger Jess. Jack, he was told, lived in Birmingham but he could see little point in pursuing him. When their mother was dying the brothers had contacted anybody they could think of who might have kept in touch with Maggie but nobody had heard from her since she walked out of her aunt's house in Aldershot. Indeed they knew she was alive only because about ten years ago she was clearly visible in a photograph of a January sales queue in London. No, he had not kept the newspaper. It was, he thought, The *Times* or *Telegraph* but he could not be sure. It could even have been "one of those Freebie things".

Molloy could only pray that Frobisher's sojourn in his shed was yielding more success than his own wild goose chase around London's commuter belt. Tomorrow they would be seeing both Ru and Em and he had no idea what they could ask them that they had not asked already, nor Fred for that matter whom they appeared to be preparing to interview as part of some game directed entirely by Anton.

Frustrated and morose, Molloy's mood changed suddenly as he was driving through Clapham and found himself resolving to go home instead of to the office. He would spend the evening with his family.

"Hallo! What a surprise!" Alice's mother looked delighted. "Why don't you take Alice out while we hold the fort?"

He wanted nothing more than an evening in, preferably a quiet one in which he and his wife could put the children to bed and then sit in whatever peace the baby allowed them. His mother-in-law read his thoughts.

"Or perhaps we could have an evening off. In fact even the whole night. We can be back tomorrow. Alice says she won't need us much longer anyway so she can get some practice."

"That is one great idea. You could do with a break."

Alice looked over the bannisters. "Mum, can you…..Oh, you're back early!"

Molloy grinned up at her. "I can do bath time."

"What brought this on? Did you put something in the Inspector's tea?"

"Haven't seen him all day. He's shed-bound. Sadly I haven't heard from him either which probably means no progress."

"They said on the news that the show is cancelled for this year but there is going to be a Christmas Spectacular in which all the couples who have got this far will dance and maybe the winner will be chosen by public vote. Just like on *Je Ne Sais Quoi*. Nobody seems to know whether that is going out with a bang or a signal that they intend it to return next year after all."

Molloy postponed any consideration of how that might affect their investigations. It would now be a month before the dancers were assembled and the studio in normal use again.

"We can stay in or go out. But if we stay in your parents can have a well-earned rest."

"In. No contest. They are only staying another couple of days so we need the practice."

Molloy grinned, savouring the prospect of an utterly normal evening. He hoped Frobisher wouldn't ring.

CHAPTER TEN

IN WHICH FROBISHER RETREATS TO HIS SHED

Frobisher had erected a trestle table in the annexe. Once the room had opened on to the small garden and housed his tools and the children's bicycles but he had blocked up that exit, opened the room on to the kitchen and the only evidence of its previous function was the row of small plants, the results of Barbara's annual propagation, which stood along the window ledge.

Today the table was covered with his diagrams and tabulations. He began with a drawing of the dressing room corridor.

Cobb and anybody on the other side of him would have had a long walk to get to Jess's dressing room and would also have had to pass the hair salon, the door of which was always open. Matt, next to him, would not have had to pass hair but would have had to pass three dressing rooms and anybody who happened to be on the corridor. Em would have had to pass merely Ru's room and he alone of all the dancers would have known whether anybody was with Jess or whether she was in her dressing room alone. By the same token he would know when she had gone to hair and make-up.

Anybody on the other side of Cobb would have had no reason to be in that part of the corridor at all. That did not mean a desperate person might not have taken the risk but it would scarcely be the product of a calculated crime.

Of those in the frame Cobb appeared to have known that the lights were out in the corridors as well as the studios, Em had been alone on the corridor with Jess after stage call and Ru had forgotten something as major as the singers drowning out all sound. Only Matt seemed to raise no suspicions. Em had a temper but was unlikely to be expert in the art of killing and there had been no struggle.

That left the possibility that someone hid in the store room, but if so how did he escape? The fire door had been unopened. The lift went only to the next floor and there opened both on to the upper dressing room corridor and onto the audience side but it was deactivated once stage call was announced. The only route would have been through the studio and that appeared to be where Helen's throat-clearer was heading.

Who was walking along the corridors in the dark and why? Could it have been somebody with a perfectly legitimate reason to be there? Someone who was moving cautiously rather than stealthily in the dark? Someone making for the fuse box? If so why wasn't he visible when the door opened? Having heard Helen scream he would surely have been there investigating? Or was he there and his presence taken for granted? Or was he in the kitchen and then just became part of the general melee when everyone was crowding out of the door and on to the corridor?

It was, thought Frobisher, possible but unlikely. If it had been someone mending the fuse, he would have said so and everyone had been questioned about their whereabouts when the lights went out: the hair and make-up artists, the crew, the runners, caterers who might have been collecting up unused crockery, stage door hands who might have left messages in dressing rooms, anybody and everybody who might ever have had the most tenuous reason to be on those corridors and nobody had admitted to being there.

So he was there for illegitimate purposes but that did not necessarily mean murder. A thief? Some friend smuggled in by a dancer? Someone who had been hiding in the store cupboard for whatever reason? A journalist looking for scandal?

If he was connected with the murder then how? It must have been done by stage call or Jess would have left her dressing room so that meant he had already done it and was using the lights failure to escape but then why cause the lights in the studio to go out?

He needed darkness only on the corridors and could have escaped through the fire door. Presumably he wanted to ensure nobody would come looking for Jess and bump into him or that anybody who did come would be slowed down by the darkness.

No, because he wasn't heading for the fire door but for the studio or at least for the kitchen. So if he was the murderer he needed to fade back into the normal scenery, into some expected activity which meant that he was connected with the show and for that Frobisher was unfeignedly thankful. A stranger hiding in the store cupboard and evaporating from the scene would have made their task well-nigh impossible.

So was the man in the dark the murderer or the murderer's accomplice? Was he both killer and computer fiddler or merely the latter? And was it all somehow mistimed? Should the lights have gone out earlier to cover the killing and an immediate escape?

Remember Anton's old lady, Frobisher told himself. It could not be absolutely certain that the lights in the studios and those in the corridors had gone out simultaneously. Could they by some wild chance be unconnected? Supposing the murderer was hiding and then heard Helen pelting along? He knows she will soon be running back and he doesn't want to be seen so he doesn't come out until he hears her starting up the stairs and then he creeps out and throws the lights. Just switches them off. No need for computers or fuses.

Frobisher liked the theory for its utter simplicity but it begged big questions. Why should the murderer hide when he knew that any minute someone would come looking for Jess? He would have been eager to escape the scene as soon as possible not hang round. Because he needed the lights failure in the studio to cover his return? He was depending on darkness to suddenly re-appear where he should have been and although he could have plunged the corridors into darkness any time he relied on the computer to produce the same effect in the studio. He was not going to move about while there was any risk of being seen. So he gets to the studio in the pitch black and waits for the door to open and people to fall out and then switches the light on in the ordinary way being at that point not in the least afraid to be seen.

Cobb? He *could* have been on the other side of the door when it opened but he had certainly arrived for stage call and by then the murder was over. Anyway, if he had tried to leave through the studio door when all the lights went out he would have been seen unless the corridor lights were also out which would have meant an accomplice. And why should he leave at all if the murder were already done?

"But suppose it wasn't?" said Frobisher as Barbara appeared with a cup of coffee.

His wife looked askance at the scattered diagrams and timetables. "Suppose what wasn't what?"

"Lawrence couldn't be precise."

"Indeed?"

"We've all been taking it for granted that Jess had to have been murdered before stage call because otherwise she would have come out of her dressing room but supposing she had been delayed on purpose? And Em went back."

"Did she?"

"But it doesn't even begin to explain the lights..... or does it?"

"I don't know."

Frobisher suddenly became aware of his wife's presence and started.

"How long have you been here?"

"A little while. We've had quite a conversation."

The Inspector smiled ruefully. "Sorry, I was deep in thought."

"I know. Well, I hope you solve the mystery of the lights."

If only, thought Frobisher. If only. Stirring his coffee he began to examine the possibility that Jess might have been deliberately delayed and then murdered after stage call. It seemed to fail at the first hurdle. Even if somebody had got out of the studio unseen during the period of darkness, murdered Jess and returned unseen why would she have waited in her dressing room?

And where did Beautella come into all this? The cards with her name on bore exactly the same print as those with Jess's name on. Whoever had murdered Jess had wanted them to think Beautella was a possible murder victim, that the computer error was no error at all. The cards had been placed to be found before Jess's body was discovered but the ones with Beautella's name on had been strategically placed to be found only when the judges reached her score sheets. A distraction? A terrible warning to Beautella to keep quiet about something? Or a genuine attempt at murder? But for the cards it might have been just a cruel practical joke or even a genuine computer error.

As for motive, Bronwen Ahmed had a slight one and could just have used the lift which would still have been active if the crime was over by stage call, but she was suffering from a broken bone, was in a wheelchair and could hardly have slipped back into the audience without being seen. She was weak from an operation and would surely never have managed to strangle a much fitter, stronger, larger woman.

If Fred or Cobb were found to have DNA matching Jess then there would be a motive but she had looked like neither and he thought it a far-fetched notion. Both men were more than intelligent enough to know that the police would take DNA samples and if they were planning a murder would have planned it to take place well away from the show. But if the threat of exposure had come out of the blue? If the murder were not planned? He could do nothing except wait for DC Forbes to tell him the result of the tests he had sought.

The re-examination of the DNA headed a list of matters now being checked. DC Forbes was almost wholly occupied with the task of tracing Maggie Woods. Jess's ex-husband was now back in the country after a business trip and it was essential that he and Molloy talk to him about whatever Jess might have confided of the circumstances of her adoption and the contact with her birth mother.

It was also essential to eliminate any possibility that the man creeping about in the dark could have been doing so for reasons utterly unconnected with the murder. All the dancers must be given the third degree over whether they had smuggled anybody onto the corridor for whatever reason: a lover, a dare, a journalist. Anything. He would guarantee confidentiality unless it proved connected with the murder. They must find out precisely when anybody had first looked in the kitchen after the studio door was opened and if anybody had been there. Each and every CV must be examined for computer expertise. They must find if anyone had a grudge against the show.

The list filled several pages and Frobisher leaned back in his chair, trying to make his mind a blank into which inspiration might suddenly float. Instead he began to drift into sleep. Presently his head fell forward on to the desk and he dreamed of Jess dancing, whirling like a dervish, an accusing dervish with a mask of death.

Throughout the day he took various calls as the results of his juniors' work was reported. Ahmed had extensive training in lighting and Langdon a little. The Fabulous Flying computer was normally kept at the company's premises but had been brought in to the studio the week after the murder as that was when Beautella had been supposed to fly. When the plan was postponed, it had not been taken back because it was not needed. It was kept in a secure cupboard by night to which both Ahmed and Langdon had a key but it was often lying about by day because Beautella's height phobia had led to an abnormal amount of practice. The lighting computer was a fixture and could not have been removed.

No employee was under any disciplinary threat. So if there was a grudge it must lie elsewhere.

Through it all Frobisher re-visited and re-visited the evidence and, stubbornly, it yielded nothing. He found himself peering even at the list of dances which the competitors had undertaken on the night of the murder. Surely this was irrelevant, he thought, but something began to form itself in his mind.

Fred and Em had waltzed, Cobb and Beautella had danced the Charleston, Jess and Matt the American Smooth, Hal and Leonie the Samba, Belle and Bruce the Salsa and Ru and Tatum the jive.

He stared at the list, not knowing for what he was searching but suddenly convinced that it could tell him something.

His efforts went unrewarded and he turned from the list to study yet again a set of points he had noted from the various statements which he had not been able to remove from the office.

Engrossed, he did not notice Barbara enter with sandwiches and a flask, which remained untouched until the front door slammed and Zoe's demanding tones penetrated even his preoccupied ears.

They needed a breakthrough, he thought as he yawned, stretched and spotted the sandwiches, and it seemed as if only a Divine miracle was likely to produce it. Then Anton phoned.

CHAPTER ELEVEN

IN WHICH ANOTHER DOOR OPENS

"I'm very sorry to disturb you, Inspector, but I cannot reach Sergeant Molloy. They tell me he is in Southampton and I have made a discovery which I think may interest you."

Nobody should have told him where Molloy was, reflected Frobisher, but he let it pass being more interested in the discovery and in a mood to give credence to anything which held out the prospect of moving a few centimetres forward from where he was mired in his marsh of uninformative material.

"Could I ask you to join me at the FBC studios?"

"*Now?*" Frobisher was astonished.

"Please. That is if it is not too much trouble."

"Ok, but it will take me a while to get there and it's rush hour."

"I have some things to do myself. Shall we meet in, say, two hours?"

Frobisher tried to repress excitement. "Is this discovery really going to take us somewhere?"

"I wouldn't want to be too rash but I think it might take us quite a long way."

Please be right about that, begged Frobisher in his thoughts. He debated whether to ring Molloy but decided that could wait until he had examined Caesar's find for himself.

Meanwhile he had time for a quick shower and change of clothes. He was in the very act of opening the front door when Jonathan arrived home.

"Dad! Great! Oh, are you going out?"

Frobisher bit his lip, hating the disappointment on his son's face.

"Yes, but perhaps not for too long."

"Right," Jonathan's tone was spiritless and Frobisher was tempted to tell Anton his discovery could wait till morning but he knew that he could not now wait that long. If he was to have any sleep that night he must find out this evening if there really was a breakthrough or if the dancer was wasting their time.

"We must go to that kitchen behind the studio," Anton told him when they met at the FBC gates.

"You have already been there today, sir?"

"Yes, don't be cross. I told them I had your permission and it can't much matter now, surely? I mean, the scene has been thoroughly trampled many times over."

"And who told you DS Molloy was in Southampton?"

"Er…pass. Did he make any progress?"

Frobisher grinned reluctantly. "No. He would have rung if he had."

"Thank you for your trust, Inspector. I hope soon to repay it."

"I hope so too," muttered Frobisher as they entered the studio and the lights came on dimly. These were the sensors which, once the stage lighting was engaged, were automatically deactivated by the computer. Once the computer was off the lights reverted to manual operation.

They made their way out into the corridor where Anton located the switch by the studio door and lit their path to the kitchen.

"We all think that Cobb could have been on this side of the door but it seemed unlikely because that would have meant opening the door and sliding through when everybody was trying to find it and, as far as he knew, the corridor would be lit in which case everybody would see him. But we also know that he was the first person Em saw when she opened the door and that nobody heard him say a word during the blackout. So let's put those two things together: he couldn't get out through the door but he may yet have been on the other side of it."

"So how did he get there?"

For answer Anton bent down and opened the door of the kitchen's only double unit. It was empty and shelf-less. To Frobisher's amazement he crawled in, pushed the back and it swung open to reveal the studio.

"Not quite Narnia," observed Anton as he extracted himself from the confined space. "There are dozens of these cubby holes in these old studios. It was obviously a cupboard used for equipment from the studio side and some bright spark saw a double use for it when that tiny kitchen was installed. It swings both ways but you would never know it was there because it was designed to look like part of the wall. Actually, Inspector, I would stake a year's salary that hardly anyone working here now knew about it."

"Even so, my men should never have missed it."

"With respect, they weren't looking for much up here. They were focussing on Jess's dressing room and then after the Beautella incident on the area around the computers. Maybe they didn't miss it but just didn't think it important enough to flag up."

"It isn't on the plans."

"Probably because nobody was aware of it, when the latest plans were drawn up."

"So how did Grainger find it?"

"Probably the same way I did - by accident."

Frobisher raised his eyebrows.

"Ok, I was looking about, not really knowing what for but actually more interested in that fuse box than this cupboard, when it suddenly occurred to me that just possibly the murderer would need to know what was happening in the studio. Was it still in chaos and darkness or had some emergency lighting been found? Were they all talking over each other or was it quiet? Were they looking for the door or just standing waiting for someone to find some illumination?

"So I tried to press my ear to the wall and the easiest way was via this cupboard. I asked a friend to ring my mobile - which I then left in the studio - and stuck my head in here to see if I could hear it and when I pressed right up against what I thought was the wall it gave way. He may have tried something similar. Or he may simply have found it on the other side by pushing his foot against the wall to do up a lace or something. The possibilities are endless."

"Yet just now you were telling me that nobody would know it was here."

"Even if they did it would not seem very remarkable and it might not be consciously registered in their minds."

"Look, I agree this is interesting but what are you suggesting? That Grainger crawled through here while the lights were out and then stood outside the studio door in the dark clearing his throat? Why, for heaven's sake? He was there when Helen was sent to find Jess. The lights were all still on both inside and outside the studio. Jess was already dead by the time they went out so for what purpose would he or anyone else crawl out into the kitchen and then mingle with those falling out of the door? Anyway he might have been seen if the lights had suddenly come on while he was getting through the supposed wall. Why take that risk?"

"No risk. He would have said he fell over amidst all the confusion in the dark or even that he knew the aperture was there and that he was going to open the studio door from the other side. And before you ask, he could have produced the same arguments if he got covered in dust."

Frobisher grinned. "Yes, that was one of my objections but you still haven't told me why he should be crawling about between the kitchen and the studio after the murder was already committed. I now think it far more likely that some stage hand knew this existed, came through precisely in order to open the door from the other side, cleared his throat in the darkness frightening Helen Brown witless and then was forestalled by the door flying open and so many dancers stumbling out. He had acted naturally and thus thought no more of it."

"Except that until Helen told us the lights were out in the corridor, nobody knew. Yet you are suggesting he did and never thought to mention it when he found out murder had been done. It's no good, Doctor Watson, no good at all."

"Then tell me, Mr Holmes, why did Cobb Grainger crawl out of one door in order to walk in another almost immediately?"

Anton shook his head bemusedly, looking so crestfallen that Frobisher laughed.

"Cheer up! If he did use that hatch behind the unit then he will have left plenty of DNA behind especially as I do not think he was wearing gloves for the Charleston."

"I suppose I may have messed up fingerprints for you but he didn't need gloves. He had a large spotty handkerchief as part of the act and anyway he has no reason to deny ever having used the hole in the wall. It was there for all to find and need not be connected with the murder. Yet I'll swear it is. I know he was on the other side of the door."

"The good sergeant agrees with you but neither of you can tell me why."

"No, but all will become clear eventually. It must. Are we still on for Fred tomorrow?"

"Yes. If there is any delay after Ru and Em we will let you know."

They went home via the Pig and Pen but Frobisher was glad he had not bothered Molloy. Sharing Anton's view that the discovery was probably significant, he still could not see how.

Nor could he see what he was going to ask Ru. He had been the last person to see Jess alive and had forgotten about the singers. Having the room next to the murdered woman he had the best opportunity to know when she was alone and was best placed to slip between his and her room unobserved. He might, with the element of surprise on his side, have been strong enough to strangle her.

"But motive is there none," muttered Frobisher to himself.

He faced the same difficulty with Em. She alone was on the corridor with Jess after the others had gone to stage call but Jess would have been a match for her in any struggle and there was not a shred of a motive.

Yet on any analysis these two were more viable suspects than Fred and Cobb who only appeared in the frame at all because of the absurd notion that one of them might be Jess's father or because

Cobb was so profoundly dislikeable and because he believed Fred had lied. Cobb could not have walked to Jess's room without passing the hair salon and Fred was even further away. They were in the frame only because of hunches, not solid or even flimsy evidence.

As for Matt, he could more than any of them have walked into Jess's room without exciting suspicion and he had been in almost daily contact with her since the competition began. When he thought of Matt something stirred just below the surface of conscious thought but he could not identify it. It had first happened, he was sure, when he was looking at that list of dances but try as he might he could not pin it down.

Bruce and Belle could be eliminated if the Beautella incident had anything to do with the murder because neither was there that week during which the computer was reprogrammed. That left Tatum but her dressing room was not on the same floor. Em, Ru and maybe Matt, Frobisher repeated to himself over and over again as if were a mantra.

Em lived in a tiny house near the river at Barnes. Molloy counted three cats and had to wait for an elderly Yorkshire terrier to be removed from a chair before he sat down. Frobisher noticed him glance anxiously at the seat but there was little hair on it. Em obviously kept her animals well-groomed.

No sooner were they all seated with coffee than the postman rang the doorbell and Em got up to sign for a packet that had come by recorded delivery. As she walked back into the small sitting room she was inspecting a clutch of envelopes and was clearly expecting a missive that was not there, for she gave a snort of exasperation and tossed the rest on to the sideboard. There was something bad- tempered about the gesture and both detectives thought of the smacking incident. Em was prone to displays of anger. Had Jess aroused her ire?

"When you turned back from going to stage call, Miss Carstairs, were you aware that Jess was not with you?"

"Not really. She could have already gone up there before final call so even if I had noticed she wasn't there, it wouldn't have meant anything."

"Did she usually go with the rest of you?"

Em frowned. "To be honest, I'm not sure. There is a lot of coming and going and professionals moving into different rooms. People walk around chatting and don't necessarily know who else is there or not."

"Would Matt have looked for her?"

"No. His dressing room was a bit further along and they would meet behind stage. That was what Fred and I often did. It was chance whether or not we saw each other on the way."

"So nobody would have noticed?"

"Maybe Ru would know if she had or hadn't left her room, just because he was right next door and you can hear everything through those walls but even if he had noticed she wasn't leaving, so what? We all went up independently, Inspector. Sometimes hair and make-up hang round checking us as we go and sometimes they just wait backstage. There is no set pattern other than the requirement to respond to stage call."

"I know this is difficult, Miss Carstairs, but try to remember. When you were going back to your room or coming out of it again, was there anything, anything at all that might have caused you to think you were not alone on the corridor? The smallest rustle, just the sense of someone else about? A door closing in the background? Anything?"

Em screwed up her face in a conscientious effort of memory. "I don't think so. I only waited a second or two, just to let Cobb get far enough ahead so I wasn't really aware of being alone. The corridor just didn't feel empty yet. Does that sound silly?"

"No. It sums it up very well. Do you hear the singers practising?"

"Who doesn't? What a racket!"

"Do they take you by surprise or do you begin to expect it?"

Em frowned again. "Pass. I think I just accept the sudden noise rather than expect it."

"Let me put it this way. If you were arranging a phone call would you say 'avoid seven nineteen because of the singers'?"

"No. Certainly you could never be that precise because they do their scales any time from about ten minutes prior to stage call, but, no, I don't think I would factor them into any arrangements. It would just be bad luck if they started up when I was on the phone."

"Would you even warn somebody it could happen? Might you say 'we may get a bit of a noise in a moment'?"

This time Em did not pause before shaking her head.

"You have had the same dressing room throughout?"

"Yes, the celebs do."

"So think back. Did those singers ever bother you? Before you got used to them?"

"I don't think so. I can't remember them doing so. I do recall being startled the first time I heard them, though."

"And the second?" Frobisher could not prevent himself leaning forward in his chair and Molloy saw the answering surprise in Em's eyes as both detectives watched her thinking.

"I gather you attach importance to this answer, Inspector, but I am afraid I have no idea what it is. I just got used to them but I haven't a clue when."

"When you were on your way to stage the second time, did you look behind you?"

Again Em made a visible attempt at memory, frowning, shutting her eyes in concentration but as both detectives had expected all that resulted was a shake of the head.

"Can't remember. I suppose as I came out of my dressing room I may have looked along the corridor to see if anyone else was going up to stage. That would have been quite natural but I couldn't swear to it one way or the other. All I know is I was alone, along the corridor and up the stairs and then I caught up with the tail end of people going towards the studio."

They were learning nothing, thought Molloy.

"Less than nothing," agreed Frobisher as they made their way to their car. "And I don't suppose we'll be any luckier with Ru. They have all wrung their memories dry."

Ru made a similar observation as he handed round coffee in his small Docklands flat. Molloy took his mug warily, noting that the entire flat seemed to be tiled rather than carpeted or floor-boarded, and fearing the effect of dropping it.

Frobisher was also noting the décor with distaste. The walls were decorated in an Italian style and the furniture was painted too. The overall effect was both chilly and formal but also over-powering as if someone had re-created the Sistine chapel in a box room. The sofas were large and covered in cream corduroy, the curtains of heavy blue brocade.

"Nice place you have, sir," was Frobisher's diplomatic comment.

"Thank you. I painted the walls and furniture myself. When I am not dancing, I am a frustrated artist."

Molloy smiled inwardly but kept a straight face as the Inspector, after a few more pleasantries, began his questions.

"Sir, when we did the reconstruction, you had been in that particular dressing room for only three weeks? And on the night of the murder for two weeks?"

"Yes. That's right."

"Yet you were already so accustomed to the singers that you forgot to mention them?" Frobisher was careful to keep his tone curious rather than challenging but he saw Ru tense.

" I had forgotten how loud they sounded in that room, yes, but I had been used to hearing them for weeks. The room I was sharing with some of the other dancers before that was right above them on the upper corridor. We all got used to it. Even so, I should have remembered that when they start their caterwauling you can't hear yourself think."

"I am going to ask you to relax for this next question, sir, and don't think too hard. Don't try to remember any particular night. Just tell me who you might reasonably expect to see on that corridor other than dancers or make-up artists. Never mind when you have seen them. Just tell me of anybody who might be there."

For a second Ru looked bewildered, then his face cleared. "Tamara, the celebrity booker who used to call on all the celebs in the course of the day to make sure they were all happy. But even though you have told me not to think of any particular night, I can tell you that she wasn't there when Jess was murdered. I remember that she did her rounds that afternoon during band call because she came out of Em's room rolling her eyes towards the heavens."

"Do you know why?"

"I suspect Em was in one of her moods. She could get quite ratty sometimes. Then, of course, you sometimes get journalists doing interviews but not between the show and the results. The press chap, Stuart, was often about. So was Bronwen Ahmed occasionally."

"Why?"

"She probably found spending every Saturday night alone a bit tedious. There are no children to look after. Or maybe she wanted to keep an eye on Rashid. May have felt threatened by his being surrounded by all those gorgeous young women week after week ."

Yet it was a middle-aged woman who might be falling for him, reflected Molloy.

"Then again," Ru was continuing. "If I am a frustrated artist she could be a frustrated dancer. She used to be quite an athlete but she's had a series of miscarriages and is now more or less forced to live like a couch potato. Poor old Bronwen."

"What do you mean, sir, by 'quite athletic'?"

"She was a tennis player. Came close to representing Wales."

Bad luck, thought Molloy. Not martial arts then.

"I gather last time she was there she had a broken leg?"

"Yes, she was wearing one of those surgical boot thingies. Great invention, that. I had one when I broke a foot. You can take them off to shower and sleep unlike that plaster stuff............."

Rupert's voice suddenly trailed into silence as he heard his own words and the same thought occurred to all three. To shower, to sleep or to commit murder?

"She had better be next on the list after Fred and Jess's ex. Also we must find out exactly when she had broken the leg and if it was nearly healed, which the boot might suggest, and why should she need a wheelchair rather than depend only on crutches?" Frobisher sounded suddenly energised after the morning's frustration.

"Yes, sir, and I think Ru moves up a bit higher on the likely list. He was pointing us in the direction of Bronwen Ahmed and all that stuff about being used to the singers is a bit of an afterthought, given how devastated he appeared to be at the time that he had forgotten them."

"And we come back again to his being the only one who could know exactly when Jess was alone. But why? Where's the motive?"

Molloy shrugged. "I'll also try and find out the reason for Em's foul mood that afternoon. Meanwhile should we see Bronwen rather than Fred? We're only really giving him priority because Anton wants to play some daft game at his flat."

"Given his form so far, it probably won't be so daft. Nevertheless, I can't help feeling we're on a wild goose chase with him and Grainger. Jess's father indeed! There isn't a scrap of evidence."

He was reinforced in that view when they got back to the office to find the DNA results. Nobody tested was any relation to the deceased, but Bronwen Ahmed was at a hospital appointment and he decided to keep the meeting with Fred.

Em had a temper, Ru seemed keen to point the finger at Bronwen Ahmed, Bronwen had half a motive, Fred had known Jess years ago and Cobb was hated by just about everyone. None of it amounted to anything and the AC was getting impatient.

Anton rang Fred's bell a few minutes after they arrived. Their host look puzzled.

"Who on earth is that?" he muttered, getting out of his chair.

The detectives heard Anton's cheerful tones, saying he was passing and on the spur of the moment thought he might drop in to see if Fred had heard any more about the future of the show. If it was inconvenient, not to worry.

Fred told him the detectives were in his living room and anyway he knew nothing about the future of *Lively Toes*. But if Anton wanted to discuss it they could fix a time.

They heard Anton prepare to depart and then suddenly ask if he could be a real pain and use the bathroom. He would let himself out. Frobisher grinned at Molloy as they heard Fred agreeing and asking if Anton remembered where it was.

Fred came back and firmly shut the door, evidently not wanting his unexpected guest to hear their conversation. That, thought Frobisher, would help Anton's clandestine purposes and he hastily refused Fred's offer of tea lest their host wander back out to get it.

He had no idea what Anton wanted in Fred's flat but having co-operated thus far, he had come equipped with the means of drowning out the sounds of any search. Recalling that Fred had no television, he produced an Ipad and played back Cobb's impromptu dance while Beautella was trapped near the ceiling. He asked Fred to watch it carefully and kept the volume as loud as he could without exciting comment.

The dancer dutifully concentrated on the re-play and Frobisher could hear no sounds from anywhere else in the flat. His attention was recalled by Fred's snort of derision as Cobb threw an anxious glance towards the ceiling.

"Bloody play-actor! He was loving every moment of it."

Frobisher pushed his luck and played the dance a second time. "Right, sir, now is there anything in that performance which might suggest to you that it was not impromptu? That it could have been rehearsed?"

The detective casually placed the Ipad on top of his brief case, still playing. Fred obligingly watched it through again as if with a new purpose.

"No, nothing. It is basically a series of unconnected moves. Beautella could tell you if there was anything there she had not taught him."

"She says not other than the tap."

"It is very amateur tap and he has a good ear. The judges would give him two for it but the audience wouldn't realise and, in the circumstances, it is unlikely anybody would care."

Frobisher switched off the Ipad. He could hear nothing from outside the room as Molloy asked the next question.

"Did you know that Jess was adopted?"

151

"Adopted? Was she?"

"Indeed. You said that when you first knew her she had been about to go to University but changed her mind and her parents were not pleased. But Beautella says Jess told her she had been going through 'a bit of a bad time'. Do you know what that bad time was?"

"Probably the rows with her parents."

"She didn't mention anything else?"

"It was thirty years ago, Sergeant."

"We have reason to believe that around that time she was looking for her birth mother. You were a vicar and mentoring her on her future. Are you sure she didn't mention it?"

"I was an *ex*-vicar and my advice was limited to career options. If she had mentioned something of that importance I would have remembered."

"This is very important, sir. I know it was a long time ago, but can you remember anything at all that might have indicated a general unhappiness rather than just arguments with her parents?"

Fred thought. "Well, I will keep trying and let you know if anything occurs to me."

"Thank you. There isn't anything else for now, but I would be grateful if you would keep this conversation private. The Allwards are sensitive on the subject of the adoption and if it proves irrelevant, there is no need for it to be in all the papers."

"I am not a gossip, gentlemen."

Seconds later they were moving through the hall to the front door.

There was no sign of Anton.

CHAPTER TWELVE

IN WHICH FROBISHER IS INSPIRED BY PENGUINS AND BEAUTELLA BY A BOTAFOGO

"How's it going?" Barbara put a cottage pie on the table, gave Zoe's hand a playful slap as her daughter reached for it, called Jonathan for the second time and sat down herself seemingly all in one movement.

"He'll be deep in some boring book and it'll go cold if we go on waiting," grumbled Zoe as Frobisher replied to his wife's query with a single word.

"Treacle."

He was getting up to call Jonathan when they heard a light step on the stair and their son appeared. Zoe sighed theatrically and pulled the pie towards her.

"Sorry, Mum," apologised Jonathan. "I was lost amidst the penguins."

Frobisher saw Zoe open her mouth to make a cutting comment and hastily forestalled her. "School project?"

Jonathan, his mouth full of pie, nodded and Zoe subsided. The rest of the meal proceeded peacefully and they all helped with the clearing up. Jonathan returned to Antarctica and Zoe watched him go with a mutinous expression, from which Frobisher guessed that she had been hoping for his support in her choice of the evening's television. Both he and Barbara had resolutely opposed television in the children's bedrooms but the age of the computer was making the ban almost irrelevant. Zoe would doubtless spend the evening on social media if her parents' choice of viewing prevailed and would catch up with her programme later.

"Finished your homework?" He tried to make the question neutral rather than challenging.

Zoe shrugged.

"Well, you had better do it now. Then you'll be free. I'm off to the shed for a bit."

"What sort of a place is this?" snapped Zoe. "One in the shed, one at the bloody North Pole. You won't let me go out in the week and then you expect me to live in a morgue, just like all those mouldering old bodies you spend so much time on."

Her parents answered simultaneously. Frobisher murmured mildly "South Pole" and Barbara demanded a cessation of swearing.

"I've had quite enough of it. It doesn't make you big if that's what you think."

"Swearing! It's not as if I said…."

"Enough," interrupted Frobisher before the word was out. "You can go to your room and I shall want to see your homework before any television."

As his daughter, looking at him angrily, hovered between compliance and defiance, the revelation hit him. "*Penguins,*" he breathed. "Of course. *Penguins.*"

Hurrying through to his "shed" he heard Zoe saying "He's mad, Mum. Mad, mad, bl-, blinking mad."

He found his hands shaking as he located the list of dances on the night of the murder and a few seconds later was phoning Molloy. Alice answered.

"He's bathing Kathy. Can he phone you back?"

"No," thought the frustrated Inspector, even as he said yes, of course, no hurry.

Molloy's call came within seconds.

"Clearly that wonderful wife of yours has the gift of interpretation," remarked Frobisher cheerfully. "Do you remember who was dancing what on the night of the murder?"

"Roughly," answered Molloy in puzzled tones. "Fred and Em the waltz and Jess certainly the American Smooth, Bruce and Belle the er...Salsa, Ru the jive, Hal and Leonie er, er, oh, yes the Samba and Cobb the Charleston."

"Spot on, Molloy and from this you deduce what?"

There was a short silence before Molloy said uncertainly "Am I missing something?"

"Maybe. We assume that whoever did it took the flapper band along with him. The men wear tight costumes for the Latin dances. How was any of them to conceal it? But Fred, Matt and Cobb were variously in dinner suits or tailsuits and Ru was dressed as a teddy boy. Any of them could easily have hidden it."

"Well done, sir. Of course that presumes it was a man. The same arguments would apply to the women. Most of them wore next to nothing for the Latin stuff."

"Indeed, but for now I think we can concentrate on the penguin suits."

Molloy refrained from saying that they had never suspected Hal or Bruce anyway. His superior's brainwave did little more than confirm they were right in their principal suspicions but he still chided himself for not having thought of it. Fred, Matt, Cobb, Ru plus Em and Bronwen remained the main players but none of them could have anything to do with Jess's adoption, which was all that would occupy them tomorrow.

Jess's former husband lived in a small three bedroomed house in Kingston upon Thames. Molloy's first impression was of clutter with shoes, boots, fleeces and anoraks spilling away from the pegs in the hall, books piled around the floor in the small sitting room and the kitchen showing a glimpse of food stacked around the units for which clearly there was no room in the cupboard. A trampoline filled the back garden and the front seemed taken over by padlocked bicycles.

Molloy recalled Mrs Allward's unkind remark that Jess had married a pauper. Presumably she would have regarded this house which estate agents would have described as "entry level" as proof and would have expected a man of fifty to be further up the property ladder and able to provide better for his children but Molloy reckoned otherwise. Divorce rarely left one better off, the property was in a good location and David Fletcher must have stretched himself to three bedrooms in order to accommodate visits from his children who would not at that stage have been candidates for permanent residency. Henry Allward had described him as a good dad and Molloy agreed.

Fletcher read his thoughts. "Afraid it's all still chaos. They brought everything with them and want to bring a lot more of Jess's stuff when you guys OK selling her house. Heaven knows where we'll put it all but sufficient unto the day is the trouble thereof. Tea? Coffee?"

Frobisher took a seat in the front room while Molloy followed Fletcher into the kitchen to help. They returned with the beverages and, surprisingly, half a fruit cake.

"Sarah made it," explained their host. "It's good. Too good, alas. She's very keen on cookery. Jess used to say she had given birth to tomorrow's Nigella."

Frobisher smiled and made appreciative noises as he sampled the offering. For a while they talked of the children, their reactions to the events in which they had been submerged, their new schools, hobbies and prospects.

"It's good of you to take the time off, sir," said Molloy as they settled down to the real purpose of the visit. The detectives knew that Fletcher kept the books for three small local businesses: an indifferently successful restaurant which survived but never really prospered, a bookshop run by an aging spinster on lines which had not changed since she first opened the small store in her late twenties and a rather tatty garage which specialised in run-down cars.

Fletcher looked cheerful enough however and Molloy thought he was probably a man who preferred to live quietly. Frobisher, making the same deduction, repressed a grin at the thought of such a world being invaded by two spirited teenagers but, recollecting the circumstances of that invasion, was quickly saddened. He wondered what Fletcher's wife was like and how she regarded the change in circumstances.

He asked Fletcher bluntly what he knew about Jess's adoption.

"Very little, Inspector. Jess told me when we got engaged and then never referred to it again. Said she thought of herself as Anne and Henry's child and but for her feeling I ought to know would never have mentioned it. She didn't tell the children and as a matter of fact they don't know now. We felt they had enough to manage as it is but of course if it's going to come out anyway....."

"I am afraid it may but I will try and warn you. That is I will warn you if it is in my power to do so but the media have their own methods and I can't guarantee that we can control what emerges when. Perhaps you should tell them before they find out that way."

David Fletcher looked miserable and Frobisher hated having to press the matter.

"Did she tell you about trying to contact the birth mother?"

"No. In a way she deceived me because she said as far as she was concerned Anne was her mother and she had no interest in her real mother. It was Henry who told me she had tried and been rejected. We went out to a pub for one of those man to man talks shortly before the wedding and he told me that he thought Jess could be fragile under all that career-girl steel."

"Try to tell me everything you recall about what he said."

The policemen were disappointed but not surprised that it amounted to no more than they already knew.

"Did she ever mention her father?"

"No. I asked her if she knew anything about him but she said she didn't and that would tally with Henry's account that her mother would not speak to her. If her real mum wasn't saying anything I don't see how she could find out unless of course he was on the original birth certificate."

"He wasn't. And you think she really did let it go?"

Fletcher looked him straight in the eyes. "I don't know. As I say I found out most of it from Henry rather than Jess, who only told me what she felt she owed me as we planned to have children. She was the most private person I have ever met and if truth be told it was a factor in the divorce – I often felt I never really knew my own wife. She could be stubborn as indeed she was in choosing dance over university, so if she had really wanted to find out more I don't think she would have just given up. Inspector, is her background relevant to what happened?"

Molloy noticed the euphemism. They had been divorced since the older child was twelve but Fletcher could not face talking about murder in connection with his wife. The reluctance manifested itself again later in the conversation when Molloy asked him if his wife had always used her maiden name.

"Always. For professional reasons. It appeared as Fletcher only on legal documents. Just as well considering the success of ... Angela Lansbury."

He could not even say *Murder She Wrote*, thought Molloy and he saw Frobisher give a slight grimace.

"We're finding it pretty difficult to track down the mother. Did your wife keep a diary? Or old address books? Anything that might give us a clue to how she found this woman? We searched her house of course and her old bedroom at the Allwards but perhaps the children took away some of her stuff for sentimental reasons?"

"No journal or daily diary that I know of. I will ask them or you can go up and see if you can find anything. They won't mind if it helps to catch the ....whoever it is."

After a series of unproductive questions on boyfriends since the divorce, past enemies and any recent emotional attachments the detectives moved upstairs. They were still there amidst the disorder when the children came back from school.

No, they told the detectives, Jess was not a hoarder and apart from photograph albums there was not much from the past. She kept a folder for each of them containing old school reports, Brownie and Cub certificates and that sort of thing but threw away all her own theatre programmes and records of dance triumphs other than some cups.

"She always said live in the present not the past. It used to drive Granny mad because she treasured anything about any of us so Mum passed quite a lot on to her," explained Sarah.

"We had her address book but the police took it. Dad was quite worried about how we were going to send out the funeral invitations but we can't do that anyway because………."

David's voice trailed away and Sarah took a tissue from its box under a heap of clothes and handed it to him.

"I'm sorry" said Frobisher. "We'll let you bury her as soon as we can but there are procedures in cases like this. Of course we'll let you have the address book even if only a photocopy. Meanwhile I am going to ask you what may sound a daft question. Did your mum have a special hiding place when she didn't want things found? Like when you were going on holiday and she was guarding against burglars?"

The tearful boy shook his head. "She used to give her jewelry to Granny to look after. That was all. She used to wrap it up in newspaper so that it looked unimportant. We would laugh about it."

"Of course if she was hiding something from us, we wouldn't know about it, would we?" put in Sarah and Molloy saw a thoughtful look cross Frobisher's face.

It had not been a good day and he hoped the Inspector would not propose a return to the office.

"I think we'll call that a day," yawned Frobisher and Molloy uttered a silent prayer of thanks.

At the tube station he bought a small bunch of flowers for Alice. He was giving them to her with a flourish and a bottle of wine he had obtained from the off licence round the corner when a text caused his mobile to ping. He wished he had not heard but having heard duty compelled him to look. *Please ring DC Forbes.*

That could wait till the morning he decided, embracing his wife. Half an hour later he reluctantly decided that *Please ring DI Frobisher* could not so wait.

Alice stood in front of him, refusing to release him from her entwining arms while he struggled to tap out the number and hold the phone to his ear. She heard Frobisher's voice and suddenly realised that her husband was no longer aware of her presence, all his excitement transferred to the disembodied voice on the other end of his mobile. She pulled a face and flounced away from him in mock dudgeon.

By the time he had finished the conversation Alice was upstairs responding to a call from Immie and Kathleen had set up a wail from her Moses basket.

"Going out again?" called Alice resignedly.

"No. We've had a breakthrough and we need it. I'll see to Kathy."

"I think you'll find you can't do what she wants. Come and settle Immie while I deal with it."

Molloy smiled and took the stairs two at a time. It was half an hour before the restoration of peace and quiet and Alice was able to ask "what breakthrough?"

"We've found a major witness."

"To the *murder*?"

"No. To matters long ago."

DC Forbes had traced Maggie Woods and an interview had been secured for the following afternoon but Alice's interest was still firmly fixed on Beautella.

"Poor girl! Is she any better?"

Beautella wasn't any better and the appropriate response to her collapse was now a matter of dispute within her family.

"She must make an effort and get on with it," was her father's attitude. "People with claustrophobia have been buried alive or shut in small cupboards by school bullies or trapped in packed lifts for hours on end and emerge to live normally. Amy must now do the same with her height phobia. Studio LaReine won't run itself."

Laura agreed with him but Sarah supported her mother who believed her daughter to be in a state of nervous liquefaction beyond her control. It was not, she observed, just the dreadful experience with the height but the fear that she could have been a victim of attempted murder. The argument might have continued for a very long time but for a chance meeting between Laura and Helen Brown.

Beautella had been taken from the studios by ambulance and had left behind everything in her dressing room, which had been locked and sealed off by police. Only her handbag had been returned and the police had now said she could collect anything else she needed but she felt unable to leave the sofa so Laura rang the FBC and it was agreed that she would be met and escorted to the room by a runner.

Despite the uncertainty over the programme's future there was still a skeleton staff working on it and all staff had been retained for the Christmas Special, now only three weeks away. Helen was one of those kept on to run errands and it was she who met Laura when the latter left work early and appeared at FBC reception one late afternoon.

It took only a few minutes to locate Beautella's possessions and as they were stuffing them into a carrier bag Helen asked how she was getting on. Laura painted a grim picture of a helpless and tearful invalid so Helen suggested she visit. She did not know Beautella well and it was quite possible that her own connection with the murder would make her unwelcome if the dancer was trying to forget but Laura was enthusiastic, saying some contact with the outside world other than the police might be just what her sister needed.

Mrs Hobbs worried that it might be too soon but Laura went ahead with the arrangements and Helen arrived on a Friday evening, clutching a basket of fruit. Beautella smiled up weakly from the sofa and Helen felt a flash of impatience.

They talked of all aspects of the programme except the murder and the flying incident because it was all they had in common. Beautella's responses were languid but she raised half a smile when Helen began laughing at the hopeless attempts Em had made at mastering the Botafogo, a complicated step in the Samba.

"I've never managed it either." Helen stood up and attempted the step herself, humming a Samba tune, failing hopelessly and giggling.

Beautella raised herself on one elbow and began issuing instructions with increasing frustration as Helen muddled the step time and again, unaware that now the blunders were deliberate as she sat up, then suddenly cast aside the duvet and began to demonstrate the step in slow motion. Finally she went over to the music centre in the corner and after rifling through a collection of c.ds. found a samba.

In the kitchen her parents looked at each other in disbelief which gradually turned to hope. When her father quietly put his head around the door of the sitting room only Helen noticed. His daughter was too absorbed in the Botafogo.

Beautella found she was enjoying herself.

"That," she panted as the music died and Helen had executed three or four perfect steps "was a revelation".

"You mean that anyone could be so hopeless?"

"No. That I love teaching more than I love performing. Even if studio LaReine doesn't survive I am going to go on teaching."

Helen looked surprised. "Was that ever in doubt?"

"Not until recently but ever since the last show I've been thinking of chucking in my hand and re-training as a secretary."

"The memory will fade but you've got to help it. I've got a problem with 7.25pm and with hearing a man suddenly clear his throat but I just immerse myself in whatever I'm doing and give my mind a rest from it all."

Beautella nodded but did not look wholly convinced. "Why would anyone want to murder me?"

"I suspect they didn't."

"Then they went to an awful lot of trouble not to. Fixing that computer and you've heard about the cards with my name on?"

"Yes, but it could have all been a massive red herring, designed to confuse the police into thinking there must be a connection between you and Jess or maybe the murderer thought you had seen something, perhaps something you didn't even know you had seen."

"Thanks a bundle. That would mean he's still after me. The police have thought of all that and they gave me the third degree but I wasn't even on that floor except for the time I was in hair and make-up."

"No, but you may have seen something somewhere else either before or after, which only the murderer knows to be significant."

"Anton says no. He thinks if that were the case the murderer would have chosen a much surer method and made sure I could never tell a soul. He thinks it could have been a warning to somebody else: a clear statement that if that person blabs he's a dead man. A sort of Look – What – I –Can –Do moment. I hope he's right."

"Anton? Has he been round?"

"Twice. The other professionals have sent cards and flowers and texts but Anton actually made an appearance in elegant person. I get the impression he might be helping the police but he didn't say so and I could be wrong. He asked really weird questions such as had I ever seen anyone coming through a hole in the wall between the studio and the kitchen. It was spooky at times."

"Then he had better be careful. There's a homicidal maniac out there."

"Thanks another bundle. Do you want to stay to supper?"

"Or we could get a Chinese?"

"OK but if we're going out I need to shower and get dressed. What's the time?"

Simultaneously they consulted their watches. "Seven thirty," pronounced Helen triumphantly. "And I didn't even notice the dreaded hour come and go. Hurry up or I'll die of hunger for a chicken chow mein."

As the front door shut behind their daughter, Mr and Mrs Hobbs stood staring at each other. Eventually Gillian said "Can you manage two lamb chops or shall we share hers?"

CHAPTER THIRTEEN

IN WHICH THE DETECTIVES MEET A MADAM AND ANTON
REVEALS HIS HAND

"She's Maggie Hawes, these days and lives in Newquay," said
Frobisher as soon as Molloy appeared in the office next day. " We
need to leave now if we want to get there by three, especially remem-
bering what it was like when we went to Dartmoor. We'll drive ourselves
again and take it in turns. A WPC from the local force will join us for
the interview given the delicacy of it. Anton will also be with us."

"*Anton?*"

"Yes. He rang me last night to say he had made a significant
discovery and needed to brief me urgently but I said it wouldn't be
possible until tomorrow as we were going to Cornwall to see Maggie
Woods. He said it couldn't wait and could he come with us and talk
on the way?"

"What was wrong with last night?"

"He wasn't going to be available till the early hours and I didn't
think that a good idea in view of the drive ahead."

"The last significant discovery turned out to be a hole in the wall
and none of us have been able to accord it any significance at all.
Why should this be different?"

"Because he was insistent on seeing me, offering one in the
morning and before breakfast today. He sounded genuinely urgent
and frustrated that a theatrical contract prevented us meeting there
and then."

"I am not sure this is wise, sir. He will try and muscle in on the interview."

"Then he won't succeed. This is police business."

Molloy refrained from pointing out that Caesar was already privy to rather a lot of police business and that last night was a Friday when, but for the suspension of the programme, the dancer would have been under contract to be at FBC and not at a theatre. He supposed it possible that he was stepping in at the last moment to fill a gap caused by illness or cancellation but still could not shake off the view that Frobisher was taking a major risk. Amateur detectives belonged in novels not police cars.

"Do we know what came out of his foray at Fred's flat when we assisted him to enter without breaking?"

Frobisher smiled. "Relax, Molloy. We will know because apparently it is all part of it. Now let's go. We pick him up at Taunton, where the show was last night. He is getting a taxi to the service station."

The journey to Taunton Deane service station was straightforward. Molloy drove while Frobisher kept his phone on loudspeaker so that they could both benefit from the briefings being relayed at intervals by DC Parkes of the Devon and Cornwall Police. Maggie Hawes was a widow who had married late in life. Now 65, she appeared to live in comfortable retirement courtesy of her late husband who had run a chain of garages and second hand car businesses, none of which had a particularly good reputation, but Ronnie Hawes had always kept just within the law, at least as far as anybody knew.

Meanwhile Maggie had her own reputation. She was widely suspected of controlling girls and of some hard drug dealing but the local police had never managed to collect enough evidence. Her own house was always clean of drugs and the girls and their clients never went there.

"She didn't look after the girls particularly well," DC Parkes told them. "The WPC you will be meeting later remembers an incident involving a very dodgy client with a knife but she wasn't directly involved in the investigation and it was a while ago."

"Sounds charming," muttered Frobisher. "OK I don't want you ringing me again unless it really can't wait. We shall have a third party in the car. If there is something I have to know text and wait till I ring you."

"Understood, sir," replied DC Parkes cheerfully.

Ten minutes later Anton was in the back, announcing that he needed twenty minutes sleep. It did not surprise Molloy when the twenty minutes became fifty. Both he and Frobisher guessed that the dancer wanted to brief them on the return journey so that they could combine information and that suited them because Frobisher wanted to immerse himself in his notes before the interview.

Neither spoke of the case, uncertain how deeply asleep Caesar really was. He came round briefly as they passed signs for Bovey Tracey and then fully as they slowed for the Tamar Bridge.

"Toll bridge," muttered Molloy.

"Don't worry going this way, sergeant," came Anton's cheerful tones from the back. "They charge you to leave Cornwall, not enter it."

"Do you come here often?" asked Frobisher.

Anton ignored the irony. "Twice a year usually. I have some relatives in Fowey."

"And you call in on the Aunt at Manaton on the way?" Molloy's tone was mischievous.

Anton sidestepped that one and Molloy smiled bleakly.

"Look, sir, I am genuinely grateful for your help so far and I am all ears for whatever wouldn't wait last night but you really must stay clear of the interview. You can either wait in the car or we'll drop you at a coffee shop or whatever but you are not welcome when we interview Maggie Woods. This is a police matter." Frobisher's tone was verging on the brusque.

"Of course it is. I'm more than happy to wait in the car. Anyway without wishing to be immodest I am sure she would recognise me and wonder what I was doing there."

"Quite. We wouldn't want her complaining to the AC. There will also be a local WPC who may also wonder why you are with us.

If she sees you to speak to you must say that we are quizzing you on some of the dancing technicalities before dropping you off at a relative's."

"Done. Don't worry, Inspector. Your ..er.. request will be carried out to the letter. I really rather want to stay on this case."

"You are not on the case, sir. We are. I take it that you would rather tell us whatever you have to say on the way back?"

"I think so now, Inspector."

Molloy thought he detected a slight emphasis on that "now". Was Anton suggesting he no longer had enough time or was he hinting that he had taken umbrage at Frobisher's tone? In an attempt at conciliation he began asking about last night's theatrical performance and Anton, judging the atmosphere correctly, gave a breezy response.

They arrived in Newquay early and Frobisher parked the car out of sight of the house, despite its having a spacious parking area in front. All three men got out and stretched their legs, Frobisher removing to a distance at which he could make a phone call out of earshot and Molloy drinking from a bottle of water.

"I think the Inspector is cross with me," remarked Anton.

"No." Molloy elected honesty. "He is just rattled because you really have no locus to be with us."

"Oh, dear. Well I think he might be excited by what I have to tell him."

"He was hoping – and so was I – that you would have told him already."

"I was going to, but……"

"But you took umbrage."

"I ….." Caesar fell silent suddenly as Frobisher strode towards them.

"WPC Fratton is already in the house," he announced peremptorily. "Let's go."

Molloy handed Anton the keys of the car.

"And don't be tempted to follow us," Frobisher called back over his shoulder. When they were level with the house the detectives glanced back and Anton waved cheerfully, calling out "Good luck!" Molloy grinned and Frobisher grunted but the sergeant sensed his ill temper was subsiding. He waved back and a few seconds later he was meeting Maggie Hawes.

Despite the briefing of the scandalised former staff of the children's home and of the local force, Molloy had approached the interview in a spirit of charity. A pregnant schoolgirl in 1966 would have felt the full force of society's disapproval and might easily have used hardness and defiance as a means of coping with it but he soon felt as keen a disgust as he saw written on WPC Fratton's face and could only hope he was disguising it better.

Maggie Hawes looked ten years younger than her true age and could probably have passed as Jess's older sister. She also looked expensive and demanding and was unmoved by her daughter's fate.

"Yeah, I read about it and guessed it was her. She told me her name and that she was interested in dancing when she kept trying to get me to see her. A right little nuisance she was."

"I'm sorry if the news was a shock," Frobisher offered the conventional sympathy knowing it to be wasted.

"No shock at all. Why would it be? She was nothing to me and I never saw her despite her pesting, pesting, pesting."

"She contacted you more than once?"

"Yeah. Little stalker! I just kept putting the phone down after a while but then I reckoned she might turn up here if I didn't speak to her. It was a right carry-on for a bit."

"Tell me as much as you can from the beginning of her first call."

"She said she was Tracey-Jane but now she was Jessica Allward and that she had been happy and wanted to tell me that all had turned out well, as if I cared. Some social worker or adoption woman or whatever it was rang and said she was keen to trace me and I told them I didn't want to know but obviously she just decided to go ahead. I honestly think if I'd known the law was going to do that I'd have left her in the river instead of by the dogs' home."

Molloy felt the shock which he saw enter the others and wondered if it was even a figure of speech or if she really might have chosen murder.

Frobisher, with no outward change in his manner, asked her to tell them what happened next.

"Well, I've told you already. She wanted to see me and when I refused and said it was better to let sleeping dogs lie she got all weepy. I was glad when she told me lived in Surrey because I thought it might stop her coming here on the off-chance."

"What else did she talk about in the course of these conversations?"

"Not much because I kept cutting her short. She wanted to know all about me but I reckoned that was my business. I even thought of asking the police to have a word."

"Did she write to you?"

"Never."

"Did she ask who her father was?"

"All the time. Don't they all?"

"What did you tell her?"

"That I didn't know. And that was Gawd's honest truth."

"How many candidates were there?" asked Frobisher bluntly.

"As many as stars in the sky, darlin'. I didn't hold back."

"Was Fred Firbank one of them?"

"Who?"

"Or Cobb Grainger?"

They knew well enough that neither had been Jess's father but Molloy guessed Frobisher wanted to see if Maggie had had any connection with them, if Jess might have had any reason to *think* either could have been.

"Eh? Oh, they're both on that dance thingy, aren't they? No, you're barking up the wrong tree. Don't recognise either name but mark you, I wouldn't remember them all."

"No," agreed Anton as he wandered into the room. "But you do, I think, remember Sam Phillipson."

In the short silence which followed Molloy watched Frobisher struggling to control his temper and Maggie her curiosity. She must have recognised Anton and was now wondering whence he had so suddenly appeared.

"Do sit down and have a cup of tea," she said in a mocking upper-class drawl. "And, no, I'm never likely to forget Sam Phillipson."

Her next words took them all by surprise. "Poor little devil."

Anton sat on the wide arm of the sofa where Frobisher sat at one end and Molloy at the other. WPC Fratton repeated Maggie's offer of refreshment but Anton barely heard her. He was looking at Maggie.

"We were round about the same age but Sam was at some posh boarding school and was only around in the holidays. I knew him because one of his sisters was at the grammar in the same class as one of my brothers and they were quite pally. Occasionally he came to our house to collect her.

"He was a right wimp and had been badly bullied when he was younger but for some crazy reason that made him determined to go into the army. I think he wanted to prove himself. I wanted him to prove himself too but not in that way, darlin'. But he wouldn't. Said it was wrong and I must wait till I was married. I ask you! When I told him it was a bit late for that he was so shocked it was funny. He was like some old Victorian nanny."

"But you prevailed in the end, didn't you?" asked Anton sadly.

"Yeah. I'll say. Mind you, I had to get him drunk first."

"Did you tell him about the baby?"

"No. The fool would have wanted to marry me. He would have gone on and on about doing the right thing. Anyway he had other things to think about. They accepted him for the army and he was terrified. Cried and cried in my arms like a frightened five year old. We lost touch when I went to live with Aunt Marjorie and that ghastly spastic of hers."

Frobisher quelled his rising temper. "And he was Jess's father?"

Maggie shrugged. "Probably."

Molloy could control himself no longer. "Did you know Mrs Forest's son died?"

"No. But he was neither use nor ornament so it may have been the best thing."

"You told Jess that Sam was her father, didn't you?" interrupted Anton gently.

"Yes. He was dead by then so there would be no comeback on me. I made her promise that if I told her who it was she would never contact me again. Never, ever and all credit to her she didn't."

"Were you surprised when you read about Captain Phillipson's death in action?" asked Frobisher.

"Yes. And pleased. Not that he died but that he got over all that fear. You did it, Sam, after all."

So one person had touched Maggie Woods' selfish heart all those years ago, thought Molloy. She'd had a brush with salvation and didn't know it. Or did she? He found himself wondering about her marriage to Ronnie Hawes.

"Could you have loved his child, had circumstances been different?" the question came from Anton.

"They wouldn't have let me, would they? Not then. It wasn't like it is now."

"I'm sorry," said Anton and there was a silence in the room as if a far-off soul had emitted a mournful cry.

The silence continued as the detectives made their way to the car, leaving WPC Fratton to help clear up the cups and explain what follow-up might ensue.

"Poor woman," murmured Molloy.

"Possibly," Frobisher's tone was robust. "But before you sentimental souls drown in empathy, just remember the thalidomide boy."

There was another silence.

"Carapace," ventured Anton.

"Which is what you will need, Anton Augustus Caesar, plus a stout pair of hiking boots if you don't tell me what has been going on because you will be walking back to London."

"My second name is a state secret, Inspector."

"Not to the police, it isn't and all Britain will know it if you don't cough *now*."

"Right," agreed Anton. "Let's begin with the Aunt at Manaton," whereupon he launched into a tale which kept the policemen in

171

thrall until they were once more at the Tamar Bridge and crawling through the toll lane.

He once really did have an Aunt at Manaton so she had been the obvious excuse when he decided to call upon Cobb as his presence in such an out of the way place might be difficult to explain. He had no idea at all what he expected to find but he still could not shake off the suspicion that Cobb was on the other side of the studio door and, knowing the detectives were due to interview Grainger, he knew also that he was certain to find him at home so he had headed to Dartmoor.

"If I had simply left it until I saw him at the studio and told him I was going to be in that part of the world and would like to call, he could have fobbed me off so I needed just to turn up when I knew he would be there," said Anton.

The visit had followed that of the detectives. Caesar had been received in the kitchen and given tea by Jane Grainger and then Cobb had suggested they talk in the study because Jane was about to have a mammoth baking session for some charitable do and indeed the dancer had heard other women arriving while he was chatting to his host. Nevertheless he had thought the choice of study odd particularly when Cobb sat down at the desk facing him as if for a formal interview.

"I reckon he was recording," interjected Molloy and the others agreed.

"Though we could be wrong. He may have just sat at the desk out of habit," mused Frobisher.

The conversation was unproductive but as he got up, rather disappointed and conscious of a long journey ahead, Anton noticed the photographs and without any expectation of anything except a glimpse into Cobb's background, began to look at them commenting politely.

"Then in one of the prep school ones I noticed this little chap with buck teeth and there was something about the set of those teeth which was familiar. I thought maybe he had grown up to be famous so I asked Cobb who he was. And he hesitated. Quite measurably hesitated. Then he said 'Sam Phillipson. He died in the Falklands and got a posthumous VC.'"

Anton was certain that Cobb had not wanted to identify him but had decided that it would not be credible if he said he had forgotten somebody who had reached that level of eminence. There was only a very small chance that he, Anton, would later come across a picture of Phillipson and associate it with Cobb's photo but in those few seconds of hesitation he thought Cobb had decided not to take the risk.

Yet Anton was also certain that it was not the photos in the papers thirty odd years ago when he himself had been but a child and unlikely to have seen them that had stirred his memory. There was something else....

He was still brooding on it when he went into the Graingers' tiny downstairs cloakroom before embarking on the long journey back to London. Here were other pictures but in humorous vein with political cartoons and shots of Cobb looking angelic in a nativity play complete with wings and halo, and dressed, aged about twelve, in the flowing robes of Laurence of Arabia in Rattigan's *Ross*.

In the same frame Sam Phillipson was playing a British army officer and suddenly Anton knew where he had seen him before: in a picture of several officers with Fred which he had seen on a visit to his flat.

Shortly after driving off he pulled into a layby on Dartmoor and sat trying to puzzle it out. Both Fred and Cobb had known Phillipson. So what? If Cobb had not hesitated when identifying him Anton would not have thought it anything more than a coincidence. Lots of people had mutual acquaintances, either past or present. It happened all the time. But here was another odd thing and one which caused Anton to sit bolt upright in his car. He was fairly certain that last time he had been in Fred's flat that picture was no longer on display among the others grouped on a table in Fred's lounge.

"So Cobb didn't want to acknowledge Phillipson and Fred had removed his picture from where anybody might have seen it. What on earth was going on? What could be the significance of Phillipson? It had me baffled."

"Damn!" the expletive came from Frobisher who was at the wheel and they all groaned at the diversion signs ahead of them on the A38.

"Ignore them," advised Anton "and get off now. Turn left towards Sigford which is just ahead of you and aim for Widecombe. Then we can get back on this road via Bovey rather than joining the queue for Newton Abbot."

"Right", Frobisher sounded resigned. "And we can stop at that inn we went to last time. What was it called? The Old Inn? We will have to get something to eat and if we are to be forced off the beaten track it might be as well to go there."

"Bound to be better than a service station on the M5," agreed Anton.

"But meanwhile go on with your story. I can't wait till we get to the inn to hear what's coming next."

"I'll say," murmured Molloy, who had been inwardly cursing the diversion not for its nuisance value but for the unwelcome interruption to Anton's narrative.

"Where was I?"

"Baffled," Molloy reminded him.

"Yes, totally. There was some feeling about that Cobb had been a bully at school, although you drew a blank on that. The picture of Sam at prep school made him look fairly timid and so I wondered if Cobb had bullied him and whether it could have been embarrassment that made him not want to name Phillipson. Perhaps Fred had simply broken the picture and the whole thing was coincidence but I just couldn't believe that. Today of course Maggie told us that Sam *was* bullied and I would take a large bet it was Cobb who was responsible.

"Anyway that was the theory I worked on. But what had any of it to do with Jess? I began to form an idea that actually received confirmation today. Suppose Sam was Jess's father? He would have been scandalously young but then Maggie was a scandalous girl.

"We knew Maggie had rejected Jess when she traced her but what if she had told Jess who her father was? The Allwards more or less implied to you that there had been not much more than a single telephone call between Jess and Maggie but now we know there were several. If they didn't know that they might not have known she was trying to trace her father."

"But," objected Molloy. "If she had found out her father was a VC she would surely have told the Allwards? She would have been so proud."

"Remember what David told us," put in Frobisher. "She was very private and cut even her husband out of what she was thinking. Perhaps she was already in that habit."

"Yes and she may have wanted to spare the Allwards. She might have thought it would make Henry feel that he was a poor specimen beside the real dad. Perhaps. Sam was dead but I think she tracked down either his family or a close friend. All she had to do was locate the papers of a couple of years earlier and she would have found plenty to go on. If she didn't try to find someone who knew him then the rest of my theory is kiboshed."

"Let me guess," ventured Molloy. "You think she traced some-one who knew him and that person told her that Sam had only gone into the army and lost his life because he wanted, as Maggie put it, to prove himself and the reason for that was that he had been bullied as a wimp all his young life. Whoever it was Jess traced then told her who the bully was and it was Cobb. Cobb grows famous and Jess begins to toy with denouncing him in public and then the perfect opportunity presents itself. So we are not dealing with an adulterous curate as we once considered but a man whose cruelty drove another to his death."

Frobisher shook his head. He was pulling in to the village car park. "That doesn't quite stack up. Remember this place is full of mud and puddles. *What the...* "

All three had jumped as suddenly Cobb Grainger's features grinned at them out of the darkness through the window on Molloy's side of the car as he rapped smartly on the pane.

"That's the second time he's done that to us and it's worse in the dark," Frobisher told Anton sotto voce as Molloy jumped out and hailed Grainger in breezy tones.

Anton smiled. "It's blown my cover, I'm afraid. I'll never again be able to invoke Auntie from Manaton."

"Good evening, sir," said Frobisher affably. "As we find ourselves meeting like this, can we buy you a drink?"

"Kind of you, but I'm afraid I'm due at home. Cocktails for the bigwigs and all that. Have a safe drive."

They watched him go.

"He gives me the creeps," muttered Molloy. "And he's a cool customer alright. Didn't ask what we were doing here."

"Perhaps he hadn't time. He sounded pretty rushed," observed Anton.

"Or maybe his conscience is clear," grimaced Frobisher.

"On that I would take a large wager, Inspector. I think we have just said good evening to a murderer, but you were about to demolish my theory?"

"Perhaps not demolish exactly but let's get to the inn first."

They walked slowly in the dark. In the distance an owl hooted and Frobisher shivered with a sudden atavistic fear. He could not have said why.

CHAPTER FOURTEEN

IN WHICH SUPPER IN AN OLDE INN SHEDS AN UNCERTAIN
LIGHT.

"I think," said Frobisher when they had all returned from the inn's washrooms, chosen their meals from the blackboard over the bar and settled in a quiet corner, "that we had better hear the end of your story first, Anton. Then we can start picking it over in detail."

He broke off as three orange juices arrived. The policemen were sharing the driving and Anton wanted nothing which might threaten his concentration. Frobisher had suggested they wait until their food had been served so that they might have no further interruptions and so for the next ten minutes they talked trivialities while in their minds dwelling only on the case and the new light Anton was shedding.

"OK, but I'm about to move on to a new chapter." Anton leant back in his chair to allow the waiter to put his grilled steak in front of him. "And talk about Fred so if you think my reasoning on Cobb doesn't stack up as you say then perhaps we should hear about that now."

"All right. First though let me say that I'm very grateful for all you have found out."

"But....?"

"I can't see it adding up to murder. The essence of it is that Cobb Grainger bullied a national hero at prep school. We looked pretty closely at his public school record and there were no instances of bullying and you haven't told me even that he and Phillipson were at the same senior school.

"So somebody appears on the scene who can justly accuse him of being a brute when he was a wee child. So what? It might cause him to wince but not to writhe. Indeed being a politician he would turn it all round and say that one of the reasons we should get tough on bullies is so that they are stopped. As he was. That he learned his lesson early and has always been grateful for it. I could write the script myself.

"What's more Maggie's evidence is that Phillipson was still a wimp when they were sixth formers so I think it likely that he was bullied at public school as well. Why blame Cobb whose malign attentions he had escaped years earlier? Phillipson goes into the army straight from school but it is another sixteen years before the Falklands War so presumably he found he liked it after all. No, sorry, there isn't even half a case against Cobb there.

"If Cobb and he were at the same public school and he secretly bullied him until the moment he left driving Phillipson into the army where he was killed almost immediately, then yes, I would buy it but not on the scenario we have now. It's just too far-fetched."

"They weren't at the same secondary school," admitted Anton disconsolately. "That was very easy to check. The obits gave me Phillipson's school and it wasn't the same as the one in Cobb's other photos."

"Never mind, we still know a lot more than we did before you set off on the Phillipson trail but before we move on to Fred would you mind telling me how you got into Maggie's house?"

"I walked in, Inspector."

"You can call me Peter, but pardon my scepticism. I can swear on oath that I firmly shut the door behind me and heard the yale click into place."

"Yes, but in places like that people often leave their back doors unlocked if they are in the house. It's not like central London."

There was something about the way Anton avoided his eyes that caused Frobisher to ask "and you found this one unlocked?"

"We don't need to know," intervened Molloy hastily. "Fortunately it was our WPC who let us in. Maggie was still in the lounge so she probably thinks you came in with us. I suppose there was no evidence of your unlaw- I mean your clandestine entry?"

"Oh no. I used a cred…"

"We do *not* need to know. Dear God. Why couldn't you simply tell us about Phillipson and leave it to us?" Despite the seclusion of their table Frobisher glanced round to make sure nobody could hear.

"I was going to," muttered Anton.

"Ah, yes. Before we had words. Well, never mind. I suppose Maggie might wonder what you were doing there at all. You are after all a famous dancer not a detective. Even so, she isn't likely to complain. The less her sort have to do with the police the better they feel."

"Fred?" prompted Molloy.

"Indeed. Fred. It didn't take much thought to work out that Fred must have been connected with the army at some stage. Remember what he said when all the lights went out? *There will be a court martial. Top brass will be furious.* Then when they came on again he called out *well done, Sparks.* Also I remember when I first saw you in the Pig and Pen and you met that poor woman. She asked specifically about Fred, referring to him as if she knew him in the past, and then I overheard you say that she was once a man and in the army."

"He was never a padre," interjected Molloy. Ever since the fiasco over the adoption certificate he had memorised CVs with almost obsessive precision.

"No. At first I thought there might have been something significant in the Aunt living in Aldershot in terms of Maggie and Sam but that didn't work because she was already pregnant when she got there and of course now we know from today that they met through younger siblings in Bath. Fred moved several times when he was first a curate and then a vicar but never to Bath. I scoured Crockfords, Who's Who and all the biogs on the web and finally narrowed it down to a little village about twenty miles from Andover where Fred was a country parson for six years. It was the nearest I could get to anything military. Fred was there between 1976 and 1982.

"The rest is pure conjecture. The army's chaplaincy centre is at Andover. Whether they still have the records or not I don't know because I haven't had time to check - and probably won't have now because next week we begin working like crazy for the Christmas show. They know it's make or break after all the chaos."

"You think Fred worked at the chaplaincy centre?"

"Probably just gave a talk or something, went out with the lads afterwards and became friends with Sam. Or maybe he never went there at all and it was Sam who came to the village. Maybe there was a popular watering-hole there or he or one of his mates had a girlfriend who lived there or, or, or, you might as well stick a pin in the list of possibilities at this stage. Indeed the photograph was of two or three men so perhaps Fred was friends with one of the others, whom he could even have known from the past. Then when Sam won a VC, he remembered the photo and framed it."

"Tell us about the photo. Did you find it that day we came to Fred's flat?"

"Yes. Unbroken and stowed in a suitcase under the bed."

"If he felt so guilty about it why not destroy it?" asked Molloy.

"Your guess is as good as mine. Perhaps he was attached to it for some reason and was just postponing the act of destruction or he may have reasoned that if nobody noticed it was missing – and only a regular visitor would – it did not warrant destruction. But I bet he would have torn it to shreds pretty quickly if he thought he really was under suspicion."

"But where is all this taking us?" Frobisher's voice had an edge of despair. "I suppose you are going to say that at some stage Sam Phillipson confided to Fred why he had joined the army more than ten years earlier? Then, when Fred met Jess she was searching for her father and told Fred who he was and that was the reason for her misery, more than the grandfathers dying, at that time. She was traumatised by her birth mother's rejection and finding out her father was dead."

"You suppose right. I don't think Fred would have told her why Sam went into the army because that would have just upset her more but it might have made him seriously angry with Cobb on her behalf. If Cobb had been identified as the culprit at that stage, that is. We don't know yet when she found that out. She might have told Fred that only when Cobb joined this year's *Lively Toes*."

"Yes, but again I ask, where does this take us? Where is there a motive for *murder* in this?"

Anton shook his head bemusedly. "I wish I knew, but stripped down to its bones, neither Cobb nor Fred want to admit an association with Phillipson and he was Jess's father…"

"Probably," said Frobisher in a wickedly accurate mimicry of Maggie's voice.

Anton looked intrigued. "That's pretty good, Inspector. Have you ever thought of taking up acting?"

"I act all the time and tomorrow I'll be doing just that when I tell the AC we are making progress. Right. Let's get on the road."

"Just think," mused Anton as he pulled out his wallet. "If Sam hadn't had buck teeth we wouldn't be on this path."

"We may yet wish we hadn't bothered," observed Frobisher grimly. "No, put that away. Dinner's on the Yard. I reckon we've all earned it."

"I wonder if we'll meet that coven again?" Molloy tried for a light-hearted note as they climbed into the car with Frobisher at the wheel.

"Coven?" wondered Anton.

Molloy described the detectives' experience on their last visit.

"Probably making for a stone circle. There is one at Hound Tor." Anton sounded amused.

"You seem to know this area very well."

"I came here a lot as a child. We weren't well off and didn't tend to go abroad but my Manaton aunt had a large house and a big garden that we could all run round in. We used to go to Fowey too but it is much further and the relatives there had a smaller house. It was OK if the weather was hot enough for the beach but otherwise it could be a bit of a disaster with four children running amok. I came to love Dartmoor as a teenager when I could go off for long walks with Dad and leave the pesky sisters behind."

"There it is!" Molloy's exclamation cut off Frobisher's response.

The huge pile of black rock had loomed up on their left, majestic against the bright moon behind it. A small figure was silhouetted on the top.

"The view is stupendous from up there," explained Anton. "You can see right out to the sea. True, all that chap will see will be the lights but it is still worth it."

"Isn't it dangerous climbing that thing in the dark?" inquired the ever-practical Molloy.

"Depends how familiar you are with it. I wouldn't but whoever that is has clearly managed. You need to mind the ponies and cows around this bit. They wander onto the road from nowhere."

"So Gardiner told us. He's from the local force."

"Let's get back to Fred," suggested Frobisher.

They did and talked of little else but Cobb, Fred and Phillipson throughout the long journey back, yet as they reached London and Frobisher dropped Anton off at Piccadilly they had managed only one significant thought between them. It came from Molloy as they were passing the exit for Wootton Bassett from the M4.

"Do you remember the children's names and how I commented that Jess had chosen such traditional ones?" he asked Frobisher.

"Yes. Sarah Jessica Anne and David Henry Samuel. Oh, yes, I see. Jessica, Anne, David and Henry after parents and grandparents. *Samuel.*"

"We can ask her ex if there was a particular reason for deciding on Samuel. She must have offered some reason for the choice if it was really after Sam Phillipson but if that was the inspiration then it means she was still actively thinking about him fourteen years after Maggie told her who her father was. There again that is not so surprising." Molloy had sounded dispirited as he made the last observation.

As they waved off Anton, Frobisher reverted to that conversation. "I can't for the life of me see that anything we have would drive anybody to murder let alone the sort of murder we have in this case, involving high risk in a busy corridor. But given that the only thing that links any of the major players is Phillipson we are going to have to talk to his family and take a DNA sample. That means we may be about to disturb a whole lot of lives for a likely red herring. Hell."

"We can start with the siblings, sir. No need to go barging in with the widow when it isn't her DNA we need. They may already know because Jess must have talked to somebody if she found out why he went into the army."

"If she found out. That is still pure supposition. Everything beyond the link with Phillipson is supposition. Even if the DNA is negative, the link is still there because Jess thought she was his daughter but where it takes us I cannot see. We are going to have to try and break Fred."

"Not Cobb?"

"No. All he has to do is tell us the truth, acting all contrite. The real mystery is why Fred is hiding his link with Phillipson, but we haven't the smallest grounds for a search warrant."

"Do we try to see him tomorrow?"

"No. First we revisit all we know about him. In particular I want to know a bit more about why he left the church. It happened some time between Phillipson's death in the Falklands in 1982 and his turning up in the church hall of Christmas Pie and meeting Jess in 1984. There might just be some significance in that but I haven't a clue what."

That, the inspector thought disconsolately just about summed up every lead they had. Had Anton not had the advantage of having visited his fellow dancer and seen the photo in his sitting room before all this began they would be nowhere. They were, he reflected grimly, still nowhere.

He was brooding on this depressing assessment when he arrived home to find Barbara distraught.

"Zoe's not home."

"What?" Frobisher glanced anxiously at his watch. It was half past ten.

"Where is she?"

"That's the problem. I don't know. She was staying at school until about seven for rehearsals for the play. She sent me a text at seven thirty to say she was still there and then another at eight to say she was just leaving. When she wasn't here by nine I was worried but then she rang to say that her friend Sue was ill and she had diverted to take her home. I've heard nothing since and it was all lies. I rang Sue's mother to see if she was still there but she never had been. Sue wasn't ill and had come home immediately after rehearsals which ended in the normal way at seven."

Anger and anxiety struggled for supremacy in Frobisher's mind.

"It gets worse," said Barbara quietly. "Sue's mother must have given her daughter the third degree because she phoned back twenty minutes later to say that Zoe left the school with a boy."

"Which boy?"

"That's just it. It wasn't anyone from the school. It was someone Sue didn't know. Apparently he was waiting for Zoe at the gate so it must have been planned."

"Does Jonathan know anything?"

"No."

"Well, just because Sue didn't recognise him it doesn't follow that we wouldn't. Not all Zoe's friends go to that school."

"I've tried all the ones I can think of."

"I don't think there is any call for too much alarm. It is probably just the latest rebellion and underneath it all she is a sensible girl. We don't let her go out in the week because of homework but other parents take a different line so Zoe is forcing the issue."

"But all those awful lies!"

"You must have tried ringing her?"

"Her phone is switched off. I've sent text after text. The first was angry but the last was just begging her to let me know she is OK."

"Give it another half an hour. She is fifteen not twelve. She'll be all right."

Two hours later he was yelling at Zoe that she was fifteen not eighteen when she returned smelling of tobacco and alcohol.

"How did you get home?" worried Barbara.

"Tube," said Zoe, with a shrug.

At least she was not slurring her words, thought Frobisher. Whatever else she had been up to she had not drunk enough to lose control but the long inquisition which followed and Zoe's profane reaction to the inevitable grounding meant he did not see his bed till two and that he slept indifferently thereafter, arriving next morning in the office feeling fit for nothing.

Molloy had fared little better having been up half the night helping Alice with a crying baby and two sick children. DC Forbes took one look at them and brought tea. The AC appeared oblivious to their fatigue but very alert to the slowness of the investigation. The Christmas Show of this ..ah.. reality programme was coming up and the press would be clamouring at the door, he told the Detective Chief Superintendent. Perhaps they should get a fresh pair of eyes on the subject?

The fresh eyes would have not much to look at, responded the Chief Superintendent. Frobisher and Molloy had left no stone unturned.

"I hear rumours that they are using some amateur. Julius Ceasar?"

"Anton Caesar, sir. The dancer."

The AC emitted something between a rumble of despair and a whimper of disbelief.

"He's been pretty helpful and none of us wants to lose him. He knows about the studios and dancing and indeed more importantly knows the personnel. The only reason we are now looking at Phillipson is because Caesar used to visit one of the other dancers and had noticed that photo. It's all in the report, sir."

"I also hear rumours that he sails rather close to the wind in helping them. That means they do too."

"As I have occasionally, sir. It can get results. This particular boat won't capsize."

"But will she ever get to the port of destination?" The AC's eyes were keen and the Chief Superintendent found himself floundering.

The day was rescued by DC Forbes who appeared bearing black coffee and news just after lunch.

"We've had quite a bit of luck with people who knew Fred in his vicar days. The Bishop who accepted his resignation is ninety and still very with it. He lives in Dorset. But better still, we have tracked down the priest who succeeded him and who had known him from theological college. They lost touch after a while but he remembers Fred well and the good news is he lives in London. Highgate area."

"Then we'll try him first. This very afternoon."

"Is that a good idea, sir?"

Frobisher stared at DC Forbes in astonishment. She blushed but stood her ground. "I know it's not my place to say so, sir, but you and DS Molloy look all in."

Frobisher gaped.

"She's right," interposed Molloy hastily. "This case is as dense as any case can be and if there really is anything of importance in Fred leaving the Church then the way I feel now, I shall miss it."

Frobisher's expression changed from annoyance to resignation to wry amusement.

"Agreed. Make an appointment for us first thing tomorrow and meanwhile we could always try leaving the office on time."

They succeeded. On arriving home, Molloy fell asleep in an armchair until gently roused by Alice at midnight whereupon he staggered up the stairs and fell into bed to sleep once more, unwoken by the crying of Kathy or the arrival of Immie who crawled in between Alice and him in the early hours.

Frobisher fell asleep in his shed with his head on the table until Barbara woke him at eleven. The next morning both detectives rose ravenous and feeling ready for anything, including, thought Frobisher one very sulky, rude and rebellious daughter. Before he left the house he told Barbara that yesterday he had made improper use of the police computer and Dean Gates, the boy with whom Zoe had spent the previous evening, was unknown to the police. Furthermore he had made enquiries among colleagues with children at the school Zoe said he attended and young Gates was definitely not a trouble-maker. Indeed he was regarded as a student with great potential. So it was all a silly teenage escapade. Nothing sinister.

Barbara looked unconvinced and kissed him with forced cheerfulness as he opened the front door, through which he stepped full of optimism. Today, he believed, would see the treacle thin out.

CHAPTER FIFTEEN

IN WHICH FROBISHER PLAYS WITH SOME LIGHTS.

The Reverend James Everleigh placed a cafetiere and a plate of biscuits on the coffee table and looked warily at the detectives.

"May I ask why you are interested in Fred? You surely don't think he had anything to do with that horrible murder?"

"We have absolutely no evidence that Fred was involved", Frobisher reassured him and that was certainly true, thought Molloy. "But we are trying to piece together the background of the murdered woman and Fred is being less than open with us. We think she may have consulted him in his priestly capacity even though he was no longer a vicar by then, so it is understandable that he is reticent but there are things we need to know and you may be able to help us."

"I don't see how I can help. I didn't know her. But fire away."

"You knew Fred well?"

"Yes. Very well. We trained together. In those days you had to do two curacies before being given your own church and Fred and I did our second curacies in adjoining parishes. Then when we did get our own livings we were miles apart, me in the city, him in the country but we kept in touch and met up from time to time. Then I briefly took over from him when he left to think things out but the life of a country parson was not for me.

"After he left the church he seemed to cut off many of his former friends there until it was just a matter of a Christmas card and then not even that. We ran into each other once by accident and had a drink but we seemed to have lost our ease with each other. The last I heard from him was a rather formal acknowledgement of my condolence letter when he lost his second wife."

"Thank you. That is very helpful. Why did he leave the Church?"

A pair of intelligent eyes held Frobisher's gaze. "Have you not asked him that?"

"Yes. He said he had become disillusioned with the C. of E. but did not fancy the celibacy of the Catholic Church."

Everleigh's eyebrows rose. "And......"

"We think there is more to it. Look, sir, I'm not asking you to betray any confidences or reveal any private conversations you might have had with Fred. As I say there are no grounds for associating him with the murder but I must ask you to trust me that this *is* all relevant and tell me what anybody who knew him at that time might have seen and deduced with their own eyes. It was not that long after his downing his dog-collar that he met and, we believe, counselled Jess Allward."

"Very well. What he has told you is true. He was fed up with the Anglican church but had reservations about other options."

Frobisher's eyes moved to a large, framed proclamation that Jesus Saves, dominating the room from the wall over the fireplace.

"You were Evangelicals?"

"I am but Fred certainly wasn't. He was an Anglo-Catholic and that makes it a cast-iron certainty that he will never reveal anything Miss Allward told him, if as you say, he was counselling her. He would regard it as confessional and therefore what Catholics call 'under the seal.'"

"Even if he was no longer a priest?"

"He may well, particularly at that early stage, have thought once a priest always a priest. However, you were asking about his leaving and as I said he told you the truth but not the whole truth. Anybody who knew him at the time will be able to tell you that he was practically losing his faith."

189

Molloy, who had been letting his eyes wander round the room, found himself suddenly gazing intently at Everleigh.

"He had a young relative. I'm afraid I can't recall his name. Bernard or Bertie or something. He too was just ordained and was an army chaplain."

Everleigh faltered to a stop as suddenly both detectives looked at him with a sudden interest they made no effort to disguise.

"Is that significant?"

"It could be. Was he stationed at Andover?"

"Training there, yes. But he had begun to agonise over his role. Helping out in field hospitals, comforting the dying, dealing with combat stress or cowardice, yes that was all fine and exactly why he had joined the army but he was losing it over telling young men that it was all right to spend their lives learning how to kill. Apparently he was briefly attached to a commando unit as part of his training and found the hand to hand combat stuff emotionally and morally unmanageable. He would never have to do it, of course, but he had to experience what they were learning.

"Fred was really rather robust about it all and talked quite freely about it. He said you didn't become an army chaplain if you were a pacifist. That there were such things as just wars so people needed to know how to fight. That fighting Hitler had been a moral imperative and the same was true of the Soviets if ever they were to try anything. Actually I always wondered if Fred was a frustrated soldier. If he had been a year younger he would have been caught by national service and I think he rather regretted missing out."

There will be a court martial. Top brass will be furious. Well done, Sparks! Perhaps, thought Molloy, Fred had carried that regret into old age.

"Anyway, Bernard or Bertie or whatever had decided to leave and follow Fred into the more conventional forms of priesthood but Fred talked him into delaying that for a while, saying he needed to be absolutely certain that he was not turning his back on a call from God."

The detectives were beginning to guess the outcome.

"The poor chap was killed in the Falklands War and Fred never forgave himself. He couldn't get over having talked him into staying in the army. He was an only child and the parents never forgave Fred either. Apparently they had never wanted him in the army in the first place and had encouraged his doubts."

Fred seemed to make a habit of upsetting parents with his advice to their offspring, reflected Frobisher sadly, but Everleigh was by now in full flow.

"Then Fred's wife died. She had been in hospital for a perfectly routine operation, some female plumbing issue. Afterwards she began bleeding and they weren't quick enough. Septicaemia set in and it was all over by the time Fred got there. He was pole-axed and there were two small children left motherless. This time it was Fred who couldn't forgive. He couldn't forgive God. That much anybody from that time could have told you but our private conversations will stay just that."

"Of course, sir. Did you know Sam Phillipson? He was...."

"*Sam?* Yes, I remember him well. He also died in the Falklands, but of course you will know that."

"Yes. Did he ever talk about why he joined the army?"

"I didn't really know him. But Fred's relative was in his unit. He came to see Fred while I was there on a visit once and we had a long chat about the young man's problems. Yes, he talked about his own motives but that really was in confidence. The reason I remember it so clearly is that it seemed ironic when........." Everleigh stopped suddenly as if realising that he was about to say too much.

"When he won a VC. Quite. We know about the bullying and that Phillipson thought of himself as a wimp, which is why he became a soldier. He told a girlfriend he wanted "to prove himself" and joined straight out of school. Sir, I am now about to take *you* into *my* confidence and tell you what I hope you will never reveal unless and until it ever becomes officially public."

"My lips are sealed," Everleigh spoke gravely but Frobisher saw the flash of curiosity in his eyes.

"We are as certain as we can be that Sam Phillipson was the father of Jess Allward."

He saw the vicar trying to work it out. "I remember, I think, pictures of a widow and children after he died but in view of how you have just phrased it I gather she wasn't one of those?"

"No. The mother was a rather wayward girl and, although they were both over the age of consent, both she and Sam were in their teens."

"Well, I'm certain *that* didn't come up in our conversation, Inspector."

"No, sir. If the girl is to be believed he didn't know. Given that his siblings and hers were friendly he must have heard why she had been sent away to live with an aunt but I afraid she was promiscuous and if he had ever asked she would have told him it was someone else's. She was afraid he would want to marry her, although in those days that would have been up to the parents, given they were under twenty one."

"Good heavens! But how can I help?"

"Sir, this is murder. The past with its grudges and tragedies can always be relevant and in this case we can't find much in the present. Let me just ask you some questions and see where we get."

"All right. Carry on, Inspector."

"We know he was bullied and we are certain that it happened at prep school but what we don't know is whether it also happened at his public school."

"Yes. From the way he spoke it had gone on throughout his schooldays. He was badly teased about his buck teeth and when he got upset over that it was open season for some pretty serious nastiness. He asked his parents if he could have the teeth dealt with but by then it was too late. A mere brace wouldn't have done the trick and they didn't want him to have false teeth at so young an age. I think he said they wanted him to decide when he was older. As he still had them when I knew him he had clearly decided to live with them after all."

"Did he never tell anyone what was happening?"

"No. That I do remember. Sneaks were hated. But one of his friends had an older brother at the school, who then took Sam under his wing. So all was well until this boy left and then it all started again."

"When you met him he had been in the army for a long time. Was he happy?"

"Yes. He loved it. That was why he was helping Fred persuade the young man to stay in. Apparently he had nearly given up and in the early years was counting down the days to the end of his commission, but then suddenly he found that he was enjoying the physical challenges, that he wasn't afraid and he had a real gift for inspiring others. It all, as they say, came together for him."

"Did he name any of the bullies?"

Everleigh smiled. "I don't remember but I doubt it. Even if he had I wouldn't recall them now from that one conversation. After all, I can't even remember the relative's name and Fred must have talked about him quite a lot. As I said I would have forgotten the conversation altogether but for the VC."

"Let's come back to Fred. Do you think he ever regretted leaving the Church?"

"Sadly not," mused the vicar with a small shake of his head. "At first he did not know what he was going to do and took the children to stay with his mother but then he took up dancing and the rest is history. He married again years later but the kids elected to stay with his mother."

"Just one more question, sir. You were surprised that Phillipson was Jess's father and also at the circumstances but did Fred ever say anything in later years which might suggest that Phillipson had a secret?"

Everleigh hesitated. "I am afraid I cannot help you, Inspector."

Frobisher smiled. "You just have, sir."

A few minutes later he and Molloy were in conference in the car.

"So Cobb wasn't the only bully," observed Molloy. "That weakens the case for him being afraid of exposure."

"He doesn't know that he wasn't the only bully or probably doesn't ," observed Frobisher. "Then it looks as if Jess did tell Fred that Phillipson was her father. Our vicar was very discreet at that point. Also the relative hated commando style killing. Perhaps he explained to Fred how it was done. Lawrence said the method of death was 'expert'."

"Motive, sir?" Molloy brought them both back to earth.

"What was his motive for lying to me when I asked him if he knew any reason why anyone would wish to harm Jess?"

"Perhaps it wasn't so much a lie as a hesitation, sir. He may have thought as you do: that what had happened between Cobb and Sam was not sufficient motive for what happened. On that analysis he answered truthfully."

Frobisher snorted. "And he as good as lied when I asked him if he knew Jess was adopted. He said 'was she?' and then later said it had been thirty years ago that these conversations took place, implying that he couldn't remember."

"Do we still want to see any of Cobb's teachers or classmates now that we know what he did to Phillipson wasn't unique?"

"Probably, if only to tie down that passage in their lives. Have we made any progress?"

"DC Forbes has found one teacher who remembers the incident and several pupils. The headmaster has died. She has fixed up two interviews with a London-based pupil and the teacher who lives in Hampshire. We could combine him with the Dorset bishop. That is if we still want to see the bishop."

"Possibly for completeness sake but for now it's off to the studio. The lighting chap is there?"

"Yes and Fabulous Flying."

"We've got to begin to tackle this from the other end, Brendan. Motive is proving a wild goose chase. We must look again at opportunity, again at expertise, again at the timing and forget motive."

"We know Rashid Ahmed is the only one with enough expertise to fiddle the lights in the studio, but even his training was some years ago and may be out of date."

"We know no such thing. We merely assume it because he once had formal training but what of the others? Did any of the celebs ever have any basic training in production? Did any of their spouses or boyfriends come from that world? Are any of them real dab hands with a computer?"

"We have followed those lines, sir," said Molloy in hurt tones. "But all we've drawn is a blank."

"Well, let's hope we get something from this session."

The lighting engineer, Chris Ansell, was a man of forty five who had begun as a trainee when he was sixteen.

"Didn't need a lot of fancy qualifications then," he told them. "You learned on the job."

"Things must have changed quite a lot?" Molloy stared at the lighting computer.

"They still are changing. This is state of the art stuff but five years from now people will laugh at it and ten years from now it will be a museum piece."

Frobisher expressed suitable wonder and asked Ansell to describe how it all worked. With commendable patience as he had already described this once to the detectives and twice to the police computer experts Ansell began from scratch.

"The programme as you know is recorded as live. That means very precise timings and things have got to happen when you expect them to. Each week each pro supplies a director's tape giving the final version of their dance and we use that to work out the lighting sequences. Band call and dress rehearsal refine it if necessary in terms of timing. Sorry, I'm repeating myself. I've already told you all this."

"Pretend you haven't," Frobisher told him earnestly. "Somewhere in all this is a major clue and we haven't found it yet."

Ansell nodded. "Well, theoretically you could just programme in the sequence and the computer would do it all, but this programme is full of amateurs so I've always operated the sequence manually. Otherwise you get a celeb forgetting a sequence so that the spotlight is where he or she should be but not the dancer. Em was very prone to that. And by watching her like a hawk I could move the sequence by a few milliseconds or in the worst case by several seconds."

The detectives smiled. "Go on," urged Frobisher.

Ansell clearly felt silly, having said it all so often, but he continued. "So when it has all been worked out I print off the sequence from the computer and then tap the keys manually. The sequence sits here."

Self-consciously, he pointed to a blank space on a table bristling with gadgets next to the computer console.

"And you followed the same sequence from the same bit of paper for dress rehearsal and the real thing?"

"Yes. We always have a mock judging session at dress rehearsal. But the timing of the start for both bits of the show depends on a signal from downstairs that all the dancers are in place and then we get ready. The band strikes up and the spotlight goes first to the judges, but on this occasion there was no signal. Venetia was ad-libbing like crazy."

"You had the spotlight on her?"

"Yes, but occasionally she mentioned the band or the judges who were of course seated by then," so I was switching round quite a bit– all manually because the delay had naturally not been programmed in so I wasn't even following a sequence. I was just following the ad –libs. It didn't much matter because the recording only began when we were starting."

"And you started with?"

"The spotlight on Venetia. Then the judges, then the band, then the audience, then the first dancer to emerge."

"And to switch all the lights off, *all* of them, you would do what?"

Ansell demonstrated. "And I did not do that. Absolutely not, Inspector."

"OK, go on."

"The director decided we should start because Jess was next to last to come on. Each dancer appears individually and there is a small reprise of the dance. So there was time to get her up to stage.

It was he not Rashid who signalled that and I began the sequence. Venetia began to talk to the judges and then suddenly it was pitch black."

"Where were you in the sequence then?"

Ansell pointed. "And, as you see, if I do that the lights do *not* go out."

"What happens up here between dress rehearsal and the show?"

"Nothing. I go and get something to eat and so does anybody else who is working with me."

"So the computer and the sequence is unattended?"

"Yes. But as I told you there wasn't time to re-programme the computer and nobody could have switched the sequence because it was exactly the same bit of paper. It had a ring from my coffee mug on it."

"Do you often do that?" asked Frobisher sharply.

"Yes. There isn't much room here as you can see so I perch the mug on the corner of the sequence but never of course over the writing itself."

"And you did that day?"

"Must have."

"Sorry, sir. Can you *remember* doing so?"

"Well this is something new," murmured Ansell with more curiosity than sarcasm. "I don't exactly remember but I did have a mug up here and I can't think where else I would have put it."

"Did it always leave a ring?"

"Nearly always. I'm afraid I'm not house-trained."

"Who else would come in here? The director, producer, any curious celebrities?"

"All of those occasionally. Cobb Grainger came in once and asked a lot about it but I got the impression that he was treating it as he would a constituency visit to some factory. Duty rather than real interest. PR in fact."

"Fred?" the question came from Molloy.

"You're joking, Sergeant. Fred never shows any interest in anything except the dancing. Not these days."

"You told us nobody came in here that day. Rashid Ahmed stood at the door for a few seconds and said that Em was more scatty than usual and to be alert, which you already knew from dress rehearsal but he didn't come in and nor did anyone else."

"That's right. I asked Mike from sound if he saw anybody round here and he said no. Of course he wouldn't have been around either between dress rehearsal and the show."

Buzz Roberts from Fabulous Flying was equally patient with yet another inquisition.

"Somebody got at this computer while it was here during the week between the intended date of flying and the actual. It was locked away but somebody still got at it. Otherwise what happened could not have happened."

Frobisher glanced at a sheet in his hand.

"And you say re-programming the computer would have taken hours?"

"And then more hours. Yes."

"And nobody showed any particular interest in how it worked?"

"Beautella herself. She was scared stiff and wanted me to do it all manually. Cobb was curious but only in a cursory way. He spent more time looking at Beautella than the computer. Poor chap was in despair with her. Em wandered over at one point during the morning before band call to say she had once flown in a pantomime and had always wondered how it worked. Trevor Langdon probably showed the most interest and that was not much but he kept an eagle eye on us when we were rehearsing because he thought they should never have allowed Beautella to fly and was afraid her nerve would go. Everybody else just let us get on with it. We have done enough flying for FBC in the past."

"Ever worked with anybody from this show before?"

Roberts thought about it and then shook his head. "Not that I recall."

They were not making much progress thought Molloy dispiritedly and when they finally left the studios Frobisher uttered the same observation.

"Cobb showed an interest in both computers at some time or another", volunteered Molloy. "And he has that big, flash computer in his study."

"I have a pint of milk in my fridge but it doesn't mean I know how to milk a cow."

The sergeant smiled bleakly.

"As far as I can see the only people who would have had any chance of slipping those names into the judges' papers would have been Rashid Ahmed, Trevor Langdon who put the packs together and Helen Brown who was told to lay them out. None of them could have murdered Jess. They were all quite visibly in the studio throughout the period between the show and the line- up for the judging and both Langdon and Ahmed were there audibly – very audibly – throughout the period of darkness. By the time Helen was sent to find Jess she was already missing and we now presume dead. Otherwise why hadn't she turned up?" Frobisher shook his head.

"And Trevor is clear that he went through each clutch of papers individually immediately before handing them to Helen, who is equally clear that she went straight away to lay them out on the table. On the evening Beautella's name appeared Langdon actually laid them out himself because Helen was not yet back at work and everybody else was tied up. Again he says he checked them all thor-oughly to make sure each set was complete, just as he checked that floor management had put out water for each judge and a cushion for Serena to give her a bit more height. Everything was in order. He did not go back to the table after that so the insertion of the cards was performed in the short space of time between Langdon checking the table and the entry of the judges. Ahmed took a quick look but by and large trusted Langdon and Floor to have it all ship shape."

"The first judge on was Liz and she was under the spotlight until she sat down so she couldn't have done it. She had no handbag and the camera records show clearly enough that she wasn't car-rying anything. Then Jos, then Serena and neither of them could have fiddled with the papers because Liz would have seen what was happening."

"Do any of them have a background in magic, sir?"

Frobisher grinned. "I reckon sorcery might be a better word. But given that we are dealing with show biz that might not be such a bad idea. I'll clutch at any old straw."

"Perhaps Phillipson's sister will cast some light, sir. She said an odd thing to DC Forbes when she took her call. 'Yes, I have been expecting you for some time.' What did that mean?"

"Probably not much. If Jess contacted Sam's family when she was eighteen then she did so at a time when she was embarking on a career in dance. So if someone called Jess Allward then popped up on the screen as a dancer Sam's sister would have put two and two together. When she was murdered that same sister would have expected us to be probing Jess's background."

"She didn't come forward."

"Why on earth should she? She can hardly have information of relevance to the murder itself. What's her name?"

"Claire Higlett."

"Well, I'll take a bet, Detective Sergeant Brendan Molloy, that all we find out from Mrs Higlett is that Cobb was among many who bullied her brother, that she told Jess that was why he joined the army and then we are back to saying but even if Jess was about to expose him that is no reason for murder. We are going to be led along one big circular garden path."

"No bet, sir," murmured a demoralised Molloy.

They walked through the FBC reception area on their way to the car park. By now familiar figures to those staffing the desks they were greeted cheerily and wished good night.

"That sort of time already?" grumbled Frobisher.

"Do you need a car, sir?" asked the man at the taxi desk.

"No thanks. Ours is outside."

"Right. What about you Freddy?"

"Two please," said a female voice behind them brightly.

To Molloy's astonishment Frobisher whirled round and stared at her. Oblivious to his scrutiny, her attention fixed only on the taxi co-ordinator, Freddy was explaining the needs of her programme for guests' cars.

What on earth was the matter, wondered a bemused Molloy. Had the boss been expecting a man to answer to the name of Freddy or perhaps he had recognised her voice? She had finished now at the taxi desk and was turning away. Frobisher watched her go.

"Sir?"

The Inspector jumped suddenly and turned to face him. "Sorry, I was miles away."

"Anything to do with the case, sir? I don't remember her working on the show?"

"No. She's another programme's fixer."

"Runner, sir."

"Runner indeed. Running. Running away, Sergeant. Of course!"

"A runner did it, sir?"

"Almost certainly."

Molloy looked at him in disbelief but Frobisher put a finger to his lips and indicated that he wanted to think.

Chapter Sixteen

IN WHICH FIVE MEN LEAVE IN A HURRY

Claire Higlett received them in an empty classroom of the school in which she taught maths and physics. The blackboard was covered with incomprehensible equations - to him at least -and Molloy was glad he did not have to solve them. He had never been strong on science at school.

"Thank you for not contacting Jo," she said with a sad twist of her mouth. "We never did tell her."

Josephine Phillipson was Sam's widow and Claire's opening words confirmed the detectives in the scenario they had predicted. Jess had found the siblings easy to trace and had picked one of the sisters, as it happened the very sister who used to play with Maggie's brother.

"It was a bit of a shock to us, but I recalled Maggie very well and also the rumours which went round when she was sent away to an aunt. Sam had been friendly with her for a while but no more so than with other girls and I never heard his name in any of the speculation."

"He didn't know himself," put in Frobisher. "Maggie told us that. She was afraid he would want to marry her."

"Yes, it all fell into place and we would have been willing to accept Jess as part of the family but she didn't want that. She said she had been lovingly brought up and would always regard the Allwards as her family and, anyway, she didn't want to upset Jo who was then still relatively recently a widow. Two years isn't that long, Inspector."

"No. So what did Jess want?"

"To know. That was all. What he was like. What her real grand-parents were like. Had Sam been happy? Why the army? That sort of stuff."

"Did you tell her that he had been driven into the army because he despised himself for not standing up to school bullies?"

"Yes. But also that he came to love soldiering and that then he never wanted to do anything else."

"This is a really important question, ma'am. Did you name any of the bullies?"

"Yes. She said that they might almost have done him a favour in driving him to do something in which he was to be so happy but that nobody could think that now he was dead. I answered some-thing along the lines of hoping I never met any of them and that I would certainly tell Cobb Grainger, Stuart Plax and Byron James what I thought of them if they ever crossed my path."

"Do you remember her reaction?"

"Not really. She didn't ask any more about them or about the nature of the bullying. I think she came to hear only about Sam and wanted to take away a glowing picture so that was what I painted for her: his family life, kindness, courage, care of subordinates, all that sort of thing. Poor girl! And then to think it all ended like this."

"She made only that one contact?"

"In person, yes. I told her she was welcome to call upon us any time but asked if she would give us prior warning if ever she wanted to contact Jo or meet her half-brother and sister but she said she wouldn't. When she herself got married and had children she sent me a photo of them all plus grandparents. I think it was her way of reassuring us, of saying it was OK, that her life was good. Years later one of Sam's children, by then grown up, came upon it and asked who they were. I almost told her. Perhaps I might have done if both Jess and I were to be still around when Jo died but not now. Not now Jess is dead. Let the past lie."

"If only we could," lamented Frobisher as they made their way out through a throng of noisy children heading for home.

"We had better contact this Stuart Plax and Byron James and see if Jess ever sought them out. That will give us some idea as to whether she had confronted Cobb in the past."

"If she had then he might not have been so keen to do *Lively Toes.* I prefer the theory that she suddenly revealed who she was to him in the course of the show, threatened to denounce him and then kept him squirming over when that might be. But at least we can now test that. If she confronted Plax and James then she would have done the same with Cobb. Better ask for the alumni lists from Phillipson's school."

"No," said Stuart Plax with a regretful shake of the head. "I never heard of her in connection with poor old Sam until now. We were utterly ghastly to him. He was known as Snivelling Sam because every time we trapped him he would cry, poor little devil. It was on my conscience for years but then he actually turned up at a school re-union. I avoided him like the plague but then thought that was the coward's way out so I went across to apologise and he waved it away. Told me he was in the army of all things. The Army. *Sam Phillipson.* Nobody could believe it."

"Do you remember a Byron James?"

"Yes, Inspector, I certainly do but I don't think you'll find he had much of a conscience about it."

That was certainly true thought Molloy as James sneered his way through the interview, which Frobisher had left to him but the upshot was the same: he had never been confronted by any daughter of Sam Phillipson.

"Do you think we should tell the Allwards now about Phillipson?" Molloy wondered when he reported on the interview to Frobisher. "A lot of people now know and James is the sort who will bellow it about in the pub."

Frobisher reluctantly assented and they divided up the remaining interviews with the bishop and Cobb's teacher and schoolmates but to Molloy it appeared that Frobisher's heart was no longer in it. Instead he appeared to be chewing over some theory of his own, something to do with a runner. He knew better than to press his superior before he was ready but he was overwhelmed with curiosity. Which runners? Ed? Helen? Neither was feasible.

"Hallo, Sergeant!"

Molloy turned and found himself hailed by Beautella and Helen. He began to walk towards them.

"What are you doing here?" asked Beautella. "Are you coming to visit my studio?"

"No, I'm collecting the Christmas tree. My wife says it's the only way to remind me what time of year it is. I'd forgotten your studio was round here."

"I'm training the delightful Cobb." Beautella pulled a face. "Helen is coming to help the camera team. Just think in three days it will be the Christmas show and then I'll never ever have to dance with him again. Are you coming to the show?"

"Indeed. Duty calls."

"Any progress?"

"A little." Molloy sounded cautious and both women laughed.

The detective was pleased to see that they were visibly recovering from their ordeals as he watched them walk away with a lightness of step neither might have imagined possible a few weeks ago. He chose a tree and lugged it out of the shop to find snow in the air. Pleased he did not have far to go to his car, Molloy held the tree upright in his arms and proceeded carefully along the pedestrian-thronged pavement. A busker in a street doorway was playing *Hark the Herald Angels Sing*. What sort of Christmas would the Allwards be having, he wondered, or Jess's children?

"Burnham Wood coming to Dunsinane?" Cobb Grainger's face grinned at him through the Christmas tree. Molloy jumped but managed to stop without bumping into him.

"Good afternoon, sir. Off to Studio LaReine?"

"Yes. Thank heavens this nonsense will all soon be over."

"I'm told you could win, sir."

"Perhaps. Do you need help with that tree?"

Molloy declined and felt relieved when Grainger had left him. He hoped only that Cobb would be in custody by Christmas but the thought produced a fleeting sorrow for Jane Grainger who surely deserved better than to find she had married a murderer.

He manoeuvred the tree into the car boot and diagonally across the seats, pleased that it only just reached the windscreen and that he could close the boot firmly. Nevertheless he drove carefully back to work. The next two days would involve desk work, checking the typescripts of his interviews and comparing information with Frobisher. It should mean being home at regular hours.

"Make the most of it," advised Frobisher. "The press will be hell as we get to the Christmas Show. They will say we have let the trail go cold."

"Trail? What trail?"

"Hmm," muttered Frobisher, his thoughts all too obviously wandering elsewhere.

"Whatever this theory is you're working on, sir, will it help us in time for the Christmas Show?"

There was no reply and Molloy looked up to see his superior, coffee cup frozen half way to his lips, staring intently at the opposite wall, his gaze seemingly fixed on the "In the Event of Fire" notice. Was that a hint? Something to do with the fire door on the dressing room corridor? No, decided Molloy, the inspector was intrigued by something only he could see and, whatever it was, it was present in his mind not the room.

"I think he's on to something," he remarked first to DC Forbes and then to Alice that night.

"I wish I were too," he added as the wildly excited Immie and Conor fought over who was to put what on the tree. "The only bit of inspiration I have contributed to this case so far was there in the file all along."

"Has he given you no hint at all?"

"Something to do with the runners..."

The conversation ended abruptly as Conor pulled a length of tinsel so hard that Immie, who was holding the other end, fell forwards into the tree and hurt herself on its needles, her screams of pain and shock waking Kathy and the air suddenly filling with protest and rebuke.

It was not much quieter in the Frobisher household where Zoe was arguing with Barbara and the inspector had shut himself in the "shed". He was talking aloud to himself as he tested and re-tested every aspect of his new theory. It seemed as watertight as he could expect at this stage but he decided he would try out the timings for himself on Friday night. Then if it all hung together he and Molloy could decide how on earth to prove it and that he knew would be a veritable Everest to climb. There was no real proof and if he could not break the suspect they would never solve this case.

"What was all the yelling about?" he asked Barbara as he emerged a couple of hours later.

"The usual nonsense. Zoe was excited by the snow and said perhaps we really might have a white Christmas this year and Jonathan innocently began some learned disquisition on the odds. You can imagine the rest."

Frobisher grimaced but then fell once more into deep thought.

Friday brought more snow, which seemed to add to the air of excitement which filled the studio of *Lively Toes*. At least the competitors were excited but he detected taught nerves in the director and producers. They knew this was make or break for the future of the show.

"I think whatever happens, this is my swan song," Fred told Molloy. "I'm too old and there are moves I just can't do any more. They've kept me on far longer than I could reasonably have expected. After all when this programme was conceived we were all thinking in terms of gentle ballroom dances but each year the celebs got more ambitious and now it's all lifts and gymnastics. I'd rather jump than be pushed."

Molloy glanced at the dancer's hands.

"Yes," said Fred, intercepting his look. "Arthritis. Both hands. Knees and hips. I am just about getting by this year because Em is quite happy swishing about the floor without attempting anything too ambitious but I wouldn't stand a chance in twelve months' time."

"I'm sorry," said Molloy.

"I don't think I'll do this again," Beautella told Frobisher. "I'm closing the studio and teaching on cruise ships for a while. Cobb has put me off this show for life."

"I'm sorry," said Frobisher.

"They're all giving up," he observed when the detectives found themselves alone.

"No. Ru wants the show to survive and Ahmed is as tense as a coil."

"When it's nearly time for stage call for the judging, I may disappear for a bit," Frobisher told him. "And I mustn't be interrupted."

Molloy forebore to ask how you interrupted someone who had disappeared but he sensed rising excitement in the inspector and felt a corresponding rush of adrenaline .

"A breakthrough tonight?"

"In theory, yes. The proof may be a bit harder. Now let us loiter with intent."

They lurked in the dressing-room corridor, watching dancers and celebs go to hairdressing and make-up and the dressers flit from room to room. From Em's came a bad-tempered tirade.

"No! It's horrible! It makes me look like the sugar plum fairy. I told you I wouldn't do pink froth. You're just trying to make a fool of me."

The dresser came out in tears.

"She has the temper and she's a big woman," murmured Molloy. "Suppose Jess suddenly riled her?"

"Then where did the flapper band suddenly come from?"

Ru raced past them on the way to band call. He returned a few minutes later with an angry Tatum in tow.

"That's the second time we've missed our slot," she was saying as they disappeared into hairdressing and the celebrity booker appeared from the stairs, hurrying towards Em's room.

Ed the runner emerged from the lift with a tray of beverages in cardboard mugs. He held it carefully in one hand while knocking on Em's door.

"Oh, now who is it?" yelled Em irritably.

The celebrity booker opened the door and took the drink from Ed, pulling a face at him as he did so. Ed smiled bleakly.

"Everybody acting in character," murmured Molloy.

Cobb emerged from his room beyond Angela's salon and, spotting them, cheerfully enquired after Molloy's Christmas tree. It was relief from an unlikely quarter but after all the bad-tempered shouting Molloy found himself responding in a friendly rather than merely polite fashion. As Cobb disappeared up the stairs Frobisher grinned.

"Fraternising with the enemy, sergeant?"

Molloy grunted. "Where do you want me in dress rehearsal?"

"With me here but during the real thing I need to be here alone and I want it known. The last thing I need is somebody coming down here innocently and wrecking my experiment."

"So I watch the show instead?"

"No. At about the time the lights failed - remember it all happened during the second half so we need simply to time the whole thing from stage call and not by the clock - I want you to crawl through that hole in the wall, stand in the kitchen and count up to five, then come out to the studio door and clear your throat. It does not matter who sees you but it is crucial that the studio door doesn't open until after you have cleared your throat so station a runner on the studio side of it."

"Then I'd better go now and find that hole and make sure I can get through it quickly. You say it doesn't matter if anyone sees?"

"No, but if it's Cobb that sees then note the expression on his face."

"You don't feel like telling me what all this is about, sir?"

"It's about the solution, Sergeant."

"Or possibly not," Frobisher added under his breath as Molloy departed to find the hole. "I could just be wrong – again."

The dress rehearsal augured well, said a happy director to Rashid Ahmed. Matt and Lisa had performed an above average fox-trot, Hal and Leonie an energetic jive, Fred had held on to Em sufficiently tightly during the Quickstep for her to miss only three steps, Cobb had not frightened Beautella with any unexpected moves during the Samba and Ru had been so brilliant a matador in the Paso Doble that only the judges had remembered to watch Tatum.

Obviously it would not be the usual tense final given that indifferent performers were still left in the competition but those would be eliminated at the halfway mark and then a new hazard introduced whereby the judges would ask the last two couples to reprise any of the dances they had performed in the course of the competition and the choice would be that of the judges and the dance carried out there and then. Each couple had been allowed to nominate one dance they would not be asked to do in order to eliminate the flying risk for Beautella.

"It means," Ahmed had explained to the detectives "that they have had to rehearse every dance rather than just concentrate on the new ones. "Fred says they haven't bothered as they know they won't be in the last two but it has caused havoc for the others. Cobb has apparently been swearing like a trooper because he loves to improvise rather than just re-create but of course only the judges will know whether he is being faithful to the original and it's the audience which has the final say. He'll win unless one of the others pulls the rabbit to end all rabbits from the hat."

They were trying to do just that, was Molloy's conclusion as he watched Matt hold a gold-swathed Lisa over his head as they went into a vigorous swing in the centre of the floor and Hal and Leonie jump on to a table for the jive. It was such good entertainment that he almost forgot his reason for being there.

"Do we grab a bite?" he asked Frobisher when dress rehearsal was over.

"Nope. We stand very unobtrusively in the wings and watch every move. *Every* move. Who does what in the interval could be important."

"We haven't asked that they re-create what they did on the night."

"No, because I want everyone acting naturally and as far as possible not alerted to what we're doing. Watch the lighting booth. Ansell's gone. That's Mike going from sound as well. There goes Ahmed. How long could anybody rely on the studio being empty before the audience starts arriving or before anybody comes to check anything? This is when they all eat unless of course something has gone wrong in which case a lot of people stand round in a post-mortem. That day they all went off after about five minutes just as they're doing now."

Cleaners came and went almost immediately. Then there was a gap of about half an hour before floor management and members of production began to drift back. After that there were nearly always one or two people checking equipment until a mass meeting of production, floor and technicians about ten minutes before they started letting in an excited, voluble audience.

As soon as Rashid indicated to them that stage call was imminent Frobisher departed for the dressing-room corridor and Molloy for the wings, where he kept a close eye on his watch. After the dancers were in line in the wings he waited a couple of minutes and then imagined the lights failing and bent down to open up the panel. He looked at Cobb but, disappointingly, the politician had his back to him. Only Em had noticed his antics and was nudging Fred as he began to crawl through the hole. He was surprised to find the other side in darkness.

He stood and counted to five then felt his way out to the corridor where he turned gropingly towards the studio and conscientiously cleared his throat. From a distance of inches Frobisher emulated a high-pitched female scream.

"For pity's sake!" Molloy's heart was racing.

"Now stay there in the dark and listen," said Frobisher as he produced a torch and lit his way back along the corridor. "*Listen.*"

"Did you hear anything?" the Inspector demanded as he the beam re-appeared, heralding his approach.

"Something very faint, not much."

"That's how it was done but it begs one very big question. Let me think about it and then we can both think about proving it."

"I'm all ears, sir."

"Meanwhile we can just enjoy the show. We know now as much as we ever will. Did Cobb see you coming through the hole?"

"Sorry, sir. No."

"O.K. We'll just have to be unsubtle about it. Make sure he's sees it's open and watch him like a hawk."

"Em saw me, sir. I would think they all know by now."

"Pity. Well, let's enjoy the show."

They stood in the wings and chatted to the couples waiting to go on. The professionals trooped out from the other end of the floor and Matt appeared with Lisa urging some last minute advice on him.

"Good luck!" said Frobisher.

"We need it," grinned Matt.

As their dance was finishing Hal and Leonie did some last minute practice which caused the detectives to back away, afraid of being hit in the eye by Leonie's flying heels. When their turn came, Fred and Em stood in silence with glum resignation. The judges' comments could hardly have lightened their mood, reflected Molloy as they came off the floor. If this really were to be Fred's last show then he was hardly leaving on a high.

Cobb came to the wings, grinned at them, winked at Beautella and applauded Fred as though he and Em had given a virtuoso performance. He was in high spirits and Molloy found himself hoping the politician fell flat on his face. Frobisher was staring at Grainger intently but if the latter were aware of it, he gave no sign of discomfort. To Molloy's disappointment, he gave a faultless, whirlwind of a performance as did Ru and Tatum.

Anton and one of the female professional dancers then entertained the audience with a foxtrot to *Putting on the Ritz,* while the judges conferred. To nobody's surprise the finalists were pronounced to be Cobb and Tatum.

"No contest", murmured Frobisher, as Tatum simply could not recall the polka and a grim Ru did his best with a wide professional smile. "What friend Cobb doesn't remember he will improvise."

"And lo, it came to pass," agreed Molloy as Cobb and Beautella lapped up the cheers of the standing audience. "And next?"

Frobisher glanced at a list in his hand. "Fireworks, another professional dance, the usual interval during which the viewers' votes will be counted and then the results. At the beginning of the interval some band will perform."

Molloy thought it tactful not to mention that the band in question was then enjoying a number one position in the charts, until he caught Frobisher's expression and grinned.

"For a moment, sir, you sounded like the AC."

"Let's grab a cup of FBC coffee. I want to do our test again at the beginning of the results half because this time we will be following the real time line and can do it by the clock. That's a bit of luck because I thought it might take longer to count viewers' votes than with just the audience voting but technology can do anything."

"Don't scream this time, sir. It gave me heart failure."

Frobisher laughed and Molloy, not knowing whether or not to take that as assent, tensed himself as he stood in the pitch black and cleared his throat.

"Eeeeek!" squeaked Frobisher mouse-like, switching on his torch. "But that's twice it has worked."

Suddenly he pushed Molloy out of the way as the studio door flew open and Ed and Helen ran past them. They could hear the furious tones of Ahmed and the disbelieving buzz among the dancers.

"Not again!" wailed the director into Rashid's earpiece as he absorbed the news that neither Cobb nor Fred was present. The detectives, making the same assessment with their eyes, turned and raced for the dressing rooms. As they reached the bottom of the stairs the runners were hurrying back.

Frobisher firmly barred their way. "Have you found them?"

"No," panted a wide-eyed Helen.

"The fire door is open," puffed Ed.

"Quick! " roared Frobisher, racing for the emergency exit, which was indeed open.

"They could have one hell of a start," he raged as they fell into the car. "They must have been about during the interval or they would have been missed by hair and make-up, but God knows when. They could have been missing since shortly after the end of the main show. Indeed sometimes the men just get quickly checked as they're going on for the next act. It's the girls who get all the fussing."

Molloy was on the phone. It took a while before he could command anyone's attention but having delivered his questions it was not more than two minutes before Ahmed rang back.

"Angela saw both at the end of the main show. She looked in vain for Cobb because he was expected to win and she wanted to make sure he was all tickety-boo as she put it but she couldn't find him. Em says she saw Fred going into Cobb's dressing room after the main show and thinks he looked angry."

Shortly after he had relayed this Ahmed rang again.

"Beautella says she made no attempt to contact Cobb in the interval. Several people are saying they heard Cobb and Fred rowing in Cobb's dressing room but nobody knows what about. By the time anyone got curious the singers were in full throttle." Molloy summed up the conversation to Frobisher. "As you heard I asked him to ask everyone individually with dressing rooms in the vicinity if they heard any of it because we know those walls to be paper-thin."

"The singers don't start caterwauling until just before stage call."

"No, but this was earlier. Ahmed says the singers had made some mistake in rehearsal and were going through it again and again. It's just our luck that we spent the time in the studio instead of downstairs."

"Or we spent it having coffee if I am guessing correctly. Try telling that to the AC and the Super."

"What is certain, sir, is that at the moment we haven't heard from anybody who either saw or heard them after the first ten minutes of the interval."

The phone rang again. This time the conversation was a great deal shorter.

"That was Gate Security, sir. They both left in their own cars. Cobb first and then Fred and Gate reports hearing shouting and car doors slamming just before Cobb went out."

"Get DC Forbes and a couple of others there. We need statements from everyone who saw or heard them and tell Ahmed that nobody goes home until we have them. They are to close the gates now and when our chaps arrive nobody is to leave without being asked if they saw or heard Cobb or Fred or both. Anybody might have been passing or nipping out for a smoke or ordering cars from the taxi desk or whatever."

"Are you sure one of us shouldn't be there?"

"More than sure. Get full details of their cars."

"Have done, sir. Cobb's is a bright blue Range Rover and Fred's a dark red Peugeot."

"Do they have bright blue Range Rovers?"

"Cobb does. Should be easy enough to spot in daylight but in this…" Molloy grimaced at the snow now falling thick in the dark night.

"Quite. Do you know if we have high vis jackets and torches in the boot?"

"Certainly several jackets and I saw a torch. Where are we going?"

"Dartmoor. Where else?"

"But why should Cobb suddenly go there in such a hurry?"

"Your guess is as good as mine but I know why Fred is chasing him. I will bet a year of my salary to an hour's worth of your measly pay that Fred is planning to murder Cobb."

"But… I can't see it. What have I missed?"

"As much as I did for too long. But I wasn't expecting this. After all, victims normally murder their blackmailers not the other way round. By the way, it might be worth checking if Anton is still at the studios".

CHAPTER SEVENTEEN

IN WHICH THREE MEN DANCE WITH DEATH

As if on cue Frobisher's mobile rang. Molloy glanced at the screen and could not repress a smile. "Talk of the devil," he murmured.

"Where are you?" he asked without preamble.

"Good evening, Sergeant Molloy. Hope you're well?"

"Good evening sir and I hope you too are well wherever you may be, which is….?"

"Just passing Slough. And you?"

"Not yet joined the M4," responded Molloy, hitting the loud-speaker button.

Anton's tones floated merrily into the car. "You had better get a move on."

"Can you see them, sir?"

"I do wish you would call me Anton."

"Stop assing about, sir," fumed Molloy causing Frobisher to chuckle.

"Ok. Ok. No, I've kept well behind them. Behind Fred that is. I haven't seen Cobb since he roared through the gate."

"Do they have any reason to think you might be following?"

"Don't think so. They were intent upon each other in the car park and as soon as I realised they were rowing I kept out of sight. Before you ask, they were rowing about Jess. Fred was calling Cobb a murderer and yelling that he wouldn't get away with it and Cobb called him in turn a 'bloody madman'."

"Did anybody else witness any of it?"

"A woman getting into her car. She was just gaping at them."

"Tell him to keep us posted," interrupted Frobisher. "We need to get on to the local force, preferably your friend Gardiner, and deal with the other niceties while you're at it."

Molloy relayed this to Caesar. "Just one more thing for now, sir. Are you in your normal car? Dark grey Merc?"

"Oh, the surveillance society! Is there anything you don't know? Yes. The very same."

Molloy spent the next forty five minutes telephoning the office, checking progress at the studios and contacting Gardiner. As they were between Reading and Swindon he took a call from Anton saying that he was passing Swindon and, no, he couldn't see Fred's car.

"They're still miles ahead, sir. Do we need the hooter?"

"No. Tell Anton to keep using my phone as yours will be busy and tell him we are in an unmarked car and very unlikely to announce our presence with a siren."

"Heard that." Anton's cheerful voice came over the loudspeaker.

"If possible, sir, I want to listen to their conversation when they do meet. I have no doubt that Cobb is heading for home although I have no idea why. So, please don't let them see you when they finally come to roost."

"Roger."

While this exchange was taking place Molloy had been talking to Ahmed and DC Forbes. Three witnesses had heard Fred and Cobb shouting at each other. Two of them had variously heard "murder", "blackmail" and "Jess" but neither of those had heard much because, Cobb was running, Fred was yelling after him and their conversation was in snatches.

They were nearing Bristol before there was a long enough lull for Molloy to ask Frobisher what he believed to be happening.

"I think it goes like this: we know that Jess found out she was Phillipson's daughter and, thanks to the Reverend Everleigh's tight-lipped discretion, we can be pretty certain that she told Fred when she was being taught by him at Christmas Pie. It is reasonable to suppose that she used him as a mentor over many months and that he was indignant on her behalf.

"Sam's sister admits she told Jess the names of the bullies who drove her father into the army and thence to his untimely death. So she knew the name Cobb Grainger and it would not have taken her long to find out that he was indeed the same Cobb Grainger who was at school with Sam. Indeed given that he was already famous as an MP it is likely she found out long before he showed up on *Lively Toes*.

"We know from Plax and James that she didn't contact them at any stage in her life so it is unlikely she contacted Cobb thus, when he's asked to do *Lively Toes*, the name Jess Allward means nothing to him beyond the professional persona. However she, like everybody else, takes a dislike to him but she *un*like everybody else has it in her power to disturb that nasty complacency. So she tells him she's Sam's daughter and that she holds him morally responsible for Sam's death.

"That would explain the building tension in her which Matt noticed: she was determined to confront him."

"And to expose him?"

"Possibly, but if she had really been going to do that she would have warned the Allwards, not let them find out from the media. That doesn't mean she didn't make the threat. She would have enjoyed stringing him along week after week, with Grainger never sure when the axe was about to fall. What she did do was tell Fred.

"She may or may not have told him all the names in 1984. If she did he might just have remembered them because he had briefly known Sam and might have felt angry on his behalf but it is unlikely he stored them up all these years. Grainger has only been a household name for fifteen years or so not thirty. So I think she told him on *Lively Toes* that Grainger was one of the bullies."

"So why didn't he tell us? Why cover up for Cobb?"

"At first I thought it could just be what Everleigh called "the seal". That even though he was no longer a vicar he might regard anything she said to him as utterly unrepeatable, that she herself might have insisted on such terms. She didn't confide in the Allwards and you heard what her ex said – Jess didn't let people get close. Perhaps she chose Fred just because he had been a priest.

"That might have explained why he lied to me about anyone having a motive for wishing Jess harm and prevaricated to the point of lying about whether he knew she was adopted but of course it wouldn't explain why he hid the photo under the bed. That suggested a secret of his own and it also strongly suggested guilt. Thank God Anton was an occasional visitor there and noticed it was missing. It would have meant nothing to us. I think he tried a bit of blackmail."

"Fred? He tried blackmailing Cobb over Phillipson?"

"No. Over murder."

To Molloy's intense frustration the phone rang.

"Anton, sir. He's on the M5. Just past the exit for Burnham -on –Sea."

"Good, we're catching up."

"Go on, sir."

"Remember that Fred was at the front of the gaggle when the door opened and let's assume you and Anton are right about Cobb being on the other side. He could easily have made the same deduction and of course he knows that Jess had a hold over Cobb and so he thinks Cobb is the murderer.

"Now think of his flat. Apart from its location, everything about it is poor. Carpets and curtains worn. Chairs old and oozing stuffing. No TV. Fred has had a middling successful career not a stellar one and even that is nearing its end and he's poor and doesn't fancy eking out a living teaching in church halls or on cruise ships and anyway, then what?

"We may have to dig very deep but we'll probably find that he spent what he had on private treatment for his second wife or private education for the children or that he overstretched himself to buy that flat in central London or maybe we will find some private vice such as gambling or women but I think not. Remember what Ahmed said? He called him 'pretty devout'."

"Hang on! Does a devout man blackmail? And anyway Everleigh said he was losing his faith after the Falklands."

"That which is lost can be found. No, in the ordinary way such a man would not resort to blackmail but Fred wanted more than money: he wanted to avenge both Sam and Jess and maybe also the young relative whom Sam helped him persuade stay on. If Cobb had not tortured Sam then he wouldn't have been there to persuade anyone......."

"Far-fetched, sir, if I may say so but even if we leave the relative out of it, why should not Fred simply tell us all? Then Cobb would have spent his days in prison."

"Ok, let's forget the young relative and stick with Sam and Jess. Incidentally I'll bet that relative is in that photo too. Why else would Fred display it?"

"Because Sam was a VC and it would have made a good conversation piece?"

"Not a happy time for him to want permanently displayed. No, I think it was a family photo which the visiting children and other relatives would have expected to see. But anyway that's beside the point. Fred wanted not just to expose but to punish Cobb, to feel him squirm, to stretch out the moment of fear so he blackmailed him and for all we know salved his conscience by intending to share the proceeds with the church roof."

"And then?"

"And then Cobb wouldn't play ball. He knew we were stuck and all Fred could produce was a supposed motive going back to near infancy and a wild theory about how he could have been on the other side of the door. I expect he taunted Fred and the silly chap then believed that he, Cobb, was going to get clean away with it. After all, why not? If Cobb wasn't afraid of what he, Fred, knew then why should he fear him telling us?

"I think Fred only ever meant to prolong the anguish for Cobb. To make him think he was safe so long as he paid up. He probably did intend to tell us in the end but Cobb acted as if he could tell the whole world and Fred decided to take the law into his own hands."

"If he really believed Cobb had killed wouldn't he have been afraid of him? Do you think he took the old hackneyed course of leaving a letter with his solicitor?"

"I'm sure of it. We can now requisition it."

"And the lights, sir?"

"I thought you'd never ask....."

The phone rang again and DC Forbes made a thorough report over the speaker. By the time it was over they were near Taunton and Frobisher was still bombarding her with his own questions as they neared the end of the M5. No sooner had the call finished than Anton rang.

"I'm sure that was Fred turning off the A38," he told them. "Bovey Tracey exit. I'd have taken another route in this weather."

"Are you sure it was him?"

"No, but I'm following. I'll be able to get quite close. He can't recognise me in this muck."

"Right, Molloy. I'm going to risk a bit more speed." Frobisher swung into the outside lane. The snow was falling faster, large flakes dancing along the screen in flurries and squalls, mocking the furiously- working wipers. *Slow down* would have been police advice to the responsible motorist.

Everyone else on the road was doing just that, observed Molloy silently. He strained to see the exit signs - Torquay, Chudleigh, Chudleigh Knighton.

"Any minute now, sir."

Frobisher switched on the siren and crossed to the inside lane just as the Teigngrace sign became visible. Immediately he switched the siren off again and told Molloy to ring Anton. There was no reply.

Molloy kept trying. Frobisher, nearly blinded by a sudden flurry of snow missed the turning to Haytor and suddenly found himself with sheer drops only feet from the car as the road climbed steeply.

He forced himself to back slowly while Molloy tried not to look.

"No choice. We can't go on and hope for the best. There may not be another turning for miles."

"No, sir. It's a good job the lovely Beautella isn't with us." Molloy repressed a gasp of terror as the car gave a small skid.

It had lost them precious time, grumbled Frobisher between gritted teeth as they reached the fork he had missed and turned left.

"I can't get Anton," Molloy's anxious voice was deadened by the sudden rumble of a cattle grid and another slew of the wheels.

"Leave it. He may be there by now and lurking about where he doesn't want to be seen or heard…..*What?*……."

"Watch out, sir," cried Molloy redundantly as Frobisher swung the steering wheel and the car swerved wildly from side to side, miraculously missing the large dark shape which had materialised in front of them seemingly from nowhere.

"A cow," muttered Molloy as his superior righted the car.

"Indeed. I have farmyard GCSE, sergeant. That is police property which we have just dented and scratched to ribbons but at least we aren't in the ditch."

"No and the cow escaped… *careful*."

Molloy's last exclamation was wrought by the appearance of another large form wandering across their path.

"Before you tell me, that was a horse," observed Frobisher brightly but he slowed down until the form of Haytor Rocks was briefly visible through the snow and they saw a car with its headlights on parked off the road to their left. Molloy jumped out, went over to the car and beckoned Frobisher into the car park.

"That's Anton's. Fred's is here too, parked right across Cobb's."

The detectives peered around them and listened until they thought they discerned faint voices from the direction of the tor.

Molloy had already opened the boot and Frobisher, picking up the torch, ran, shrugging into his high visibility jacket as he went. The sergeant raced after him feeling his feet sink into the soaked peat of the moor. The voices grew nearer while they ran or at least tried to run as they tripped, fell and fought with clutching brambles.

There was something wrong with those voices, realised Molloy as he again picked himself up from the moor and saw Frobisher faltering to an unsteady stop a few feet in front of him. He caught up with him and both men stared at the spectacle in front of them as the snow slowed to a half-hearted scattering of weak flakes and then ceased altogether.

A circle of hooded figures in dark robes stood chanting in such light as the moon could force through the snow-laden skies.

"Wild good chase," Frobisher's voice was bitter with frustration when the moon, briefly successful against the snow, threw the tor into relief and lit up the silhouette of a man on each of two peaks.

Frobisher uttered an expletive between clenched teeth and ran forward. Molloy saw him stumble, collide with one of the robed figures and then several round objects fall to the earth, which as he raced after his superior he saw to be apples. An outraged cry went up from the coven as he trod on one.

"Sacrilege," he panted but Frobisher had gained ground and did not hear him.

It was uphill now and Frobisher's yells of warning came back to him on the wind. He knew the Inspector was calling not him but the men up there on the slippery rock, the men probably still wearing dance shoes. Surreally he recognised Fred's tailcoat. Cobb's Samba trousers glittered in the moonlight. Then as he was once more falling and getting up he saw a third figure. A sensible sort of chap. One dressed in a hooded jacket. Anton.

Behind him he could hear the coven and, glancing round, saw its members following him, their progress impeded by their robes, the lower ends of which they were endeavouring to hold in their hands. As he made what speed he could after Frobisher he had the absurd notion that he was fleeing from witches.

At least the snow was holding off and he could see what was happening on the tor. His breath was now coming in painful gasps. He was not unfit but a half-mile run over bogs, brambles, bushes and stones and for the most part uphill would normally have been beyond him and he could now see that Frobisher had been forced to stop and was bent double. Molloy jumped as an unseen pony whinnied, then both detectives were again running for the tor which had now become the stage for a grim, silent ballet.

Cobb Grainger knew fear. For the first time in his sixty five years he was cowering, wanting to sob, wanting to crawl away into some black hole where his pursuer would not find him. He knew the violent shivering which now beset him was not merely from the icy cold which whipped through his thin clothes.

He had rather enjoyed the chase from London despite his anxiety. Fred was welcome to come all the way to Devon if he wanted but there was no way he was going to let him into his home. He had already rung Jane to tell her to bolt all the windows and not to answer the door to any but him. But Fred had sat on his tail with annoying determination and he wondered if he would be able to jump out of the car and into the house without a fight.

He had no qualms on his own behalf but he feared for Jane. He must put an end to Fred's antics before they got there.

He thought several times that he had lost Fred on the motorway and if there had been a service station he would have turned in but nothing so convenient ever presented itself at the right time. Then he conceived the idea of pulling onto the hard shoulder. Fred would be bound to stop too and then as he was walking towards Cobb's car, Cobb would drive off.

Fred did pull in but he did not leave his car. Cobb drove back onto the motorway in a dangerous manoeuvre which left no room for Fred to follow and was rewarded only with irate hooting from the motorist he had endangered and the sight of Fred in his wing mirror catching him up a few minutes later.

He had enough petrol and hoped Fred didn't but Fred was still close behind him when he turned off the A38. Cobb let his hatred vent in an impotent roar of rage. He should have been basking in applause, lifting high the *Lively Toes* trophy, frightening that daft Beautella with an unscheduled lift in his victory dance, phoning

Jane with the triumphant news, giving interviews to the press. Instead he was here, still in those ridiculous dance trousers and now in addition to every other indignity he was realising that he needed the lavatory too urgently to be able to get home first.

Well, at least now he had the advantage of knowing where he was. He knew the moor roads backwards, could surely dare a greater speed than Fred and had only to lose him with one clever and unseen side turn.

Fate favoured him as he reached the straight run of road which led up to the turning to Haytor Vale. He narrowly missed a cow and heard the squeal of Fred's brakes. Looking back he saw the dark bovine shape standing nonchalantly in the middle of the road inches from Fred's bumper.

Cobb laughed aloud. "Thanks, Buttercup."

He had intended to turn towards Haytor Vale which would present Fred with three options but a car was coming slowly out of the turning and Cobb knew he couldn't wait. Instead he accelerated and turned into the Moorlands car park where the National Park Visitor Centre stood. Immediately switching off the lights he sat, listening. There was neither sight nor sound of the Peugeot. Fred was either still behind the cow or had turned into Haytor Vale and was now facing the choice between left or straight on and probably also wondering whether he should have turned off at all. In this snow and darkness he would never see Cobb but would try to find his house, which Cobb knew would be difficult even if Fred had an exact address and postcode to feed into a sat. nav.

He rather thought that Fred might not. The chase had surely been born of impetuosity, not planning. At any rate he could now relieve his immediate need and use the lavatories of the Visitor Centre. He would not use a torch but fearing that his glittery trousers might be picked out in the headlights if Fred decided to return to the moor road he reached to the back seat and pulled out an old, dull car rug which he held loosely round his waist.

He briefly debated whether to forget the facilities on offer and do what he had to do there and then, but he was cold and wanted shelter. He also had some absurd notion that a constituent might suddenly materialise and recognise him. He knew this was illogical but still he headed for the sign saying "gentlemen" at the side of the large café and map shop. It was to be his undoing.

As he entered the gents the light came on. Cobb froze. The light would be a giveaway to anyone hunting him. He tried to shrug off the disturbing metaphor but his needs would no longer be denied and he hastily relieved himself.

As he was leaving he heard a car pull in.

Oh, just face him down, Cobb rebuked himself angrily. Yes, Fred was strong but so was he. He stepped out, letting the car rug fall away and noticing with the first stab of real fear that, from the position of Fred's car lights, he was blocking the Range Rover.

The second came seconds later when Fred left his car and began to walk towards him.

"What price Sam Phillipson now?" called Fred sarcastically. "You killed him as well as Jess, didn't you?"

Cobb pulled the car rug back round his waist and prepared to confront his tormentor.

"That little wimp? I'm surprised Galtieri thought him worth the bullet."

Fred did not change his pace.

"I promised Jess that one day I'd see you wet yourself with fear."

"Unlikely in the circumstances. My bladder is empty and you wouldn't inspire fear in a mouse." Cobb tried to match Fred's sarcasm but was irritated by the wavering note in his voice which had so unaccountably spoiled his defiance.

"I'm not after a mouse. I'm after a rat and I don't do humane traps."

It was then that Cobb noticed what Fred carried in his hand.

He dropped the rug and ran, zig-zagging for the moor, the moor of which he knew every inch, which offered him in the snow –laden night his only chance of escape. If only there had been fog. Then he could have stood within feet of Fred and still have been unseen. Instead there was snow and snow left footprints. He listened and heard the crunch of Fred's faltering steps in the darkness. That meant Fred would hear his.

He ran on but forced himself to think. He could crouch down and listen for Fred's steps, let him go past then crawl softly in another direction. He could run, knowing that he could lead Fred into hazards of which the dancer would be unaware. It seemed Fred had no torch. He would trip every few paces. But if he outran him, then what? He could not move his car. But if he did not run he would freeze to death on the moor. They were both in danger of that fate but Fred had a jacket, perhaps some small advantage.

Suddenly his mobile buzzed and he grabbed at it with fingers that were rapidly numbing. Unable to silence it he threw it far away from him, hoping Fred would be misled by the buzzing. It landed soundlessly and Cobb felt a flood of relief.

"Hallo, Darling!" came Jane's voice. "Where are you? I've locked up everything. Is the weather dreadful?"

"Yes, darling," mocked Fred's voice. "Where are you? Not, I suspect where your phone is."

He was not as near as Cobb had feared but even so Cobb knew he must close with him, jumping on him and disarming him because the nearest place of safety would be the Moorlands Hotel behind the car park and even if he outran Fred to it, the instance he entered its grounds its security lights would betray him. There was nothing for it. He must put Fred out of action, at the very least parting him from that evil weapon.

Fred's voice came again, nearer and between him and the road.

"Hiding? Just like poor old Sam?"

"If you're so convinced I killed Jess why don't you present your evidence to the police?"

Cobb ducked down and then moved away from the direction of Fred's voice. He was going uphill.

Fred spoke from the same position. "Because you know and I know that they're stuck. They know you did it but they can't prove it."

Cobb was silent.

"And", continued Fred, this time further off. "You will say I blackmailed you".

The ice was chilling Cobb's bones. He knew he should begin to circle downhill but here he was on one of the moor's tracks and to go off it he would end up crunching through the dead gorse and heather. He began to creep up the path, knowing the only safety lay in the other direction.

Fred said no more until Cobb had moved a couple of hundred yards when out of the darkness he called "Oh, I found a path. I bet you found it first. It's taking us up, Cobb. Away from civilisation. We'll both freeze. Would it not be ironic if they found us side by side?"

Cobb glanced behind him. He could just make out the shape of the tor. If he could reach it he could shelter in one of its nooks and crannies. He turned and ran, not caring that Fred could hear the sounds of his precipitate flight.

Fred began a noisy chase. Some other sound was now audible on the night air and Fred, puzzled, paused to listen. Cobb, recognising the chanting, turned and shouted in its direction.

"Police! Murder! Police! Help!"

The wind whipped away his voice across the moor and only Fred heard but Fred was now gasping for breath himself and standing bent double while he tried to still the rasping in his lungs. He did not understand the noise he had heard, knew nothing of pagan ceremonies or witchcraft on the moor but he had recognised the direction from which Cobb's voice came and with a renewed determination he set off to find its owner.

Cobb had reached the tor when he saw the moving light in the distance. Then it disappeared again, blotted out by the snow. He forced his brain to work and decided to climb Haytor. If he could get up there Fred would have no chance. He would never be able to follow and if he did Cobb would hurl something at him. Someone always left something up there.

He began to work some life into his numb fingers as he had managed to do even while running, clenching and unclenching his

fists, pushing them inside his thin shirt, breathing on them whenever he stopped.

Then he remembered his survival training. If he could squeeze
anything out of his recently emptied bladder, it would be warm.
He might just buy enough time to get up there before his fingers
ceased to work altogether.

He got half way when he heard Fred immediately below.

"The higher you climb the further you fall."

Well if that old cliché was all Fred could manage, he must be
losing it. Cobb climbed on, not replying. He heard Fred slip and
curse and laughed silently, having no breath for any audible mirth.
Fred slipped again and was barely half way when Cobb reached the
top and sent down an avalanche of snow, a sandwich box and a full
bottle of fizzy water. Soon Fred would be past the steps and then
he would be helpless, needing both hands for the rock and so that
nasty little weapon would be useless. As it was his avalanche missed
his pursuer or else Fred had simply endured it and he wished he
had held one thing back. Instead he was now poised to boot Fred's
head as soon as it appeared.

Then in an instant the snow grew weaker and stopped as the
moon shone palely on the scene below. Two men were struggling
up the moor one on the path, one floundering in the bushes and
peat holes. They were heading straight for the tor, for him. They
were but silhouettes yet Cobb thought they could be Frobisher and
Molloy.

He was about to wave when he realised he had watched them
too long and Fred was now standing on the tor. He glanced at his
hand and backed away. Fred laughed. Cobb gave a cry of fear,
turned and jumped.

His feet slid beneath him and he knew he had twisted his ankle
but he was alive and out of reach of Fred on a different peak and
the detectives were coming.

He and Fred stood looking at each other, a chasm between
them. Then out of the gloom rose a third figure, a figure who could
not have been far behind Fred as he climbed the tor.

Fred, alerted by the sudden switch of Cobb's eyes, spun round, missed his footing, dropped the weapon, grabbed at it and seemed to pirouette as he tried not to slip on the snowy surface.

Anton reached towards him but he dodged and took a flying leap at Cobb's peak, his arms spread aloft as if he were performing a grand jete. Cobb instinctively staggered back but Fred slipped on the ice as he took off, seemed to hover in mid- air and then fell, with a cry seemingly more of chagrin than terror, into the abyss. Later Molloy and Frobisher were to wonder if the chagrin sprang from frustration at being deprived of his prey or from his last dance move on this earth failing so catastrophically.

Meanwhile Cobb, certain that he was going to land beside him, turned and jumped on to the next peak. It could only fail and as Anton completed a precision leap on to the peak Cobb had just vacated, the politician's twisted ankle became a broken one and he slid off the peak to the ground below.

Anton became aware of Frobisher bawling at him from the base of the tor.

"Just come down. Come down, will you? And stop bloody dancing!"

CHAPTER EIGHTEEN

IN WHICH FROBISHER UNRAVELS A MYSTERY

Cobb, both his legs broken, lay knocked -out beside the tor. When he opened his eyes the first thing he saw was a group of hooded figures staring at him under a pale moon. He let out a whine of abject fear and slipped back into unconsciousness.

"Must have thought he'd died and woken up in hell", surmised Frobisher in deeply satisfied tones as the paramedics took the supine figure to their ambulance.

"Broken neck," said the pathologist Gardiner had roused from his bed to inspect Fred. "Death was instantaneous."

Molloy wrapped his hands round his soup mug. The scene of crime people were in action.

"Do we need to keep them?" he jerked his thumb at the coven.

"No. We saw as much as they did. Just get names and addresses."

"Already done, sir."

"Excuse me, Inspector," said one of them. "But may we finish our sacrifice first?"

Frobisher stared. "Your sac...... No, you damn well may not. Go home!"

"Well, may we just look for the apples?"

"No. Everything between here and the road is potential evidence and you will not remove it."

"Do you suppose that was the Chief Wizard ?" asked Molloy as the coven departed with an air of barely suppressed mutiny.

Gardiner snorted. "He runs an ironmonger's by day and an art class by night. Was once on the local council. Soft in the head if you ask me."

"Because he belongs to a coven or because he served on the council?"

Gardiner grinned then picked up something in his gloved hand.

"Who would this fool?" he moved the rubber blade of the toy axe from side to side.

"I think it fooled Cobb," smiled Anton with malice in his voice. "But who just happens to have a toy axe lying about their car?"

"Someone with a grandchild who played a woodcutter in a fairy tale."

Anton stared at Frobisher in disbelief. "You know that?"

"No, sir. Just a guess. Or perhaps he saw it in props and took a fancy to it for a grandchild."

"Or," suggested Molloy quietly. "He saw it in props and thought it might serve a more sinister purpose."

Frobisher smiled. "Perhaps but tonight would have been pretty difficult to foresee. And what a night it has been. All we have to do now is go and see the murderer."

"They won't let you," pointed out Anton. "They'll need to operate on him."

"On Cobb? But Cobb is not the murderer. Fred thought so and you two thought so". Frobisher's glance took in both Caesar and Molloy. "But Cobb didn't kill Jess."

Anton stared at first him and then Molloy.

"Oh, you're good, sir, and I couldn't have cracked this case without you. You are very, very good for an amateur but I am afraid it wasn't Cobb. We would all like him to have done it but he didn't."

The others stared at him.

"So who did?" ventured Molloy at last.

"Let's go and see," suggested Frobisher.

Twenty minutes later Molloy found himself staring incredulously into the terrified eyes of Jane Grainger.

"It was always the lights that bothered me," Frobisher told his spellbound audience of Molloy, Caesar and Gardiner as they sat in the deserted dining room of the Rock Inn, where the cook, waiters and cleaners were just beginning to arrive for their day's work. Through the bar came the aroma of a very large fry-up and they had already demolished three large pots of strong, black coffee.

"In many ways manipulating the studio lights was a darn sight more risky than the murder itself. Whoever did it would have spent hours and hours on the computer. So why? What was the purpose? We got it right early on when we guessed that it was to cover an escape but if the murderer was one of the cast then just by being at stage call he or she would already have escaped. Why on earth should the lights go out *after* that?"

"We thought there could have been some mistiming," put in Molloy.

"Yes and we worked on that but what really threw us in this case was not just that the fire door hadn't been opened and the lift was deactivated, it was always that there seemed to be no motive. Bronwen might have had one but in the hotbed of gossip that was showbusiness nobody really believed that Jess was actually in love with Ahmed. Cobb might have had one but it seemed far-fetched to assume that what he had done as a child could have destroyed him. There didn't seem motive enough for one let alone two but there was and two were what we should have been looking for all along. Or as we heard Freddy say, Brendan, 'two please'."

"You said it was about runners," accused Molloy in hurt tones after he had explained the exchange to Caesar and Gardiner.

"No. You said runners after I used the term 'fixer' but what I said was 'running away'. That was why the lights went out so that the murderer could run away. And that in turn meant that the murderer was not in the line- up at stage call and Cobb, Fred, Ru, Em etc were all there.

"Yes, I think you are right that he was on the other side of the door," Frobisher looked at Molloy and Caesar. "He made that slip about how everyone had assumed there was light on the other side and he could only have known that there wasn't if he had been there. But as in the case of Caesar's old lady, the timing was split-second. It is just possible that he fell through the door and noticed a millisecond's worth of darkness before the lights came on but I don't think so, because I think it was he who switched them on. The switch for the corridor is right by the studio door."

Gardiner began to look lost but Frobisher's next words held them all.

"Motive. We've been a bit slow. What is the one good thing about Cobb Grainger?"

"That he's in hospital with broken legs," growled Molloy.

"His wife," said Anton softly.

"Exactly. Jane, who anyone with two glass eyes could see adored him and he her. They had built up a lot together: family, career, nice house, success, popularity and then along comes Jess.

"At some stage Jess tells Cobb that she is Phillipson's daughter and that what he did all those years ago drove him to his death. I suspect that if he had expressed shame and remorse or had been a nicer guy to have around she would have left it at that, but that wasn't Cobb's way. He brazened it out and she threatened to expose him. He probably laughed in her face.

"Cobb warns Jane that there might be some embarrassment on the horizon but she or he or both begin to see things differently. We know that once someone is accused of misconduct a lot of people suddenly come out of the woodwork. You see it all the time with abuse cases. And of course not only the genuine pop up but also those with pound signs in their eyes.

"We know Cobb was a bully at prep. school but there is no record of any trouble thereafter. No *record*. But that doesn't mean he wasn't tormenting other boys. It means only that he wasn't caught. We know from the chief whip that he had no staff problems at Westminster but what about life before Parliament? Did he bully secretaries? Would someone come forward to say that he made her life such hell that she left a job she loved or cried every day in the office or whatever? And then you can bet it would escalate until he was accused of putting his hand down a woman's top or making callous or suggestive remarks to a constituent. These things snowball and truth and fantasy become mixed up.

"Even if he rode it all out, minimised the true and disproved the false, he would be damaged irreparably and his friends and family would go through the wringer. No, I suspect Jane forced him to tell her all that might be said from however far back and then they decided they couldn't afford to let Jess do it.

"It all pointed to Cobb early on. He was probably on the other side of the studio door, he knew it was dark there which nobody else knew until Helen recovered her memory and he had a motive. However if he did it then he had to walk past the open door of hair, then past several dressing rooms, then do murder while the singers were carrying on, then walk back. Yes, he could have concealed the flapper band but that corridor was a hive of activity until stage call when it suddenly emptied. The risk was too great and the singers work both ways. Nobody could have heard the murder but equally the murderer couldn't hear anyone approaching the room. No, it had to be done after stage call when the murderer could move about without meeting anyone and all hands were to deck in the studio."

Frobisher paused as large plates of breakfast appeared and the policemen fell on the food with the relish of the half-starved.

"So the first challenge was to make sure that Jess did not go to stage call with the others. They will have thought up something simple because they needed only a very brief delay. Perhaps a missing key or piece of makeup or something that Jess might just look for before she left. They didn't need to steal it: just move it to an unfamiliar place in the room. But they knew they had only a few seconds before she got up and left without it. As she was sitting at her table I'd guess it was something she normally kept there.

"It meant Cobb getting into the dressing room but that would have been easy enough, because he wouldn't have had to hide it.

He could have opened the door for a runner bearing coffee or quite openly knocked when he knew she wasn't there and stuck his head round the door. People coming and going and calling on each other well before the murder was committed would have caused no interest at all.

"Jane was in the store room next door and as soon as it was quiet she slid into Jess's room, did the deed quickly and then had to get away but this was the period of maximum danger. They knew that someone would be sent to find Jess and the risk was high that Jane might meet whoever it was as she made her way back to Cobb's room."

"To Cobb's room?" The exclamation came from both Molloy and Anton.

"Yes. She didn't use the fire door and she didn't use the lift. That can only mean she used a window and there is no window in the store room."

"But why Cobb's room? Why not go through Jess's window?"

"Because she would have had to risk the window being locked and even if it wasn't she would have had to find something to stand on and clamber out all while Jess was being missed and someone sent to find her. Instead she had the key to Cobb's room and a chair was already standing under an unlocked window. I've checked the position of the CCTV cameras. One is pointed at the fire door but as far as I can see none is focussed on that block of dressing room windows.

"So she locks the door behind her, pockets the key and climbs through the window."

"Hang on, sir. We sealed off that area and nobody went back down there. I distinctly remember the report saying that all windows were found latched."

"Yes, but look at the size of those rooms. Everyone, as you must surely have noticed, hung coats and clothes and bags from the handles of the window latches which were parallel with the sills. So all Jane has to do is make sure that the coat or whatever stays on the latch while she climbs out. Then she shuts the window and the weight of the coat pulls the latch back down."

"But what part do the lights play in all this?"

"Let's start with the corridor lights. They were solely to get Jane away without being seen. The switches are at both ends of the corridors and at the top and bottom of the stairs. But she needed to be able to see if she wasn't to grope her way along or use a torch so she opens Jess's door and peers out. All is quiet so she hares along to the stairs and listens again. Sure enough she hears Helen running and flattens herself against the back of the stairwell. If she tries to get to the switch now Helen might see her so she waits until Helen comes back and races up the stairs where she starts running towards the studio. As soon as Jane knows Helen's clear of the stairs she flicks off the lights and hurries to Cobb's room probably using a mobile briefly for illumination. Once inside she locks the door and escapes through the window."

"Those timings fit brilliantly," agreed Molloy with admiration in his tone "But supposing Helen had called Ahmed on her mobile instead of running for dear life? How would Jane have got away then?"

"It wasn't very likely was it? A girl on her own with a dead body and a murderer who could be lurking anywhere? Of course she was damn well going to run. If they could be sure of nothing else they could be sure of that.

"Meanwhile back at the ranch all is chaos and confusion. I'll come back to the studio lights in a minute. Cobb is worrying himself stupid about Jane getting away and he knows about the loose panel. Anton, you are almost certainly right that he discovered it one day by accident, but once they were thinking about murder it presented another opportunity. If he got through it he could waylay Helen, perhaps, delay the inevitable moment of the murder being reported by a few more precious seconds. Give Jane a fraction longer.

"Again it all fits. Cobb wasn't heard or otherwise noticed once the lights had been out for a couple of moments. That was because he was getting through the wall into the kitchen. Helen could hear soft sounds but wasn't sure where. He emerges onto the corridor and clears his throat preparatory to calling out to Helen and the rest is the history of this case. He is in the act of switching the lights on when the studio door busts open."

There was a short silence as three minds looked for and failed to find a flaw in the smooth exposition.

"Then we come to the studio lights," went on Frobisher disguising his relief that none of the others had spotted a weakness. "They were designed to do exactly what they did: cause havoc and ensure that for a while everyone forgot Jess and that the corridor wasn't going to be filled with minions despatched to find her.

"I admit it took me a while to work out how that was done. There were only two possibilities – and we asked Ansell to go through it all again and again until he must have felt like strangling *us*. One option was the sequence: lights on Venetia, on judges, on band etc. Perhaps the lights were programmed to go out if that sequence was repeated a certain number of times but I discounted that because I don't believe that Cobb would have spent hours re-programming the computer on the off-chance that Venetia would ad-lib and Ansell would follow her in a given order of spotlights. After all they might simply have cut and started recording again when all was back in order."

"The written sequence?" Molloy and Anton spoke as one while Gardiner looked at each in turn, lost now in a tale with which he had never been conversant but spellbound nonetheless.

"Yes. It was switched twice. We know the first time was between dress rehearsal and the show because there was no malfunction at dress rehearsal. We know also that the studio is empty for some of that time because we witnessed that ourselves this week. So Cobb walks as bold as brass up to the lighting box. Then he looks round the studio ready to hail anybody who might be about. The very picture of innocence. If he is caught at this stage he simply abandons that part of the plan.

"He has a sequence with only a minute difference that Ansell, concentrating on the studio floor, does not notice. After all the sequence changes every week so he has no subconscious memory but the computer has been programmed to accept that small insertion as a command to kill the lights. The piece of paper has the obligatory coffee ring. Cobb had been up to watch Ansell at work one day and Ansell told us he was patronising but in fact he was prospecting. I suspect that on the day of the switch he went up there with two false sequences, one with and one without a ring.

"After the show was pulled all the world and his wife were up in that lighting booth because of the lights failure. Almost certainly he was among them, pretending amazed curiosity and was able to switch the sequence paper back to the real one."

"Does anybody remember his being there?" asked Caesar with sudden sharpness.

"No. There are two holes in this theory and that is one of them but ask anybody up there who came and went and some will give you some names that others don't. Suggest that Anton was there....."

"I wasn't."

"I'm glad to hear it because it proves my point. Three people say you were including the producer."

Anton looked indignant.

"Anyway it was all bru- ha- ha as my mother used to call it and nobody really knows who was where and when. They had the sense to ban access to the dressing room corridors until we came but other than that it was just a melee. Some people went off to find guests they had in the audience, the audience itself was in a state of excitement and disorder as it left, some of the cast went to the lavatories, some to the canteen, the crew stayed largely in the studio and just about everybody at some staged milled round that damn lighting-booth."

"All right, sir. How did Cobb get the names into the judges' papers? What was the point of the Beautella business and when did he ever have time to re programme the computer? Or Computers if you include Fabulous Flying? And when did Jane get in the building to hide in the store room? And when she had climbed through the window how did she get away?" Molloy gave the impression of a winded man who has suddenly gathered his wits.

Frobisher stood up and took a stack of magazines from a nearby window ledge. As he put them on the table Molloy noticed that the front of the topmost was devoted to a picture of Haytor, sunny and inviting. For a moment they all looked at it, seeing only snow and ice and death.

Then as one they cleared the plates away and Frobisher divided the magazines into three piles.

"Please check that these heaps consist of all the judges should have," he invited Molloy, who at once pulled the top of the front magazine towards him and then the top of the next.

"Exactly. You have checked each page for the headings but if the cards were near the bottom you wouldn't have seen them. I think he had watched Rashid and Langdon checking and knew that was the method they used. It was done well before the papers got anywhere near the studio."

"It was a risk, sir. One might have fallen out."

"If it had nobody would have known what it meant and it would ultimately have served the same purpose, which was to emphasise that the killing of Jess was premeditated. You see they knew that sooner or later Jess's parentage would be traced. They could not have guessed that she had told nobody in the family and must have assumed that David at least knew. Then it might come out that Sam and Cobb had once known each other as children and then the trail would start. If that happened Cobb intended to create the impression of an attempt to murder Beautella so that we would be confused into looking for a link between her and Jess. As they were both professionals we might have spent a lot of time on that."

"This is hardly keeping it simple, sir. Why take another set of risks when they had got away with murder once?" Molloy sounded doubtful.

"Cobb is a politician. He plots every move of every campaign and works out all the likely scenarios and, where possible, he tries to cover them all. Beautella would not have gone to the rafters unless he felt we were lining him up as a suspect and we were."

"But why leave that photo up? Without it we might never have got on the trail in the first place." Anton sounded puzzled but also somewhat distant as if he were trying to work something out for himself.

"Because he was cooler and cleverer than poor old Fred. He could work out that if he were to be seen in the smallest way to be hiding anything which linked him to Phillipson it would heighten suspicion. Lots of people would have seen that photo and it was in due date order with the others. He decided it was safer to leave it there. I stress again that he thought we would find out anyway so the photo posed no unique risk."

"Now to the rest. That studio is used solely for *Lively Toes* but the contestants are forbidden to enter it between Fridays in case they get an advantage by practising on the actual floor. It is pretty busy with people shifting props and checking equipment and very occasionally they let other programmes use it for practice sessions. Health and safety require regular checks and Cobb could never have been sure of having a long enough spell unseen in there to re-programme the computers except on one day- Saturday. The day after the show everybody has off and that goes largely for Sunday too. Celebs may be training in their various dance studios but the *Lively Toes* studio is a ghost town. I think that was when Cobb did it. He could have got in easily enough without passing front desk. Doors are always open for removals and deliveries and heaven knows what else. We'll need to re-trawl the CCTV for the earlier weeks But I doubt if we'll find anything. He's just too damn clever. But at least those computers will bring it home to him eventually. Somewhere, sometime, he's done some very serious computing."

"Have we got enough to arrest them, sir?" Molloy's tone antici- pated the answer. In Latin he would have prefaced the question with *num.*

"No. We can put a guard over him in hospital because there has been an attempt on his life. We can say it is for his own protection even though the protagonist is dead. But he ain't going anywhere with two broken legs in any case. As for Jane, I can question and question but I don't fancy trying to justify an arrest at this stage. We have watertight reasoning and not a shred of proof."

"You said there were *two* holes in your case, Peter? One is no definite sighting of Grainger around the lighting booth when he should have been switching the sequence back. What's the other?"

The inspector smiled at Anton. "You don't miss much, do you? The other is that for my theory to work Cobb spent two Saturdays in the studio, one fiddling the lighting and the other the flying. But this is an MP with a constituency so far from London that he can only be there at weekends and a diary booked up months in advance. How does he disappear for two whole Saturdays, even if it all began before the season of nativity plays and carol concerts and Christmas functions? When does he do his surgeries? Once, yes. He could say he was taken ill on Friday and stayed up in London but I can't see him doing that twice in three weeks without arousing comment."

It was Anton who broke the ensuing silence.

" Jane Grainger is not an MP."

CHAPTER NINETEEN

IN WHICH ANTON CONFRONTS THE MURDERERS

Rashid and Bronwen Ahmed stood in the middle of the empty studio, their arms around each other, surveying the wreckage of broken dreams.

"It should have worked," said Rashid sadly. "It was all going so well and now…" He shrugged miserably.

"Do you think they might try again in the future?"

"Not a chance, my love, not a chance. First they get a murder, then a near suicide up there in the rafters, then the great and much-trumpeted live finale dissolves in shambles with two of the dancers disappearing."

"They say Anton was with them."

"I wouldn't know. He's certainly as thick as thieves with the cops."

"Yes. Everyone is saying Cobb murdered Jess and Fred tried to murder Cobb."

"Who would have predicted it?"

"Poor old Cobb. Wrong place at wrong time. Whatever was he doing there?"

"The other side of the door? Oh, he was probably going to try and be the great saviour of the hour. He knew about the hole and thought he would climb through and open the door from the other side. It must have been quite a shock to find everything in the pitch black out there too."

"Why didn't he just tell them?"

"Because when he knew there had been a murder he must have decided the other side of the door was a bad place to be so he shut up but some of them began to suspect anyway. Then it turns out there was once something which linked him to Jess and did so in a bad light. I'm not sure what it was but it certainly set the hounds on him."

"Lucky for us." Bronwen turned and embraced him, burying her head in his shoulder.

Rashid looked dully over her shoulders at the tiers of empty seats, his heart leaden, his stomach full of ice. Many times over the last two months he had thought of his parents, dear, gentle people who had come to Britain to give their children a better chance but had never interfered in their lives and choices. Some of his friends had been obliged to marry whomever their parents directed, others had been pressured into choosing law or medicine when what they had wanted was teaching or acting.

The Ahmeds had been relaxed, saying they had not come all this way to make their sons and daughter unhappy. His brother and sister had married within the Pakistani community but when he had chosen Bronwen there had been no objection and no comment was ever made about the subsequent absence of grandchildren.

If only they had objected. Oh, why, why didn't you object? He cried out to them now in spirit. To be sure Bronwen had played a canny hand, wearing demure clothes, not drinking in their presence and speaking wistfully of her idyllic Catholic childhood in rural Wales. He should have known then that this normally mini-skirted, wine-scoffing, atheist daughter of a drunken father and downtrodden mother was someone to be avoided as a liar and arch-hypocrite but he convinced himself that she did it only for him. That she did not want to worry his parents.

How cleverly she had hinted at anti-catholic prejudice from the chapel goers so that his parents thought she understood the much greater prejudice their innocent family had suffered. In his heart he knew she was trouble but his passion told him he could change all that.

Once he had feared his parents might see her drunk but now.... Dear God, *murder*. And an innocent man suspected. Never mind that he was so thoroughly nasty – he was still innocent. Worse there were rumours that his wife was under suspicion as well. Jane Grainger ? Were the police mad? He had met her once and had thought she was everything he might have wanted Bronwen to be in forty years' time. Maybe that made him a fuddy-duddy but anything would have been better than this.

Perhaps he just liked older women. Certainly he had liked Jess. They had been discreet enough even to silence the showbiz gossips but not discreet enough to fool Bronwen, who was alive to every nuance in his expression, every tremor of desire that was not for her, every dream in which she did not feature. She had watched and schemed and determinedly caught them in flagrante. She demanded he leave *Lively Toes* and daily, hourly now he repented his refusal but it was too good for his career and for once he stood up to her. Often she insisted on coming with him, haunting the studios on Friday. He knew people speculated about the reason.

Then he would come home to find her with marks on her neck and she told him she had been practising murdering Jess.

"If I press here it really does hurt. Apparently if you apply...."

"Stop it, for goodness sake, stop it." He had once even shaken her but the fantasies went on and the horrible fascination with internet sites that taught her how to kill commando-style. He began to speculate on having her committed.

He confided the thought to his mother but she was horrified. "Oh, son, you don't want to be visiting her in such a place. It will shame you."

"There's no shame attached to mental illness," he had responded and seen his mother's eyes widen. Soon, he thought, she would be visiting him in prison because if Cobb were convicted he would shout the truth from the rooftops.

Then Bronwen told him she had worked out how to do it. At first he had humoured her, playing along, certain it was all a sick game, that at the point when she was supposed to kill she would laugh manically and turn away. Gradually he had sunk deeper into the mire, plotting the timelines, giving her the code to reactivate the lift.

She stood over him that Saturday while he reprogrammed the computer and again when they had plotted to terrify Beautella. It was easy for him to enter the building and the studio any time. He simply registered at the front desk in the usual way, occasionally going straight back out again, on other occasions sneaking back in through routes that only those who knew the building could have devised. They were used to seeing him about and if, when he called goodnight they could not find his name in the book, they assumed a careless colleague had forgotten to note it.

Switching the sequence had been a piece of cake. He had nipped up and warned Chris about Em being more scatty than usual but had not entered the booth or gone near the computer. From the doorway he could see that the piece of paper Chris was working from had a coffee ring in the usual place. Switching it back had been risky because everyone was milling about the lighting section, demanding explanations. So he pretended to knock the sequence on to the floor accidentally and went scrabbling about between legs to retrieve it. Chris was still fending off increasingly agitated questions and nobody paid him any attention as he performed the switch, crouched down with his hands under the console table.

He had resisted at first when Bronwen wanted to frighten Beautella but she knew the police were looking at her because they had heard rumours about him and Jess and, as Frobisher had correctly surmised, a second victim would confuse the detectives. Ironically the cards with Jess's name on had been his only attempt to derail Bronwen's plans. He had put them among the judges' papers, expecting them to fall out when Helen picked them up. There would be immediate questions, Jess would be sent for and she would not be sitting in her room waiting to be murdered.

But they didn't fall out and reports of their later discovery caused Bronwen to look at him oddly.

Right up until the end he believed she would not do it, but on the night he found himself sending Helen instead of Ed. Ed would move quicker, knew where Jess's room was and might not panic quite as much as Helen. He needed someone out there scared and uncertain. It was the director not he who gave the signal to start the show. He delayed in case they then renewed the effort to find Jess and was grateful when the lights went out as planned.

Yet he still expected to see Jess appear, perhaps flustered from a confrontation with his wife, but still alive. When the lights came on he looked at the audience and his wife was there at the side, in her wheelchair with her surgical boot raised in front of her and her crutches propped against the wall. She could not have done it, surely? But he knew she had.

Had he but known it the police had mapped out a fairly accurate picture of the killing albeit with the wrong person in the role of murderer. Bronwen had not hidden in the store room. She had taken her place at the side of the audience, put her crutches and handbag in their normal place and had begun greeting members of the crew and floor management as they came and went up and down the gangway. Then during a lull she went to the lift. Nor did she leave by a window but came back up in the lift, which was already deactivated, using the code Rashid had given her. As she expected all the lights were out and she settled back into her place where she was visible when the lights came back on.

She had been bobbing up and down all the time greeting people, occasionally wandering up or down a few steps in order to do so. Her boot made her highly visible and everyone knew she hadn't just sat still throughout so what with that and all the confusion of the lights failure, everyone thought she had been there all the time. The only real risk was that someone would hear the lift but she thought not. The doors on the first floor opened also on the opposite side, away from the corridor and into a tiny foyer leading immediately into the auditorium. The audience was voluble and buzzing with the lights failure and anyone in the corridor on the other side would be there to find Jess not worry about why the lift was working when it should not have been.

Rashid held her now and tried to blot out the future. Perhaps it would be all right. Cobb had not done it so somewhere there must be a flaw in the police case. His defence team would find it and all would be well.

"I'll never let you down again," he whispered. "Never. I swear it."

"No, you won't," agreed Bronwen equably. "Not now. Not now you know what I am capable of."

As Ahmed, appalled by the threat, stepped back and looked at her, he saw the horror swell in her own eyes as she stared over his shoulder. The producer swung round and saw Anton Caesar standing quietly by the judges' table.

"Every word," he said in answer to their unspoken question. "I never thought I would hear myself say this but poor bloody Cobb. I suppose in another age you would have just let him hang."

Bronwen reached in her shoulder bag but Rashid put out a hand to stop her. His brain was working furiously. What had they actually said? That Cobb was in the wrong place at the wrong time. That there was some link between him and Jess. Oh, yes, Bronwen had said it was lucky for them. None of that amounted to evidence.

"I have called the police," said Anton to Bronwen who had now produced a small spray can from her handbag. Deodorant? Hairspray? He guessed she intended to aim it at his eyes and, while he was blinded, kill him by whatever means.

He began to move along the judges' table, then suddenly with a leap and a swing he was on it and over it. Something hissed past his right ear, its perfume identifying it as hairspray.

"Not another, Bron. Let's just run for it," cried Ahmed.

"Fool! Go round and cut him off."

Ahmed began to obey but he was still protesting. "Let's just run."

"Not till he can't tell."

Anton jumped back on to the judges' table and ran for the gangway between the tiers of audience seats. He spun round suddenly
and aimed a kick at Ahmed who was close behind him. He missed
but the producer staggered backwards and fell. Anton turned again
and saw Bronwen rushing up a side gangway on his left to cut him
off. A glance back showed Ahmed getting to his feet, despair and
fear in his eyes. Anton turned and ran along a row of seats to his
right. Ahmed gave chase but just short of the end of the row, the
dancer spun round and delivered a high kick between the eyes.

Rashid gave a cry of agony and then a roar of rage, charging
after Anton like a maddened bull and he realised that a reluctant
attacker had become an angry one. He got to the end of the row
before Bronwen but only just and he felt another hiss of spray.
Sprinting down the right gangway, he ran towards the wings then
swerved at the last moment so that his pursuers were carried by
their impetus into the curtains. It bought him time but when he
tried to open the studio door which led to the dressing room corridor it was locked and he heard Bronwen's triumphant laugh.

He stood with his back to the door as they confronted him, the
hairspray poised in Bronwen's hand. She was holding something in
her other one too.

"You dropped this. There is no 999 call on here."

"He doesn't need 999," snapped Rashid. "He will have their
direct numbers."

Bronwen looked disconcerted, then threw the phone across
the floor. Anton watched both as they began to move towards him.
With wildly flailing arms and as big a bellow as he could muster he
charged Rashid, knocking him off balance. He had in mind the
other door but Bronwen had expected that and was between him
and it.

He feinted a turn, then made straight at her, knocked the can
from her hand and lifting her up carried her across the studio. He
was used to carrying female dancers but not struggling murder-
esses. After only a few steps he turned again and swooshed her hard
along the floor at Ahmed who sidestepped as Bronwen landed in

a heap. Anton raced for the door and then the lights went out. He moved away cautiously and listened. Presently the strip lighting would come on but instead all the lights returned.

"Power cut," muttered Ahmed who had crept towards the door as Anton crept away from it. "Where is he?"

"Did he get through the door?" Bronwen was rubbing herself cautiously.

"No we'd have heard. Bron, let's run."

"Try under the judges' table."

From his not very secure hiding place behind a drum kit, Anton calculated the distance to the stairs. He could forget the main door because Bronwen wasn't leaving it but one of the doors at the top of the auditorium might be unlocked. When Ahmed was looking the wrong way Anton broke cover and ran for the stairs. He outpaced the pursuit easily enough and the door was not locked but as he shot through he saw to his despair that the route down was full of decorating equipment. Instead he ran round, through the next door and back down into the auditorium, jumping from the last steps and heading for the now deserted door. It opened as Helen and Beautella walked in and the scene froze.

"Oh, hallo. We've just come to say goodbye to the studio," Helen greeted him rather inanely.

She looked round mystified by the atmosphere in the room. What was that awful mark on Rashid's face and why was Bronwen so dishevelled? And why were they all panting as if they had been running a marathon? Uncertainly she moved closer to Beautella.

It was on the tip of Anton's tongue to say "Murder. Run." But they would probably be pursued and terrified and they were the two most vulnerable girls in the whole of the large *Lively Toes* team.

Instead he said brightly "Well, now we are here, let's dance. All three of us. Just do whatever moves you like. It's a good way to remember the studio."

Anton suited the action to the word by going to the centre of the floor and pirouetting. Helen stared at the Ahmeds. Anton had said "all three of us" so the producer and his wife must be excluded but why?

Only Beautella entered into the spirit of the proposal, running to put on a c.d.

The only music Anton wanted was the blare of police sirens. He grabbed Beautella and began to foxtrot, wondering what the Ahmeds would do. From their point of view the odds had changed from two to one to three to two. Were they seriously going to try murder now? He thought, as he watched a muttered conference take place, that they must surely flee.

The music changed and Beautella began to jive, her face full of innocent pleasure. She jumped up on the judges' table and when Anton looked round to where the Ahmeds had been they were no longer there. Nor was Helen.

"Helen!" he cried and sped to the door. It was locked and too late he recalled that Rashid had the keys of the studio. He began to bang on the door with his fists and shout impotently.

"What is it?" Beautella stared at him with anxious eyes.

"They've got Helen. Kill that music." Anton ran up the stairs to the doors at the back of the auditorium. Both were locked. So that was why he had suddenly gained ground as he fled from them. Rashid had been locking doors to reduce his quarry's room for manoeuvre.

"Anton! Please! What's happening?"

"Bronwen Ahmed killed Jess and Rashid helped her. I told them I had called the police and now thanks to my utter stupidity they have taken Helen as hostage. They will use her to get away."

"Did they have guns or knives?"

Anton looked at her in surprise. "No. But...."

"Then how will they threaten to kill her?"

"The way Bronwen killed Jess. Expertly."

"They have a flapper band?"

Anton blinked.

"My dear, don't you think Helen would have yelled if they were taking her by force? "

"They may not have taken her by force. They may have just asked her to go along and help with something. She didn't know they were murderers."

"We both knew something was up. Helen wouldn't have just gone off with them. She didn't. She has been sitting over there for the last five minutes."

Anton whirled round. "Oh, thanks. As if I haven't had enough shocks for one day. Before you two rolled up I was quite literally running for my life."

The door rattled and a key grated in the lock. All three tensed and Beautella moved closer to Anton.

"Oh, good afternoon, sir." came the bright tones of Frobisher. "We have just made two arrests. I trust that this time we have got it right."

Helen had spotted Anton's phone. Picking it up, she handed it to him and they all watched while Anton looked at the screen and pressed a command. He handed the text to Beautella and Helen peered over her shoulder.

Wrong two. Studio. ASAP. NOW.

"It was that ASAP and NOW, sir. A bit emphatic you might say. I left my family in a Pizza Hut." Molloy was smiling.

"I left my wife and daughter in Oxford Street. Most willingly," added Frobisher. "What happened?"

"I came to collect the things I had left behind when I went haring off to Dartmoor. They told me at the desk that the Ahmeds were here and I didn't come in quietly but I'm wearing trainers and I don't think they could have heard me. I was just walking through the wings when I took in what they were saying and listened. Then I texted you and thought I should make sure they stayed here so I rather foolishly showed myself. Bronwen decided the best thing to do was kill me too."

"She kept her nerve," Frobisher told them. "They didn't run but tried to walk out of the front door quite naturally. If we had arrived a few seconds later they would have got away with it and we would now be in manhunt territory."

"I don't think she believed I had called you. Rashid did but Bronwen was calling the shots."

"As she may well have done throughout. We won't know until one of them coughs. Meanwhile I am going to have to explain to my bosses why I saw fit to put a perfectly respectable and very prominent politician under police guard and told his lovely, impeccably-mannered wife that she was suspected of murder," said Frobisher grimly and then, turning to Beautella. "Have you any vacancies for assistants or general dogsbodies in your studio ma'am?"

Chapter Twenty

IN WHICH A SENIOR POLICEMAN IS APPEASED AND A
POLITICIAN PLAYS A CLEVER HAND.

"It should have been obvious to us all along," Frobisher admitted to the Detective Chief Superintendent on Monday morning. "Rashid was the only one who could move about and unlock computers and cupboards with ease and arouse no suspicion if anyone happened to see him. He could come and go from the building in a way none of the dancers or celebs could and if I was looking for two people then that couple should have seemed more likely than the Graingers."

"Hindsight is a wonderful thing, Peter. You put together a pretty accurate picture of how it was done and the Phillipson issue was certainly playing a major role. It convinced Fred that Cobb was the murderer and led first to blackmail and then to Fred's own lamentable attempt at murder."

"I don't think he was going to murder Cobb, sir, although I did at first. If you are going to do murder, you don't use a child's toy axe. And now we have Grainger's own account of what happened. He has been remarkably forthcoming since being told we had charged the Ahmeds. Gardiner interviewed him again this morning and we're preparing the report now."

"Then tell me what is going to be in it right away because I am due to see the AC any minute. The media are all over this like a rash: high drama on the moors, police chasing stars still in their dancing clothes, a prominent politician in hospital with serious injuries, a well-known TV personality dead, the producer of *Lively Toes* arrested and charged. It'll run and run."

"Yes. Right." Frobisher could hardly have sounded unhappier but the Chief Superintendent wanted his report.

"According to Grainger Jess revealed her link to Phillipson in week three of *Lively Toes* but he had no idea until last week that Fred knew as well. He had heard something vague about Jess and Fred having met when she was a girl but had no reason to connect that with Phillipson.

"Jess tried to blackmail him into good behaviour towards Beautella by saying that he hadn't changed and she was prepared to tell everyone that he had driven a war hero to his death. Predictably he laughed and told her to carry on. Small children can be ghastly, he admitted. So what?

"And, yes, Ahmed was right about why Cobb was on the other side of the door. He had found the panel by accident on his very first day in the studio, interestingly the same way Anton found it – from the kitchen side. Apparently he couldn't get any hot water from the tap and was looking for pipes to see if they were warm. He thought nothing of it at the time.

"On the night of the murder he did indeed think that he would solve the muddle by opening the studio door from the other side and the rather dim emergency lighting on the floor enabled him to go straight to the panel. Then of course it was all dark. He didn't know where the switch to the kitchen light was so rather than fumble around for it he groped his way out on to the corridor and then it occurred to him that Helen was out there somewhere so he was going to call her and, as we guessed, cleared his throat first."

"As *you* guessed, Peter."

"He admits that when he knew there was a body and a concussed runner he decided not to say anything about his own presence there, but over the next few weeks he knew we were looking at him pretty carefully and he discussed with Jane the possibility that Phillipson might have something to do with it and also as we guessed they feared an avalanche might grow out of one not very significant pebble.

"He also noticed that Fred had grown quite nasty towards him and then it came to a head between the Christmas show and the results. Poor old Fred was utterly convinced that Cobb had murdered Jess and he now saw him about to win *Lively Toes* with all the celebrity that would involve. He started yelling at him that he knew all about Phillipson and why Cobb had murdered Jess and that he was going to reveal all, on air, during the results filming.

"Cobb tried unsuccessfully to calm him and thought about calling in the show's bosses but he knew Fred had nothing to lose because he had been telling everyone that this was his last show. He admits that Fred tried blackmail but he reckoned that if he paid Fred would take that as an admission of guilt and go straight to the police. He says he doesn't think Fred was interested in the money, just proving that Cobb had killed Jess. So I was only half right about that.

"Cobb made the mistake of laughing at him and Fred went ape. Whatever else happened Fred must not be allowed to denounce him on air and Cobb knew one certain way to achieve that: the show mustn't happen. If Fred called him a bully and a murderer on air it would be banner headlines and lead all the news bulletins.

"So Cobb decided simply to go home and work out how best to handle what Fred might do if the show was pulled. He knew that he was the likely winner and that by leaving he would throw all into chaos so he grabbed his coat but Fred snatched it from him telling him he wasn't going anywhere. Whereupon Cobb left anyway, using the fire door.

"At first it seemed a bonus for Cobb when Fred followed, shouting wildly. With two of them missing the show would certainly be wrecked so he thought it quite funny when Fred, having failed to stop Cobb getting into his car, followed in his own but it also led to a drastic change of plan.

"You see, sir, I was wrong to assume Dartmoor. Cobb had intended to make for his London house in Lord North Street, change, phone Jane to explain what was happening and then drive slowly to Devon while he thought things through. He hadn't murdered Jess and he wanted to work out how best to convince Fred of that but when he saw Fred sitting on his tail, he feared a commotion outside his home which might have led to the very headlines he was trying to avoid. He was also trying to think up a convincing lie to explain to the TV people about why he had simply walked out without telling anyone but first he must neutralise Fred.

"So he changed his mind and headed for the country. He says he fully expected Fred to give up but he didn't and then he began to feel disturbed about what Fred might intend so he rang Jane and told her to lock up well and let nobody in. He thought he might see off Fred in a fight but Fred was strong and seemingly fit and it was not a foregone conclusion. They were after all both drawing the old age pension and well past pugilistics. That can only mean that he did not know how plagued Fred was by arthritis."

The rest of Cobb's account took them through what had happened when he finally stopped the car up to and including the wild gymnastics on the tops of Haytor, which the detectives had seen with their own eyes.

"I hate to think what he'll do, sir. He's got a lot of clout and we accused Jane of murder and him of being an accessory before, during and after the fact."

"But not formally. There was no actual arrest and we can thank God for that. But I imagine he will give us grief and with Fred in the morgue and press everywhere there is no knowing what will come out."

Frobisher swore.

"I agree," said the superintendent cheerfully. "But at least we got 'em in the end."

Frobisher swore again when at 2pm he received a message to say that Cobb was being discharged that day. He had no internal injuries of any consequence and was insisting that his broken pelvis and legs could be nursed privately at home. He was leaving the hospital shortly before 6 and had agreed to make a brief statement before getting in the ambulance to be taken home.

"Six o'clock," fumed Molloy. "In time for the news."

"Live coverage for a certainty. A press conference about police incompetence. Can't Gardiner arrange it better?"

"No, sir. Whenever he leaves there will be rolling cameras. And pity poor Gardiner – he will actually be taking the brunt of it. The bigwigs won't be present and he is not of a rank to go issuing major statements. He will have to prevaricate and that never looks good."

Another message was hardly more encouraging. The AC would be grateful if they would join him in his office to watch the six pm news and it would also be helpful if Anton Caesar were to be present.

"Perhaps he wants to give him my job," groaned Frobisher bitterly.

At the appointed hour they reported to the office of the AC who shot Anton a curious glance which said that celebrity was a phenomenon which confounded him. Molloy's own look was directed keenly at the superintendent but he could read nothing from his expression. Then he switched his gaze in horrid anticipation to the screen from which was emanating the signature tune of the FBC news programmes.

Cobb emerged from the front door of A and E in a wheelchair pushed by Jane, his broken legs sticking out in front of him encased in plaster. Beside him walked Gardiner and paramedics.

By the doors of the ambulance Jane turned the wheelchair to face the huge throng of eager reporters. The screen was briefly obscured by flashbulbs, then it filled with Grainger's features.

"I just want you all to know how hugely proud I am of our police. I owe them and their swift reactions my very life. They have throughout this investigation been courteous and thorough, so thorough that at one point they even questioned my charming wife as if she could have done murder!"

The cameras switched to Jane who smiled modestly.

"Of course that is a joke. They always made it clear that they were just doing their duty and by doing that duty well they have apprehended a murderer and her accomplice………"

"Clever sod," swore the superintendent, *sotto voce*. "That photo will probably appear on his election address: the victim of serious crime praising the police. Yuk!"

"Certainly clever," murmured Anton. "If he had grumbled the police would have had to defend themselves and hint that our Cobb may be somewhat less than a very parfait knight. As it is they will now thank him profusely."

Someone was asking about Fred.

"Fred was an utter gentleman and had known Jess for years. I am afraid he took her death very badly and kept suspecting people who clearly could not have been responsible......."

"He suspected *you*, just you. Liar!" Molloy forgot himself and earned a warning glance from the superintendent. So Fred was to be portrayed as some deranged old fool who had met a tragic and ill-deserved fate.

When the press conference was over and the shots of the departing ambulance had faded from the screen, there was a wondering silence in the room.

It was broken by Anton. "Politicians! Lying toads! They know how to turn anything on its head."

"Devils," murmured the AC. "But we may on this occasion be thankful that they are often very *clever* devils. And so have you been, sir. I suppose you wouldn't like to join the Yard?"

Anton smiled. "I think I prefer grand jetes, double whisks and botafogos. Your own manoeuvres are quite beyond me."

THE END